THE
BARD'S
TALE

Stories and Recipes from the
Black Dragon Inn

Edited by Daniel Myers

DEDICATION

For my mother, Kathleen Locke.

CONTENTS

INTRODUCTION

A couple of years ago at a convention, Brian Pettera came up to me with a solution.

Stephanie and I finished our dwarven and halfling cookbooks and were considering doing more, but we just couldn't get a handle on a fantasy cookbook oriented around humans. Dwarves and halflings were fun, but the whole human cookbook thing just wasn't working.

That's when Brian suggested I edit a fantasy anthology with added recipes that I would have used in a human cookbook. Since the recipes would likely be centered around taverns, the stories could be about bards. Honestly, I think he had me at the word "bard".

The first time that I remember encountering a real bard was back around 1997 when my wife and I went to a library in Charlotte, North Carolina to see a story teller named Jackie Torrence. I was expecting to see something like a school teacher or librarian or the like read fairy tales to a couple of dozen kids. What happened though was as far from that as possible while still retaining the same basic form. Jackie sat, surrounded by a huge crowd, and told story after story about growing up in the rural south. She was amazing. The tone of her voice and the rhythm of her words held the audience spellbound.

A few years later I met a bard of a different type. Vince Conaway is an incredibly skilled musician who plays the hammered dulcimer. What makes him different from similar musicians is that he does it for a living. For part of the year he travels the United States, playing at renaissance fairs, and for the rest of the year he travels around the world. He plays for tips in public squares throughout Europe and South America, charming the locals by learning their language and doing his best to stay on the good side of the local police. Somehow he has managed to take the life of a travelling medieval musician and make it work in our modern society.

With Brian's suggestion and those two performers in my thoughts, I sent out requests for stories and what I got back surprised me. It turns out that when you ask a bunch of writers for "fantasy stories about or told by bards" you're going to get back an amazingly diverse collection. Yes, there were the sort of high-fantasy tales I expected, but there were also post-apocalyptic fantasy stories, and dark fantasy, and cautionary tales as well.

What binds them all together is the Black Dragon Inn. It's an old tavern at an old crossroads, timbered and plastered and full of food and drink, and song and story. It's hard to tell if the road is asphalt or cobblestone. In the distance that could be a dark forest or a ruined city. None of that matters though. Come inside. There's a mug of something warm and strong waiting for you by the hearth, and the cook has made something special for supper.

The Bard's Tale

NIGEL THE BARD

Maxwell Alexander Drake

Some say stories are an escape from reality,
allowing us to forget our troubles for a while.

I say stories are an extension of reality,
Showing us what life is like
on the other side of the fence.

But a really good story,
one that holds you captivated all the way to the end,
those can change the way
you perceive the world around you.
And if you're lucky, you just might find you are
not the same person as you were when the story began.

- MAD

Dawn came upon the land like a splash of cold water thrown into a bum's face to revive him from his drunken stupor. It wasn't a nasty, overcast morning. Nor one that someone would wish to sleep through. But rather, one most people wouldn't want to see quite so early.

There was one traveler who did not seem to mind. An aged bard strolled along, skillfully stepping between muck filled ruts in the cobblestone street. He was no stranger to this town, for he traveled through every so often playing his music and telling his tales of far off lands and distant adventures. His steps were that of a wanderer simply passing through, and yet they had purpose, as if he sought something very important. And to him, it was. To him, it was the most important thing in the world at this moment.

After hunting for quite some time, his gray-bearded face lit up as he spied that which he sought. A not overly large, yet not too small rock lay resting lazily under a low-branched tree. He scuttled over and eyed it for size.

Yes, he mused, *this shall be perfect*. He sat on the stone, dropped the small rucksack he carried to one side, and rested his lyre gingerly on the other. He spent the next few minutes adjusting and readjusting himself to get comfortable. When he was satisfied, he leaned over and plucked his instrument from the ground. As he started tuning the lyre, a group of blurry-eyed children gathered around.

The old bard leaned toward one of the younger boys. "What is your name, son?"

Swallowing a lump that had suddenly appeared, the boy looked about for support before answering. "Blackspoon, sir. Edoard Blackspoon."

"Well then, Master Blackspoon, if you would be so kind." The bard pointed to a large, three-story building down the street. "Run and ask the Innkeeper of the Black Dragon Inn what he's fixen' for supper, and what it will cost for that, and one night's lodgin'." He watched the boy run off to fulfill the day's first task.

A few minutes later, young Edoard returned. "The Keeper says roast duck stuffed with fruit and herbs, hard rolls and sprouts. He says the meal, and a night's stay'll cost ya six silver bits, sir. That includes a bottle of house wine or tankard of ale." The young lad puffed out his chest and smiled, thrilled to have remembered the innkeeper's words.

"Well done, Master Blackspoon." A laugh laced through the bard's words. "Well done indeed." His features took on a seriousness. "Now then." Leaning back, he let his gaze meet with each and every child. "You heard the lad, six bits. I'll need a total of six silver bits to begin me tale. Ya wouldn't want poor ole' Nigel to starve now, would ya?"

All the children sprang up to go fetch what they could. When they returned, they found old Nigel playing a happy tune on his lyre, singing a song about a princess in a castle and a knight in shining armor. They gathered 'round and sat very still, enthralled with the music, trying to capture every word the bard sang.

When Nigel finished, he returned his lyre to the ground next to him. "Well, let's see what y'all collected, shall we?" All the children pressed forward, placing the coins they had collected into the old man's outstretched palm. Every coin was copper, though he expected nothing more. When they finished filling his hand, he began to count. "Three, nine, that's one silver. And, another. And, hmmm..." He tsked. "This amounts to only five silver bits."

The children glanced at each other, a hopefulness in their eyes, as if their collective desire could magically produce the missing coinage. One of the older girls stood and curtsied. "That's all we have, sir."

"Well." Nigel scratched his head. "I'll tell ya what I'm gonna do. I enjoy these stories so much, I'll pay *myself* the last silver, just so I can listen in on them as well." A wide grin washed over his face. "How's that sound?"

All the children clapped their hands and giggled. "That would be wonderful!"

Despite himself, the glee the children's expressions warmed Nigel's tired heart. *Besides,* he thought, *I'll make more than enough to cover my costs when I ply my stories to their parents later this eve. Even better, I'll have a cozy fire at my back instead of a simple tree.*

Not that he minded. Nigel had done this his entire life and could think of no other trade he would rather do besides traveling the world telling stories to those he met.

"All right, all right." The bard raised his hands to settle the group down. "Gather 'round close now, for this first story I'm about to tell ya is most... *terrifying.*" He nearly laughed out loud at the sight of the younger children's eyes opening wide, and had to give himself a moment to recover.

"In Rornsar and the Seven Lands can be found the village of Lyslarr. And this is the tale of how its only inn, the Lordly Lion, was plagued by *ghosts.*" The bard wiggled his fingers as he said the final word, then paused long enough for several of those gathered to begin fidgeting with anticipation.

Finally, he leaned closer, as if starting a conspiracy. "It all happened like this..."

Roast Duck Stuffed with Fruit and Herbs

Every morning at the Black Dragon, just after the second batch of bread is done baking, the cook puts a dozen ducks into the oven to roast. Most inns don't sell many ducks at lunchtime, especially so far away from Thelera-Thelos, but The Black Dragon never has any left over. Erek's choice of stuffing and the way he uses it to make a sauce for the duck has proven to be irresistible. He'd make more, but twelve is as many as the oven will hold.

1 whole duck (or chicken)
1 apple
1 cup grapes
1 Tbsp. parsley
1 tsp. sage
1/2 tsp. savory
1 clove garlic
2 Tbsp. pan drippings
2 Tbsp. wine
1/4 tsp. ginger
1/4 tsp. cinnamon
1/8 tsp. cloves
1/8 tsp. nutmeg
1/2 tsp. salt

Place whole duck in a large roasting. Peel, core, and chop the apple into quarter inch pieces. Place into a large bowl along with grapes, herbs, and garlic, and mix well. Stuff into the duck, cover, and roast at 350°F until done - about 2 hours. Remove stuffing from duck and place in a saucepan over medium heat. Add pan drippings, wine, spices, and salt. Bring to a low boil and simmer for about 5 minutes. Serve hot.

THE HAUNTING OF THE LORDLY LION

Ed Greenwood

Yarlin held up his tankard, squinted at it critically, then peered into the gloom in the direction of the innkeeper. "Uld, is this the *best* you can manage? Ale from Talask, yes? Aftertaste of old toadstools."

"*Distinct* aftertaste of old toadstools," Tarth agreed gloomily, from across the table.

Bald-headed Old Uldrace padded out of the shadows of the dim and silent feasting-hall to loom up over the five old men like a Valduthan gate-titan and ask quietly, "And how often do you dine on old toadstools, any of you?"

"A figure of speech," Yarlin replied gently, "not a lance at your guts, Uld. You know we'll bide with you 'til the end."

"Which isn't a long way off," the innkeeper said grimly. "Another month, lads, mayhap two, and then I'll have to close the doors of the Lion and head for Valduth to seek work. No one wants to stay at a haunted inn."

He turned away. "So enjoy your old-toadstools-Talaskan. It's the last cask in my cellar."

The five topers listened for the soft thud of the door closing behind their host before anyone spoke again.

"There," Old Mrekh said bitterly, "goes a broken man."

"Time was when the Lion was reckoned the best inn between the Rorn Throne and the Talaskan border," Iltagh growled, "not just the only inn in Lyslarr."

"Yet it *is* the only inn in Lyslarr," said one-eyed Donnur, "so when Uldrace gives in, we'll have to ride to Immer's Well or farther to get drink that doesn't come from a sideyard Lyslarran still."

"Hunh," Tarth grumbled. "If I have to bruise my bones as far as Immer's Well, I might as well keep going, and fetch up at shining Valduth and see the King and all—and these metal titans that spring out of his gates and make him not need half as many soldiers as kings did in *our* day. And while I'm there, drink enough that I'll see a lot more than titans."

"The crowding," Yarlin muttered. "The high prices. The *noise*."

Old Mrekh gave him a sour look. "This silence is so much better, hey?"

He looked—they all looked—at the empty feasting-hall all around, with its high hammerbeams and pikes hung up on the walls and moth-eaten stags' heads. Their table was the only one that had a lit candle-lamp and that lacked a thick cloak of dust. It was the only table that had seen use for three months now, thanks to the ghosts.

Five wraithlike warriors in armor those phantoms were, their eyes sad and terrible, ablaze with helpless rage as they came gliding silently from the shadows with drawn swords in their hands. And everyone knew the touch of those phantom blades, no matter that they were more smoke than steel, would drive living men mad or drain much of the life out of one, leaving victims wrinkled, gray, and sickly.

So everyone fled, and word spread, and no guests came to stay at the Lion. The old men of the village still spent evenings muttering over their tankards, but even they had dwindled down to a final five. Five former soldiers of Rornsar, all, spending the king's monthly silver to slake their thirsts.

"It's magic that's done it," Old Mrekh said bitterly, ignoring the roll of Yarlin's eyes and stifled sighs from Tarth and Iltagh. "Magic and those who work magic have brought Rornsar low, and lesser realms, too. In our grandsire's days it was all thews and sharp swords and vigilance, not creeping spells here and sly sorcery there. This haunting stinks of magic, and someone who works magic is to blame. Only once all such have been found out, and killed, will the lands be free."

"This is a song you've sung a time or two before," Yarlin muttered. "Have done, Mrekh. "'Tis not as if any of us can *do* anything about even the most feeble spell."

A floorboard creaked then, far across the room nigh the entrance, and the topers all peered hard into the gloom.

And then a voice they'd all heard before, in years long gone now, spoke quietly out of the darkness. "Did someone mention a song?"

Old Uldrace had heard that tread, and now came through his door in haste with a lantern unhooded, to spill out golden light across the feasting-hall. Whereupon he stared hard, then exclaimed delightedly, "Be welcome, Lord of Song, in my humble house!"

"Flaeryn!" the old men at the table said in pleased and surprised chorus.

"What brings you to Lyslarr?" Yarlin added.

"My wandering legs," was the amused reply. "But tell me, what brings the Lion to this dusty calm, on a night when the yard without should be full of wagons and this hall warm with hearthfire and noisy with cheer and custom?"

They all stared at the bard for a moment, as if he was himself an apparition. Lords of Song seldom stopped in places as small as Lyslarr, these days. The bards of today were too grand for that, despite being but pale shadows of the True Bards of bygone days—the likes of Valandar, Thorast, and Lelaskyn the Tall.

Yet Flaeryn was held by most to the best, or among the best, of those harping now in the Seven Lands. He at least still called in at inns and taverns, rather than traveling in coaches surrounded by well-armed outriders, and going from palace to palace, and high house to high house. And like the lesser minstrels, he still told jests, sang songs, and recounted old tales to all within earshot, not just to the privileged few in grand chambers behind closed and guarded doors.

"It's the ghosts, Lord Flaeryn," the innkeeper answered him sadly. "The Lion is haunted now."

The bard spread his hands with a wry smile. "As long as I've traveled Rornsar and the Seven Lands, and longer, the Lordly Lion has always been haunted. Nigh every inn and tavern is, you know. I see wraiths most folk cannot, when they come drifting out of the shadows to watch and listen. The music draws them, like moths to a flame in the night."

So it does, a cold and baleful voice agreed, out of the darkest corner of the room.

And as Uldrace shrank back and the old men around the table cowered down in fear, silent undeath came gliding through the air, chill moonlight kindling where the moon could not reach. That fell radiance shaped five helmed and armored men from the waist up, naked swords raised ready in gauntleted hands.

Behold us, bard, and tremble, ere you die, the tallest and foremost of the wraith-warriors hissed.

The bard drew himself up, faced the ghosts as they drifted nearer with swords raised in slow menace, parting to encircle him, and chanted in a loud, rich, and calm voice:

Then did the false knights
For traitors' gold
Poison their daggers
Steal nigh the Lion's best beds
And bring death to the Kingsmen
Sir Mordelm
Sir Darmon
Sir Sareld
Sir Amarand
and
Sir Rulorlar
So they never reached Forar's Bridge
And held it not against the foe
Wherefore the army of Talask
Streamed unheralded into fair Rornsar
Sweeping to the gates of tall Valduth
Where great was the slaughter.

When the Lord of Song fell silent, echoes of his voice seemed to roll and rebound about the dark hall, for the space of a breath or two.

During which the tallest ghost came to loom over Lord Flaeryn. *That is not a lay we enjoy hearing, bard*, it said coldly, as its sword swept up on high, ready for a butcher's felling stroke.

"You surprise me not, Sir Mordelm," Flaeryn replied, with no trace of fear, his eyes on the dark face within the helm and not the ghostly blade. The wraith towering above him seemed to flinch at the sound of its name, and its sword came not down.

"Nor you, Sir Darmon," the bard added, turning to face the ghost to his left. It quivered in midair and froze. "Or you, Sir Sareld," Flaeryn added, still turning to his left. And in likewise he named each ghost, and each naming caused a wraith to halt in the air and lose a little of its moonglow— as a glow kindled about the head and shoulders of the bard, and he stood a swordsbreadth taller.

"So tell me now," he asked, in a voice that was gentle yet now seemed filled with the thunder of muted power, "why you've grown so restive now. What irks you so?"

We are oathbound yet, singer!

"That war was long ago, and Emdevarr, the king you swore to serve, is the long-gone grandsire of King Malarnthryn who rules in Valduth now. The bridge you could not guard still stands unguarded, and is still the only span across the deep gorge of the Sarl, but the lords of Talask are no more and the two lands mere old rivals now, not armed foes. So, why now?"

Mordelm's reply was scornful. *Bards trumpet what they like, and ignore the rest, and those who come after never know what was neglected or left out. Our oaths were to guard the bridge AND LET NO HARM COME TO IT.*

The smallest, most slender ghost spake then. *Carters who stopped here when last season was young spoke of King Malarnthryn's plans to destroy the bridge and so sever all possibility of the ambitious satraps of fair Sarthrae, beyond ruined Talask, sending swords on the sly to invade Rornsar.*

The bard shook his head. "Sir Amarand, did not rumor run as wild as winter winds in your day? Tell me now: did you believe every word of it back then? Or knew more than one word in fourscore turn out to be true?"

They were not the only bearers of such tidings. Mordelm's hiss was colder than ever. *We heard it, and heard it again, and it gnawed at us. It gnaws at us STILL.*

"Aye," the bard said wryly. "I've noticed." He strolled to the table, caught up a tankard from a nerveless old hand—Tarth's, as it happened—sipped from it, made a face, and set the tankard back down. "Yet the bridge spans the Sarl yet, and there's no talk in the Castle High at Valduth of breaking it or hurling it down."

He strolled back to stand once more at the center of the ring of motionless ghosts, and asked, "So tell me now, do you want to be released from your vows, and know rest?"

Yes, one of the ghosts—Sir Rulorlar—sobbed.

The other four wraiths recoiled and sought to move away from him, yet clawed the air in vain, pinned in their places like condemned men impaled on a castle gate. Their hissed chorus was as fierce and frantic as storm-driven waves on a shore. *No! No!*

Sir Darmon burst out, *We loved our king, and have tarried in the chill gray twilight between life and death for so long now that to forsake our vows would make our lives all empty waste and mockery!*

Flaeryn nodded. "I quite see that." Then he turned back to the sobbing Rulorlar. "Yet you cleave to your different choice?"

Yes, that ghost sighed.

"Then," the Lord of Song said gently, "I release you from your vow."

And the shade of Rulorlar, looking astonished, drifted floorward . . . but faded away to nothingness before reaching it.

You—You— The remaining ghosts gasped in dumbfounded disbelief, staring at the empty air where their fellow had been—and then staring at the bard.

Mordelm found words first. *Only King Emdevarr can release us from our vows! How is it that you can bind and unbind?*

Flaeryn grew a wry smile and uncased his harp. From the bottom of its case he drew forth spare strings and wax and from behind them something solid wrapped in cloth, which proved to be a rough stone the size of his palm. Setting it on an empty table near at hand, he drew a hand across the strings of the harp, adjusted the two that had slid out of tune with the rest, and began to play.

The tune was slow and soft and unfamiliar. It sounded very old, and betimes swelled to echoes where no harp should have been able to awaken echoes.

And the stone on the table began to glow.

"Tell me, true knights of King Emdevarr," the Lord of Songs asked, his voice quiet yet cleaving his harping to reach the ear as clearly as a thunderous shout, "would you like to guard Forar's Bridge *at* Forar's Bridge?"

The ring of ghosts quivered as if stirred by a high wind, then rushed up close to tower over the bard. At that, the old topers at the table erupted in a sudden scramble, in a clatter of upset and falling chairs.

We BURN to do so, Mordelm hissed.

Ghostly eyes flared like flames within those dark helms, and the topers moaned and trembled in fear from where they were now crouched under their table.

"Then join in the song," the bard bade the wraiths now ringing him close. "You'll find it simple."

He lifted his voice in what sounded like a man talking mournfully at a funeral, more than singing:

Life's but a brief song,
Unlife but echoes
We come from shadow,
We return to shadow,
All we know is shadows,
All our strivings shadows
Only mountains endure
Yet be more than shadows
Be song, be flame.

Flaeryn raised his hand in a signal, marking the cadence of the song with his fingers, and then opening his fingers in a welcome. As he repeated the verse, the ghosts joined in, one by one, their voices cold and clear.

Life's but a brief song,
Unlife but echoes
We come from shadow,
We return to shadow,
All we know is shadows,
All our strivings shadows
Only mountains endure
Yet be more than shadows
Be song, be flame.

The bard let his hand fall, and murmured, "Aye, be flame."

In eerie silence, their burning gazes fixed on him all the while, the ghosts dwindled down into the stone. And were gone.

It drank them in, pulsed once or twice, then settled down to a steady glow that was brighter than before.

And Flaeryn sighed and started to put his harp away.

The old men peered uncertainly at him from under the table. Beyond it, he saw Uldrace had found a handaxe from somewhere, and was now lowering it uncertainly in trembling hands.

"The Lion," the Lord of Song assured the innkeeper gently, "is still haunted. By gentle Florimel, the dog that noses doors open, the unsleeping pantry maid, and all the rest. Just not by five murdered knights who perished under this roof with their oaths unfulfilled."

Yarlin led the slow and cautious crawl of old men out from under the table, to peer warily at the stone. "Just how did you... how did they come to be, ah, sucked into yon rock?"

"Magic," Old Mrekh snarled, still under the table. "Fell magic."

Flaeryn smiled and inclined his head in a slow nod. Then he turned to Uldrace.

"Keeper of the Lion, may I ask a favor of you? The loan of a horse?"

The innkeeper blinked.

"It's a long ride to Forar's Bridge," the bard explained. "I'll return it, I vow—or thrice its price, if some misfortune should befall it."

He picked up the glowing stone. "And I think I can promise you that these ghosts will trouble you no more."

Old Uldrace stared at the Lord of Song. "Who *are* you?" he whispered.

Years agone, Old Mrekh had been a scout and a leader of forays in the night; he could move silently when he wanted to. Out from under the far side of the table he'd stolen, and over to the wall to pluck down an old pike, then sidle closer, as soundless as a stealthy butterfly.

Now he sped, uttering no war-cry as he came charging at Flaeryn from behind, the still-wicked point of the pike lifting to take the bard under the ribs as the Lord of Songs heard and turned.

There was no blood. Even as men caught their breaths sharply all around, Old Mrekh stumbled right through his target, pike and all, as if the bard wasn't there.

Lord Flaeryn never even glanced at his would-be slayer. He smiled wryly at the aghast innkeeper, and then at the old soldiers beyond him, and told them, "I am, as you can see, somewhat ghostly myself. We're bound to the land, we kings of Rornsar. I was King Emdevarr for so long that I fell into the habit of it, and never wanted to give it up. So on the day when the poisoned daggers of false nobles took my life, I never did."

They stared at him in dumbfounded silence, mouths hanging open in a silent, frozen chorus of astonishment.

Hefting the glowing stone in his hand, the bard asked gently, "That horse, please? Staying solid—particularly when I must become a wraith in great haste, then fight my way back to solidity again, as now—is exhausting, but I find it's another habit I've grown quite fond of." He turned and gave Old Mrekh a smile and a nod, and added, "No hard feelings, old soldier. I'll spread the word that the ghosts with swords are gone from the Lion for good. And that Forar's Bridge stands not unguarded."

And hanging his harp back up on his shoulder, he walked out of the Lordly Lion into the night.

Out of the shadows, the echoes of his harping stirred and rose, until the feasting-hall filled with the music of an unseen harp.

Long after Old Uldrace had fetched his best horse, and the Lord of Song had departed, the harping lingered in the dark feasting-hall.

As one by one, long-cold candles lit themselves, their flames dancing to the tune.

Pear Custard

In the side yard of the Black Dragon Inn is an old pear tree, and every autumn it produces bushels of golden-yellow pears. When those pears are ready for picking, the guests at the inn are usually treated to a dessert of sweet pear custard. If they're very lucky, and if the cook is in a particularly good mood, the custard will be topped with rosewater scented whipped cream.

4 to 5 pears
1 cup white wine
1/2 cup sugar
4 egg yolks
1 tsp. cinnamon
1/4 tsp. ginger

Peel and core the pears. Cut them into small pieces and place in a saucepan along with the white wine. Bring to a boil, and simmer until pears are soft - about 15 minutes. Allow to cool and then grind with mortar and pestle (or in food processor). Mix with remaining ingredients in a saucepan. Heat until it boils and becomes very thick - it will resemble oatmeal in texture. Serve warm or cold.

VOICE OF THE REVOLUTION

Sarah Hans

I'm not sure what to expect when I climb the steps to Ivan the Inspiration's porch and knock on the front door. Certainly not the hulking caretaker who looks as if she's been bred by a lost tribe of mountain giants, who answers my inquiry with a grunt and ushers me inside as if I've been expected. Certainly not the small, cramped house, dimly lit and dusty, every available space stacked with books and magazines and crumbling newspapers.

Perhaps most shocking and least expected, however, is Ivan himself. He is seated in a wheelchair, as he had been in the photo stills from his last interview fifty years ago, his nonfunctioning legs covered with a plaid blanket, gazing out at the sun rising over the beach. Even the sweater he wears is the same, though perhaps a little more threadbare. And the face he turns to me, smiling, is just as appears in every history book: handsome, friendly, sad, with a single scar running down one cheek, a tell-tale shimmer of metal behind the parted flesh.

"Welcome," he murmurs, gesturing to a chair. As I sit, I realize that the little table that separates us has been laid out with a small but impressive breakfast: a pot of tea, a bowl of oranges, bread so freshly baked it still steams, a little ramekin of butter and a dish of real, actual honey.

"My name is Darius Greensword," I say, my mouth watering despite my best efforts to stay professional.

Ivan laughs, and the sound sends a chill of frisson through my chest. "Please, eat. Daisy will be disappointed if you don't; she doesn't get to cook often."

I help myself to bread and butter and honey. Daisy the hulking nurse appears with a little carafe of real milk, and I pour myself tea with milk and honey and marvel at the authentic flavors, at the luxury.

"Being a war hero has some privileges," Ivan tells me in his mellifluous voice.

We watch the sun hoist itself over the horizon, sparkling across the ocean and gilding the sky gold and pink before the colors are obliterated by morning brightness. I finish my breakfast and savor a moment that tastes like honey and butter and tea with real milk, the sun warm on my skin.

"This place truly is paradise," I offer. "I can see why you chose it for your retirement."

Ivan nods and smiles his famous smile, an indulgent, paternal smile that inexplicably makes me feel warm behind my solar plexus. Suddenly I understand why, one hundred years ago, people fought and died at his side. I understand the love and loyalty he infamously inspired.

"You were expecting me," I say, wiping my hands and taking out my recorder.

"Not you, specifically. But someone, yes. Someone with questions. It has been one hundred years, has it not?"

"Since the Grand Revolution, yes. And it seems appropriate to revisit your part in it, on the hundredth anniversary."

Ivan looks out across the ocean and I swear his expression is suffused with sorrow and regret. It's not possible, I tell myself, but still...

"Regrets?" I ask.

"I see no amount of butter and honey and tea can deter you from your purpose," he replies.

"I'm a reporter to my core, I'm afraid."

He nods once, slowly, and fixes me with an implacable stare. For a moment, he doesn't move at all, and I'm reminded that he's human only because the government has declared him so. No human could be so immobile, without breath or blinking or even a stirring of hair. Then he moves again, and I feel a chill of fear, and I wonder if he's developed a tic, or if he's trying intentionally to frighten me. It seems rude to ask, and I'm not sure I want to know the answer, anyway.

"What do you want to know, Mr. Greensword?" Ivan's famous hands appear, and when he steeples his fingers his brass fingertips click against one another.

I stifle a gasp, but the words tumble from my mouth before I can stop them. "Your fingers really are..."

"Brass? Yes. The polymer flesh was not intended to play instruments. It wore away within hours when I picked up that first ukulele."

"But with those brass fingertips you were able to play for hours on end."

"Days, even."

"Days? You never grew tired?"

Ivan's smile wanes a little; I daresay it becomes rueful. "I don't become tired, Mr. Greensword. I require charging periodically, but my battery cells can last for months without a charge and years without replacement. I daresay my longevity and inexhaustible nature were in large part responsible for my ... popularity."

"You became a rallying symbol for the revolution."

"I suppose you could say that."

"That's what the history books say."

He shrugs noncommittally. "Then it must be true."

"Tell me about that. About the revolution."

His fingers click together in a staccato rhythm, a soft timpani drumbeat. "You already know that part. Everyone knows that part."

"Many people born since the end of the revolution don't know your story as well as you might think. All we know is what we learned in history class."

Ivan smiles indulgently and leans back in his chair. "I was created to be a glorified music box by Declan Smythe. Of course, humanoid music boxes of a similar nature had been produced for decades before my model was introduced, but Smythe's work was a revelation. In addition to being a programmer and inventor, he was an accomplished musician and composer himself. He added something to the mix that previous developers had not thought to add, something that made my generation of synthetics superior to all others: emotion. Our performances were like nothing humanity had seen before, perfect in every way. Where previous models could only mimic the quality of real human performances, we could produce true, heartfelt emotions.

"And so we conquered opera houses and theaters across the globe. Our acts were considered unique expositions, examples of humanity's most impressive accomplishments. I sang with some of the greatest *chanteuses* of the era: Beverly Roden, Veronique Dubois, Jin Ying." Ivan's eyes glitter as he recites these names, and I can almost see the reel of his glory days replaying behind his irises.

"But all things must come to an end, and so our time in the spotlight was short-lived. A mere five years after our introduction the first bombings began, and every living human who could fled the major cities. I was abandoned in a theater in Atlanta, Georgia. The theater was evacuated just before a performance, and I was left in the green room, already dressed in my tuxedo."

I interrupt to ask, "Why didn't you evacuate with the stage hands and the other performers?"

The look he shoots me is surprised, and maybe a little angry, but I'm not sure whether it's because I interrupted his story, or because I asked a forbidden question. "No one informed me." His tone is full of genuine heartbreak. "They left me behind like a common prop."

I am stunned into silence for a moment.

Ivan picks up the story from where I interrupted him. "The bombs started falling and I didn't know what to do. Wartime procedures weren't part of my programming. Luckily, however, I had centuries of stories, films, music and epic poems stored in my hard drive which I could reference. So I gathered the theater's most valuable items— jewelry, rare instruments, that sort of thing—and went into the basement."

"How long were you in the basement?"

"Three hundred years."

"Three hundred forty-six years, correct?"

"And four months, eighteen days, nine hours, fifteen minutes, forty-five seconds." Ivan's brass fingertips click.

"How did you survive all that time without power?"

"I brought all my battery backups into the basement with me, and they were fully charged. I ran essential systems only, to conserve what little power I had."

"And you watched movies."

"In a manner of speaking. I watched films, listened to operas, memorized poetry, and read novels. All the greatest works of human history are here." He taps the side of his head. "Well, the greatest works of the English-speaking world, anyway. I also know quite a few Italian and French operas, and even a few Spanish and Chinese ones. Declan Smythe uploaded those so that I could perform them."

"Why do you think that Smythe uploaded so much information into your databanks?"

"That's a question you'd have to ask him. He never revealed the reason to me but … I'd like to think he was preparing. He was a very wise man."

"So you think he knew about the war."

"I think he knew that I would be eternal, and that most of the works of art created by man have been lost to the vagaries of time."

I pause, contemplating the wisdom of this statement. "Tell me about what happened on that morning, the morning you were found."

Ivan nods and fidgets with the blanket in his lap. "I was buried under the rubble of the theater. I was dug out by treasure hunters, looking for loot now that the remains of Atlanta were no longer dangerously radioactive. A man named Reuben Firesworn and his teenage sons pulled me out. They were shocked when they discovered me, I can assure you! They didn't know what to make of me at first, especially when I started speaking to them in an ancient tongue."

"Ancient tongue?"

"English had evolved quite a bit in three hundred years, especially without any electronic means to contact far-away speakers."

"So they couldn't understand anything you said. Could you understand what they were saying?"

"Not at first." He chuckles. "But I speak eight languages. It took some time, but I was able to learn."

"And you taught them the old language."

"I did. They took me back to their encampment in a junkyard, and there was some heated debate about what to do with me. I feared being scrapped for metal parts, so grabbed some scrap metal and wire and constructed a ukulele while they debated."

"Why a ukulele?"

"It is a small instrument, relatively simple in construction compared to others. I needed something I could build quickly. Eventually, despite Reuben's best efforts, the group decided to take me apart. Luckily when they came for me I had completed the instrument and began to play and sing. My voice moved them all to tears, though they couldn't understand the meaning of the words. My singing and playing convinced them I was more valuable whole than as parts, and after that they treated me like a human member of their tribe rather than a machine."

"What song did you play?"

"'Imagine,' by a twentieth century composer named John Lennon. Perhaps the most emotional rendition of it the world has ever heard."

"Why do you say that?'

"I feared for my life. I wasn't just playing for my supper or for enjoyment. I was playing for the right to exist." His words are heated and he clenches one fist in emphasis.

"What did you do after the song?"

"Made friends. Tried to find my place among the looters. I helped them weave nets, repair weapons, and make food, at first. But eventually I found my place as a teacher and entertainer. During the day I taught the younger members of the tribe writing and reading and mathematics and, of course, music. We built instruments from scrap we found around the junkyard, and the most enjoyable part of my day was teaching the little ones to play. During the evening I performed the greatest ballads known to mankind. My fingertips wore away, but I didn't miss them, because without them my playing only improved."

"How did you sustain yourself?"

"Declan Smythe was a very wise man, and programmed me with any number of documentaries and instructional videos. I built a windmill and a small generator and recharged all my battery cells. One had expired during my encasement underground but the rest were still usable, with modifications. Naturally, my tribe wanted to know how I accomplished this feat, and so within a year we had their entire encampment electrified. Of course, the windmills had to be taller, and this attracted other looters. Some came to fight us; others came to join us. Our numbers swelled."

"How many people?"

"When I joined there were a handful of families, about 48 individuals, give or take. People died and were born all the time, and new members came and went, so the numbers fluctuated. At our peak we played host to four hundred twenty-nine people. But many of them were sick, hugely pregnant, or small children, so they were useless in the final battle."

"Tell me about the final battle."

Ivan hesitates, staring into the distance for a few seconds. He's once again eerily motionless. Then he says, "Our group grew large enough to attract the attention of the Peoples' Land Army. That's what they called themselves, but don't be tricked, Mr. Greensword. They were nothing more than bullies, men with weapons who banded together, using those weapons to harass and intimidate other groups. They claimed to be the last remnants of the government collecting taxes, but in truth they were doing little more than stealing from communities that had little left to steal." He ejects these words through gritted teeth, his fingers clenching the armrests of his wheelchair. "The Land Army slaughtered the men and women of my tribe, and my tribe slaughtered them in return. Our numbers were too great for them to defeat us easily, but their firepower was too impressive for us to defeat them. It was a feast for the carrion birds on both sides. When the smoke cleared and the fighting stopped, there were no warriors left. The village and the Land Army were destroyed, utterly. So the responsibility to care for the helpless fell upon my shoulders."

He turns to look at me, his gaze intense. "Do you know what that kind of responsibility is like? I wasn't built for that, I wasn't programmed for it. I was crushed by the grief of losing my newfound family, and I had to find a way to rebuild." He shakes his head. "It was too much. I couldn't bear it. So I picked up a guitar, threw my battery cells in a wagon tied to my belt, and started walking."

"And the remnants of your tribe followed."

He nods. "Those who could. Mostly children. They followed me right on my heels and sang in those clear, sweet voices of theirs. They were parentless and homeless, and still they sang. They would have followed me over a cliff, and there were times I considered leading them there, to their deaths. For surely this life was too cruel. Surely it would be a mercy to simply end their suffering now. But in the end, I couldn't do it. My programming wouldn't allow it." His smile is rueful. "When I started walking, I had no goal. I only wanted to express my pain and heartache in the way that came most naturally to me."

"Instead, you ended up saving civilization."

"In a manner of speaking. As we walked we gathered more and more people. And, to my great surprise, we gathered androids and robots, too. Many had been dormant for years. Others, like me, had been adopted by clans of foragers and looters who had eventually been wiped out by the Land Army or disease or the monsters that roamed the radioactive forests. When they heard my song, they were drawn to me, like moths to the proverbial flame. And it was they who cared for the children. I walked slowly, because walking too quickly damaged the quality of the song. This also had the benefit of making it difficult to leave anyone behind. My followers would stop to rest, so the androids could gather vegetation or hunt, and then once the children were fed, or once they had slept, they would catch up to me. There were nearly as many androids as there were children. The nannybots were, of course, the most valuable in those circumstances, but there were other models that proved surprisingly useful, especially mobile units who could carry several children at once. And so we became a teaming ocean of man and machine, living in harmony, caring for one another, and sweeping across the continent. Word spread of our walk, and those who couldn't join us would offer us alms. As if we were on some holy pilgrimage."

"What route did you walk?"

"I followed the remnants of streets and freeways. Eventually a team of teenagers walked ahead of me with machetes, cutting a path. If we came to a place with a collapsed bridge or an impassable body of water we would turn around and go back to the next fork in the road, and go a different way. Always singing. If I backtracked, people would take the opportunity to touch me as I passed. And it was on one of those backtracks that I realized our numbers had grown into the thousands."

Imagining the scene makes me breathless and my voice is a whisper when I say, "Thousands of followers."

"Thousands of voices. All raised in whatever song I chose. It was a powerful moment. And that's what broke the spell. That's what made me realize I could change things. I could return us to civilization. I could prevent what happened to my tribe from ever happening again. And then I had a goal: to find us a new home."

"Did you have a destination in mind?"

"Not precisely. I was determined to walk until I found somewhere untouched by the devastation. It took four years of walking, but eventually I found a city nestled in a valley, abandoned but not radioactive, some of the buildings still intact, surrounded by what had once again become arable farmland. By that point my followers numbered in the tens of thousands. We needed a lot of room." He smiles at the memory.

"New Atlanta," I say.

"Yes. When I stopped singing and turned and announced that we had found our new home, my followers were shocked. They had followed me out of desperation, but after four long years they'd lost any hope there was a destination. They were in it for the journey. A few even picked up instruments and resumed walking. Years later they would return with yet more new citizens for our growing civilization. Those young troubadours became some of my most trusted lieutenants."

"How did you determine who would be in charge in New Atlanta?"

"Democratically elected government, of course. Even if I had not been elected president four times, there would be no other way."

He says this in such a matter-of-fact tone that I have to laugh. "No, of course not. Now, as you know, the civilization started in New Atlanta has grown several million strong, and much of North America has been reclaimed. Many people credit you with saving humanity. What say you to that?"

Ivan chortles. "I didn't save anyone. I simply gave them hope, and reminded them of their own accomplishments. I knew humanity had been great once, and I knew it could be again. I simply believed in them. In *you*, in *us*. Besides," now he waves one brass-tipped hand dismissively, "it's not as if ours was the only society to be resurrected. I hear China is doing quite well."

"Not as well as we are, and many people credit that to your influence. But..." after this moving, enlightening conversation, I'm loathe to bring up the topic my editor sent me here to mention, but I think of my assignment and press on. "There are those, especially fiscal conservatives in the senate, who would like to see the war heroes who still remain stripped of their privileges and even their status as humans."

"And that is why I agreed to do this interview, Mr. Greensword."

"What do you have to say to those representatives who believe supporting immortal war heroes has become too costly?"

Ivan is thoughtful for a moment, picking at his blanket, before propping his elbows on the armrests of his wheelchair so he can lean toward me. "We earned our humanity. I'd like to see even one of those illustrious representatives do the same. Carry a child on your back for four years. Walk from one end of the country to another, searching for a homeland. Fight off monsters and the Land Army. Risk your own existence for the benefit of a species to which you can never truly belong. Watch children die despite your best efforts, of hunger or disease or monster attacks, or because they threw themselves between you and tanks driven by men who claim to be more human than you are." He pounds the table with one fist and the teapot rattles.

I can only gape at him in surprise. No words will come to my lips.

When next he speaks, Ivan's voice has been transformed. It's several octaves higher, and I realize with horror it's the voice of a child. "You have to live, Ivan. You have to live because you're forever. If you die, we die. All our stories, our songs, our memories. You have to live." He utters a rattling gasp, the child's final breath, and I feel like vomiting.

Ivan's eyes narrow and his regular baritone returns as he growls, "I have hundreds of those voices. I have recorded all their songs of despair and horror as they lay dying, freezing to death in the winter, wasting away from dehydration in the summer. Weeping over the disfiguring mutations of a newborn babe, or the radiation burns covering the body of a small child. Crying because there is no food for their growling, distended, empty bellies. My android brothers and I remember when no one else can, when no one else wants to.

"Do you not wonder why I have never had my legs repaired? Because those who lost their lives in the battles with the Land Army, those who died on the four-year trek across the continent, those who lost limbs and loved ones in those first perilous days of New Atlanta, they can never get back what they gave up. Humans don't get to repair themselves and go on. Humans have to suffer. I am human, Mr. Greensword. And perhaps I am more human than any man who was born such, because I choose it."

I blink at him in panic as he bares his teeth at me. The rumors about his madness are true, I realize, glancing toward the exit.

Daisy the nurse appears and places one firm hand on Ivan's shoulder. His face returns to its usual serenity and he leans back into his chair and gazes out across the ocean, his eyes blank. She nods her head to me and I scramble to gather my things and hurry from the table.

We make our way through the dark labyrinth of the house.

"There's so much I didn't get to ask him," I confess as Daisy opens the front door.

She shakes her head, her expression stoic.

"Why doesn't he have those troubling memories removed? He could be free of them, and he could conquer the theaters and opera houses of the world again. Even with broken legs…"

She shakes her head again, as if dismissing my question, but after a moment she answers me. Her voice is deep and rumbling but surprisingly melodic. "To remember." She reaches down and places her hand on my shoulder just as she did with Ivan. Her grip is powerful and instantly quells my questions, as if by magic. "If you were the only one who remembered all those people, all their stories, would you choose to forget?"

"Those memories are driving him mad," I reason.

Now she nods and pats my shoulder as if I'm a particularly clever dog. "Because he's human." She gives me a gentle shove out the door and closes it behind me before I can ask her any more silly questions.

I stand on the porch for a moment, considering all the arguments made in recent days for why Ivan's citizen status should be removed, for why his war hero privileges should be revoked. I came here believing he was little more than a glorified music box, a databank dressed up like a person.

Now I'm not so sure.

Milk and Sugar Bread

On most days the bread served at the Black Dragon Inn was bought from the baker's shop down past the mill, but for special occasions the cook will sometimes get up extra early and make braided loaves of slightly sweet bread.

    2 tsp. yeast
    1/2 cup warm water
    3 1/4 cups flour
    1/2 cup sugar
    1/2 cup milk
    3 Tbsp. rosewater
    1 Tbsp. butter
    3 egg yolks

Mix yeast with warm water (about 100°F), and a pinch of sugar, and allow to rest until it is active - about 10 minutes.

Meanwhile, combine milk, rosewater, butter, and egg yolks in a saucepan and mix well. Heat gently for about 5 minutes, but be careful not to let the eggs overcook and form into clumps.

When the yeast mixture has a little bubbly froth on top, combine the flour and sugar in a large bowl and add the yeast. When well mixed, add the mixture from the saucepan and stir until it forms a soft dough. Turn the dough out onto a floured surface and knead until smooth and elastic - about 10 minutes. Place back into a greased bowl, cover, and let rise in a warm place an hour, or until the dough has doubled in size.

Punch down the dough, divide into three pieces, and form into braided loaf. Cover and let it rise again until doubled in size. Bake at 350°F until golden brown - about 20 minutes.

REMEMBERING WELL

Donald J. Bingle

Thank the gods, the tale was finally concluding.

"'I die happy and with honor,' sayeth the hero, 'for I knowest thou art mortally wounded, vile worm. My quest is, thus, complete and, having died in battle, I shall be welcomed to the Gilded Halls of Tenbokah and be much celebrated by my brethren left behind in Lusifaria.' And, with a last, beaming smile, our hero closed his eyes and slept the peaceful sleep of the fallen. Whereupon all lived well in Lusifaria and prospered, though they mourned him for all of their days."

Artinius stifled an audible groan and set his tankard of warm mead back onto the raw oak planks of his table at The Unbridled Stallion, attempting to salvage his mood by licking a dollop of honeyed liquid from the edges of his moustache. By all the gods, where did they find this alleged bard? And, once they found him, who cast the spell of confusion that must have led to his hiring? He was but scant improvement over the prior performer, a young bard apprentice who liked to punctuate his childish jokes with pratfalls and magicked farts, whilst shuffling through a small stack of pieces of parchment. The whole spectacle made Artinius ashamed of his profession, yet confident that he could secure a position, himself.

Truth, more than a year had passed since he had last been in the city and a few months more since he had last performed here, but nothing had changed at the establishment ... except the quality of the entertainment. The tables still bore stains he could remember, the barmaids still required corsets cinched tight to shove their sagging breasts up to meet the scooped hem of their low-cut, sweat-stained, blouses, and the meat was still charcoaled at the surface and blood-red at the bone, with plenty of gristle and fat between.

Still, The Unbridled Stallion had once been known for the quality of its itinerant entertainment, but nothing he had seen tonight met the standards of those days of yore. Had he somehow stumbled in on some kind of 'amateur night?'

Finally, he caught the eye of Gus as the tavern's proprietor lugged in a hind-quarter of blackened beef. Apparently the owner was filling in for an absent cook. Artinius half-extended his arm and waggled a finger for the big fellow's attention and got a nose twitch in return. A few moments later, Gus was hauling him out of his chair like another side of beef and squeezing him hard around the shoulders for a trice.

"Artinius, you scoundrel. Not hide, nor hair since solstice a year past. Heard you were working the southern trade route, far as Estinia. What brings you here?"

Artinius did his best to smile back as he returned to his seat. "An old horse, bound soon for your cooking shed, I fear."

Gus furrowed his brow for a moment, as if to explode in anger, but merely leaned down to meet Artinius' ear. "Only in the stew, my friend; never as a main course," he whispered, before bellowing in laughter. "I have an end cut of prime rib straight from the spit, should you be looking for more substance than mead for your stomach."

Artinius dropped his left hand to his belt and jangled his money pouch. Two lonely coins clunked together with the dull thud of base metal. "I'll have to venture the stew, I fear, unless you have a job for a true bard."

One of Gus' eyebrows wandered up. "A true bard? Is that one who speaks the truth? Most of my customers come here to forget the truth of their lives."

"Nay," said Artinius, with a weary shake of his head. "A bard with skills and training, one who enraptures his audience, enthralling them with words that take their minds off their troubles and the quality of the tavern fare, educates them in the history of the world, and transports them to lands of wonder and delight."

Gus sucked on a tooth for a moment. "So, you didn't like the last fellow? That hero death scene was pretty good, seems to me."

Artinius almost shot warm mead through his nose. "Good? It was an obvious and non-credible fabrication."

"How so?" asked the big guy. "Coulda happened that way."

Artinius scowled. "Sit. I'll explain." Artinius knew from their long history that although Gus was simple, he genuinely cared about his customers and was eager to learn. He simply needed to be taught. Artinius finished the dregs of his mead with a swallow. "Nobody dies like that in real life. Beaming a last smile? Closing his eyes and going to sleep? Dying happy and with honor?" He gave Gus a hard stare, but the guy just shrugged as he threw his leg over the back of the spare chair at the table and sat, so Artinius continued. "The hero's left arm had supposedly been torn off, he'd been pushed off a bluff onto the rocks near the dragon's lair, and burned with fire, all before the dragon punctured his breast plate and chest with its teeth ..."

"... as he stabbed the dragon with his sword," interrupted Gus.

"... as he thrust his sword at the roof of the mouth of the dragon." finished Artinius. "The hero wasn't happy and beaming. Not possible. At best he was grimacing while breathing ragged, shallow breaths, blood foaming at his lips, his bowels loosing into his trous beneath his plate as he died a miserable, lonely, stinking death. And how does our alleged hero know the dragon is mortally wounded? A dragon is tough to kill. It breathes fire. The roof of its mouth must have the strength of a bricked fireplace."

"Gods, you're depressing," murmured Gus. He grabbed the mead off a passing barmaid's tray, refilling Artinius' tankard, then swigging a mouthful of his own straight from the wooden pitcher. The big fellow wiped his mouth with his sleeve. "It coulda happened that way, I suppose, but I like my guy's way better. And who's to know?"

"Exactly!" shouted Artinius, thumping his tankard down hard and spilling some of its sweet nectar. "No one could possibly know. This story can't possibly be told. The knight dies without telling his tale to anyone. The fight was in the desolation of The Forbidden Mountains, from which no one has ever returned. There were no witnesses, save the allegedly 'mortally wounded' dragon, who would not be giving history this spin if he lived to tell it. No one in Lusifaria knows, or possibly could know, if the knight is dead or alive and, if he is dead, whether he died in battle or in bed from wasting disease. It's all just made up. There's no history to it at all."

Gus fluttered one greasy, beefy hand at him. "So, you don't like this guy's style. It's a matter of individual taste, that's all."

"Don't give me that, Gus. The guy before was no better. His stories were short and stupid. His magic was crude and lame. And he seemed to have trouble remembering what he was doing or what he was going to do next. Very unprofessional. He just filled the frequent pauses sorting through a bunch of small sheets of parchment. What was that all about?"

Gus looked up from his mead suddenly, both eyebrows now high on his forehead, above the sticky ring of froth where the far side of the pitcher had touched during one of his quaffs. "What do you mean?"

"I meant what I said. What's the parchment all about?"

"He has notes on the parchment about his various stories. He was reading them to remind himself what he wanted to do next in his act."

"He reads?" Artinius wasn't an idiot. He knew people who read, of course. Priests, mostly. A few wealthy businessmen and bureaucrats. Magicians, of course, but only those who practiced spells much more advanced than bards ever managed.

"Of course he reads. Almost everyone in town has been taking lessons for the better part of a year. The acolytes at the new temple, opposite the jewelers' row, give lessons for free. And the Baron has declared reading as an economic boon to the city. He reduced taxes by two percent for any who can demonstrate a capability when the tax collector comes to call. Everyone's taken to it. I find it a help in my business, too." He winked an eye at Artinius. "Helps me keep track of supplies and whatnot. Don't have to remember every deal I make with the stables ... er ... I mean, stockyards."

Artinius furrowed his brow. "A city in which everyone reads? How bizarre and fantastic. You mean no one memorizes anything anymore?"

Gus emptied the rest of the pitcher into his gaping maw. "Why would they? Takes time and effort. Instead, you can just grab a piece of parchment and a quill and write down anything you need to remember. It's right efficient, it is."

Artinius found himself shaking his head as he thought it through. "But, if you should lose the parchment or it should be destroyed by fire, then all is lost forever, because no one remembers."

Gus looked about, either making sure that things were running smoothly without his constant supervision or, perhaps, trying to spy an approaching barmaid with another pitcher he could filch. "Loss is always a risk. If you should drink yourself blind here tonight and ... after settling your tab ... fall off your chair and knock your noggin and die, how many tales are lost forever inside your head?" He lunged suddenly and snagged another pitcher from the tray of a barmaid a full row away. "Writing's easy to copy. Do it, meself, when I'm taking lessons at the temple. Easier than memorizing. And you can disperse the copies most anywheres."

Artinius frowned. Memorization did take a lot of effort, especially for the longer, epic tales. It was the reason most were rhyming and rhythmic, to help the teller remember the tale. He shoved the thought away. This was all very interesting, but he came here to get a job. "But, certainly, your clientele craves to hear the classics, to learn some history. I see none of that in tonight's performances."

"I suppose there's some nostalgia, especially among the older folk, but I can't imagine the young farm lads got any use for the historical stuff anymore."

"They don't care about history?"

Gus chortled. "Youngsters never do. Think they know it all and they'll live forever. Besides, they've got no attention span for it these days. The thing about writing is that everything you want to know is available in a writing somewheres—whether it be the temple or the City offices. What's the point of listening to an epic history for an hour or two, when if you ever need any information about it, you can just look it up, slappity-dash, in a minute or three?"

Artinius looked at his friend in shock. "But how will they know they need information about the tale if they've never heard the history in the first place? And what about poetry and the art of the performance? This writing fad could be the death of history and artistry both."

"Time's change, Artinius." Gus stood up from the table and began to turn toward the kitchen.

Artinius realized the conversation was at an end. His friend was leaving to attend to business. "But, certainly, Gus, some of your patrons appreciate the old ways of entertainment and learning." Artinius tried his best to keep any hint of desperation from his voice, but to his practiced ear he knew an overtone of begging had tinged his words. "You have multiple acts. Some variety in tone and context would certainly be welcomed by the crowd."

Gus turned back to face him and rubbed at his upper lip with his right hand. "I always did fancy 'The Quest for Lady Trillium's Favor in the Realms Most Dire.' It was right pretty ..." He stopped and quickly looked from side to side, as if checking to see whether anyone heard what he had said. "... meaning it had plenty of action and some sexy bits, too." He paused. "Sunday evening crowd skews older. Food and board through Monday noon, and any tips you get from the floor, for a performance of 'Lady Trillium.'"

'The Quest for Lady Trillium's Favor in the Realms Most Dire' was one of the finer pieces Artinius had ever performed, to be sure, but he hesitated to take up Gus' offer. The requested tale was beautiful, no doubt, but it was a four-hundred quatrain epic poem. One that he had not performed for more than a decade.

His stomach growled.

"I'd be happy to include some excerpts from 'Lady Trillium' in my performance ..."

Gus shook his head. "The full epic or nothing at all ..."

"It's ... it's four-hundred quatrains ... I ... I'm not ..."

"... not sure you remember it?" Gus fixed him with a stare. "If only it were written down some place."

That clinched it. "Not at all. I was just going to suggest an intermission in the middle. Should increase sales, of which I think I should also get ten percent."

Gus turned his head away, but Artinius could still see his eyes roll before he turned back to Artinius. "Five percent, but only if you make it all the way through without forgetting."

"It's a deal," declared Artinius.

"It's a bet," replied Gus."

Thank the gods it was only Tuesday evening. Plenty of time to practice his performance and no other responsibilities or distractions to get in his way.

'Twas mid-morning Wednesday, his fast broken, when he gathered himself for a first run-though—a quick dash through the quatrains, without emphasis or emotion, just to cement the words firmly in mind. He stood at the end of his bed, facing the wall, and began to recite. He rattled off the first twenty-four quatrains in a fluid rush of words, falling headlong into the cadence of the poetry, words and images springing forth like the splashing of a babbling brook over a tumbled fall of rock.

How could he forget the glorious words of the poem? He had first recited it as an apprentice more than forty years ago at his first featured gig. He remembered each word as vividly as he recalled his first night jitters, his efforts to time the stanzas to match the rhythmic clatter of dishes being washed in the kitchen stage right, and boosting the volume of his young, clear voice to drown the catcalls of some farmboys at a table near the door. Much time had passed since he had last performed the work, but his confidence was still strong.

Even without effort, his voice sang as the dawn chorus with wonder and beauty and melody, until the twenty-fifth quatrain, when a sudden hush came over the scene, as if the step of a hunter had snapped a twig, causing the forest to silence and cover, as his memory faltered. It was a transition sequence, he knew, betwixt the history and exposition of the opening and the coming description of Lady Trillium, all gossamer and flowers, dappled sunlight playing along her features as she walks through the forest idly musing about how love falls upon one unseen, like the dew at night ... No, he was skipping ahead. Something about the Lady's appearance at the palace fête. Yes. Yes, that was it.

He slowed again midway through the description of Lady Trillium herself, faltering til he remembered that he had once appropriated the section and recited it, as if his own thought, to a maiden fair he had once pursued. He did not remember the quatrains so much from his memorization of the epic poem, as he did recall the memory of that lusty pursuit and all that followed. The heat of passion had burned the winning words of woo upon his mind with a clarity and meaning that poetry could only mimic.

Ahh. The thoughts of an old man. Yet, even a dying ember still burns hot and remembers well the light.

His lustful lies of lyric love propelled him forward through the capture of Lady Trillium and to the first stages of the quest, but he bogged down in the swamp, in the midst of the battle with the Scumwraiths of Torrador. He felt as if the Scumwraiths were sucking at his boots as he attempted to trudge onward, hesitating and halting and pulling words one-by-one. True, the meter and rhyme helped, giving him clues by limiting the infinite realm of what might come next to what could come next, but as midday turned to afternoon, he found himself scrolling through the alphabet, letter-by-letter in an attempt to match words to rhyme ... beating, cheating, greeting, heating, meeting, seating ... until he discovered, rather than remembered, what must come next.

The shadows had marched across the room and were fading in the gloaming when he finally finished, firing off the last ten quatrains in a flurried rush to finish. He was faint from standing, his voice rough from use, his mind weary from searching itself without rest. He wanted nothing but to eat and drink and rest, but this was no time to falter. He splashed some water on his face, not bothering to dry it off before he began once more from the start, trying to impress the epic poem in his mind now that he had fully recalled the words, before they would fade to grey dust as his dreams pursued brighter fare in glorious slumber.

At midnight, he finished the second run-through, then made a point to start up again a third time, silently in his mind, before he fell upon the bed and embraced a welcome sleep, hopeful that his mind would continue on in practice without his body.

On Thursday, he recited the epic tale in its entirety a full six times, stumbling on numerous occasions each of the first five, but pausing only a dozen times, without misspeaking, on the sixth. He ate a small bit of bread and cheese with lukewarm water betwixt each of the iterations.

On Friday, his second attempt was flawless, though merely a monotonistic regurgitation lacking yet in any art. On his third and fourth passes that day, he slowed the pace and punched up his enunciation, rewarding himself with several spoonsful of cool stew and a swig of mead at the end of each pass.

On Saturday morning, he added pauses for emphasis, cozying up to the rhythm of the piece. Sometimes he would stop and go over a quatrain again and again, until he felt that it had made the transition from exposition to art. In the afternoon, he added a tinge of voice for each of the characters. Nothing so bawdy as shouts or falsetto, but merely a hint of differentiation to enhance character. He ventured to the bar for his first full meal of the week in celebration, but grabbed his plate and pint in haste and retreated when the entertainment began.

On Sunday morn, he slept in, then ate a hearty breakfast in an empty tavern before retreating to his room for one final rehearsal. After, he dressed in his best performance clothes, sipped a cup of hot water and honey to coat his throat, and waited for the tap on the doorway that would herald his appointed performance.

Artinius gazed out at the crowd, a moderate conglomeration of farmers and artisans, most nearly as old as he, along with a few itinerant traders, what looked to be an adventuring party, a few of the other bards he had seen—and detested—only a few nights before, and a quartet of robed men at a table in the alcove near the door, backlit in silhouette by the light shining through the real glazed glass window behind them. Gus, himself, was front and center, eager to hear the poem or, perhaps, to pounce on any faltering in Artinius' presentation.

The murmurs of conversation fell to a hush as he began. His eyes played over the crowd as he performed, noting the usual crowd reaction patterns for such epic recitations. Some—most—sat rapt, listening to each word as if precious. Some closed their eyes, in pleasant concentration, not sleep. Some nodded in cadence to the rhyme. Some whispered well-remembered and favorite phrases from prior tellings of the tale. A few, of course, had shorter attention spans, or, perhaps, less appreciation for art. They turned away from the stage and sipped their mead or chewed their food, quietly and respectfully, at least, but uninterested still the same. A few conversed in low tones, but hushed when other patrons nearby glared or cleared their throats. One or two rowdies—his fellow bards in this particular instance—rolled their eyes and made as if to heckle, but Artinius did not tolerate such rude behavior. With a simple motion of his hand—no somatic component necessary—he cast a minor silence spell upon the offenders, forcing them into quiescence or frustrated departure.

The four hooded figures near the window were more curious, but Artinius' need to concentrate on the remembering of his tale prevented him from paying them too much thought. He could not see them well because of the contrast of light behind them, but each would tilt his head down and lean almost imperceptibly toward the table for a few moments, then back, in sequence. One, two, three, four. One, two, three, four. As if dancing, with him providing the music.

Before their odd behavior could distract him further from his performance, from his bet, he turned his head away from them and concentrated instead on his friend and employer, Gus. It lessened his fears and warmed his words to tell his epic tale to someone he knew would appreciate it and would see it through to the very end, listening to every line and to every emotion and nuance between the lines.

The words came easily to him this way. He remembered everything, every detail of his epic tale and every detail of his performances of it. From the jitters of that first time telling, to his numerous performances of it over the years long past—in bars and taverns, on stages and in palace halls, in tents and meadows fair. Even the brief intermission for more food and drink did not distract him from his performance or his audience. As he started up again, he watched as Gus, grizzled and grumpier than most, sat and listened, enraptured by the story, by the words. The big guy's eyes wrinkled at the funny bits, flew wide during the action, grew intent at the more risqué rhymes, and moistened as sacrifice beget tragic loss.

Artnius' chest tightened with pride as he turned toward the denouement as the epic tale whispered to a close. Tears ran down Gus' cheeks as Lady Trillium granted her favor to her dying suitor, who had rescued her from the Realms

Most Dire. As he finished the last quatrain, he noticed that his own cheeks were wet as well.

As the crowd thundered applause, he grew light-headed and the weight of pride pressed down further upon his chest. And suddenly, he was borne away from the world of words to the world of reality as the pressure on his chest grew painful and more painful still. He cried out inarticulately as he fell, the applause faltering amidst gasps from the crowd.

Gus rushed to his side, calling loudly for water, as the pain pressed down on Artinius, darkness flickering at the edges of his consciousness, but Artinius knew that a sip of cool water would not help. He knew what would come next. So, it seemed, did Gus.

"Flawless, my friend," Gus whispered urgently at his ear. "You have won your wager and your audience."

Artinius did his best to smile. "Ahh, but you have won your point, too, my friend." He struggled to maintain his composure, his dignity, for a few final moments. "I die. And 'The Quest for Lady Trillium's Favor in the Realms Most Dire' dies with me."

Gus tilted his head to one side, like a puzzled hunting dog. "Did you not see? Your words will live on."

Artinius' eyesight was growing dim, but still he flicked his eyes about the room. "See? See what?"

"The scribes," replied Gus, tears now streaming down his cheeks. "The scribes by the window. They wrote down every word."

"So quickly?"

Gus managed a smile that Artinius would bet was no better than the grimace he knew was all that he, himself, could manage. "There's four of 'em, y'see. Took turns. First one, first line of the quatrain. Second one, second ... Well, you get it. Right?"

Maybe this writing thing wasn't such a bad idea after all.

And, with a last, beaming smile, Artinius closed his eyes and slept the peaceful sleep of the fallen. Whereupon all lived well at The Unbridled Stallion and prospered, though they mourned him for all of their days.

Hen or Coney in Civey

*One of the benefits of being near many small farms, the
Black Dragon Inn has a ready and inexpensive supply of
rabbits to serve to the customers. The cook likes to stew
them with onions and a little wine to make a flavorful
gravy. He also doesn't skimp on the spices, so on the rare
times when rabbits are scarce and he's forced to make do
with chicken, the customers don't complain.*

4 lbs. chicken or rabbit, cut in large pieces
1 medium onion, chopped
2 Tbsp. olive oil
1 cup red wine
2 cups chicken broth
1/4 tsp. salt
1/2 tsp. black pepper
1/2 tsp. mace
1/4 tsp. ginger
1/4 tsp. cloves
1/4 tsp. cinnamon
1/4 cup red wine vinegar
3 to 4 slices bread

Sear pieces of meat briefly in a large pot and set aside,
using olive oil as necessary. Sautée onions in remaining oil
until tender. Return the meat to the pot and add wine and
spices. Bring to a boil and simmer for one hour.

Remove meat from pot and set aside. In a separate bowl
combine bread, vinegar, and some of the broth from the
pot. Stir until bread falls apart and turns to mush. Strain
back into pot and discard the bread solids. Return pot to
heat, bring to a low boil, and cook until gravy thickens
slightly. Return meat to pot and serve hot.

MAD MADDIE

Kelly Swails

You've all heard the story of Mad Maddie, the woman who has killed more of the Risen than any person alive today. Others tell stories of her bravery and heroics. They talk about the time she beheaded three Risen hungry for her flesh with nothing but a shard of broken mirror. They tell the story of how she earned the name Mad Maddie or maybe they explain about how she blew up an entire stadium filled with the undead. They usually sing one of the dozens of songs written about her as their words lift her onto a pedestal made of legends. No one talks about her beginnings. No one tells why some paintings of her feature high-heeled shoes on her feet. That job is left to me.

Mad Maddie—or Madeline, as I like to call her—lived what could be called a normal life. She grew up in a small town; went to a small school; played sports in school; left the small town behind to go to college in a big city. She used the internet and toilets that flushed. She had a job and paid her taxes. Her story is the same as thousands of other women before the Rising. What made her so different than the others that gave up and died?

Leaving the house scared Madeline so much she didn't do it. Agoraphobia, it's called. Oh, she wasn't always like that. As I said, she lived a normal life until one day she realized her life wasn't normal at all. It happened gradually. Her job allowed her to work from home two days a week, then three, then she took a job didn't require her to go to an office at all. She used delivery services for her food, clothing, and office supplies. She watched movies through digital rental services. She stopped going out to see friends and instead invited them to her house. We're such nomads now and so it's strange to think that someone would stay in one place voluntarily. For Madeline, it wasn't by choice; she wanted to leave. She felt secluded and alone and afraid of what she had become, but an even stronger fear of what lay outside her door made her stay.

If any other storyteller were to tell his tale—if they would allow themselves to believe it enough to tell it, of course—their inclination would be elaborate on just how she had become so scared of the outside world that she chose to withdraw from it. A roving band of rabid wolves, perhaps, or a sexual assault. Neither of those occurred. She didn't almost die in a car accident or get mugged or anything of that nature. Their story would be grand and majestic. The truth is she kept having panic attacks when she shopped or ate at restaurants or rode the train. The attacks embarrassed her, and so she gradually stopped leaving the house.

It all worked according to plan until the Rising. Society hummed along more or less efficiently until humanity got taken out of the equation. Some say the plague started in Africa; others, China; still others, the Middle East. In the end it didn't matter. The dead rose and started eating the living.

Madeline had heard the reports, of course, but during the early days of the Rising the establishment called it an odd strain of the flu. No reason to be panicked; just isolate yourself until the epidemic wanes, which of course didn't faze Madeline in the slightest. The day that Madeline began her evolution into Mad Maddie happened well before the truth went viral on social and conventional media.

Picture the scene: a bright, sunny spring day. Warm enough to let you pretend winter doesn't exist with just enough chill in the air to remind you that you can't ever truly escape her grasp; she just lets you run around for a bit until she freezes your bones again. Madeline had ordered a few pairs of shoes online, and they had just been delivered. She had made a deal with herself, you see; every time she ventured more than ten feet from her front door, she bought a pair of shoes, and not just house slippers and ballet flats, but shoes to wear while living life. Hiking boots. Oxfords with a stacked heel to wear to the office. Navy pumps. That day's delivery included two pairs of strappy heels. A friend had gotten engaged and Madeline wanted to attend the wedding. Last week she's walked all the way to her mailbox without breaking into a sweat or feeling faint, so she bought two pairs.

The closet full of shoes represented her hope that she would live a normal life again. She had no way of knowing that the definition of normal had changed. She didn't realize that her friend was already Risen and so the wedding festivities had been stricken from the calendar. She couldn't have known those red strappy heels would save her life.

Madeline had just opened the shoe boxes when she heard a horrific scream coming from the street. We've all heard that scream a thousand times; it's deep and primal and it sets your soul on edge like nothing else can. It's not just the sound of death. It's the sound humans make when they realize they are, in fact, prey.

Madeline opened the door and watched the delivery man get attacked by two of the Risen. She tried to comprehend what she was seeing and couldn't. Think about the first time you saw the Risen attack the living. It seems like such a long time ago, but we were all naïve once.

The Risen may shuffle and stumble, but when presented with fresh meat, they are decisively nimble. One of the Risen bit the delivery man on the arm; the other went for a thigh, both of which served to disable the man in quick order. Still, Madeline wanted to help, so she ran from the house. As soon as her feet hit the sidewalk—close enough to smell the blood and see the bitemarks—she froze. Her head swam as the largeness of the world pressed on her. Her heart pounded and she wanted to run away but couldn't. Her mouth dried as she tried to take another step. Her vision tunneled and she stumbled, scraping her knees and hands on the rough sidewalk. She knew she was close to passing out, and if that happened she would be next.

She would tell me later that a panic attack prevented her from saving that delivery man. She knows in her head that's not true, that even if he'd escape that man was doomed from the moment the Risen had broken his skin. In her heart she believes she failed him. Mad Maddie has saved thousands of lives. Madeline couldn't save one, and it haunts her.

Madeline's panic ebbed as the delivery man slumped over and the Risen devoured their meal. She stood and backed up—slowly, so as not to disturb them—and once she got inside, closed the door and locked it. Her hands left bloody prints all over the door. The two Risen smelled her blood, of course, but the noise of the lock sliding home reminded them of her presence, and they shambled to her front door.

Madeleine watched them through the small window beside the door; she only backed away when they crossed the front porch and started banging on the door. It was just a matter of time before they made their way in. She ran for the back door, opened it, and put one foot on the wooden stairs that led to the freedom of the back yard. The familiar sweaty nausea overcame her and she cried out. She couldn't leave. In that moment her sanctuary became her prison. She would die at home, which over the past few years had become her most dreaded fear. Dying at home meant the panic had won. Dying at home meant that hope had died long before.

I believe that is the moment Madeline become Mad Maddie. She slammed the back door, and once the dizziness subsided, she grabbed a butcher knife and waited. Risen culture was part of the visual and written mythology of the time—they called them "Zombies"—and so she knew she had to disable the brain, and quickly, before being scratched or bitten. She attacked just as the Risen breached the front door. She lunged for the first Risen, and with everything she had, put the knife through its skull. He went down like a bag of wet sand, gore and muck oozing from the wound.

She stepped away, breathless. The other Risen pushed open the door and tripped over his friend. Madeline's small living room didn't give her much room to maneuver and so she tripped over the coffee table as she backed away. She narrowly missed getting grabbed by the Risen's craggly, knarled hand. Her hip throbbed as she scooted toward the kitchen. She'd already used her only butcher knife, but there had to be something other implements she could use. She got to her feet and rummaged through some drawers. Steak knives, too flimsy; tongs, useless; corkscrew, potential. She grabbed it as the Risen entered the kitchen and attacked.

Madeline didn't hesitate. She thrust the corkscrew at his right eye. Its metal point pushed through the soft tissue but stopped just short of the brain. His eye popped but he didn't slow down. Madeline pushed him away and ran for the living room. The Risen followed, the corkscrew sticking out of his face. Madeline's living room served as her home office; her only weapon would have been a pair of scissors, but they were in her bedroom because she'd used them to remove tags from three shirts that had arrived the day before, fifty feet too far to do any good. She reached for the only thing that could conceivably penetrate the Risen's other eye: the strappy heels that had been delivered minutes ago. She ripped open the top box, tossed the tissue paper aside, and grabbed each shoe by the foot.

The Risen stopped his charge as though he were appraising the situation. Madeline filed this information away for later. When so many others in the media—and later, around campfires—insisted that the Risen were mindless creatures that couldn't think or assess or formulate plans, Madeline remembered that day in her living room. When the Risen saw the four-inch spiked heels in her hands, he paused. He wanted to eat, yes, but he had a self-preservation instinct, which made him and the other Risen much more of a threat.

On that day Madeline used that instinct to her advantage. When the Risen paused, she launched herself at him. She pushed the heel of the shoe in her right hand into his right eye; the eye popped as the heel squished its way in. The shoe met resistance, but she pushed harder, and after a second the heel penetrated its brain.

The Risen froze but didn't fall. Thinking fast, Madeline pulled out the corkscrew and shoved the other shoe into his left eye. When it hit home the Risen twitched before collapsing onto the ground. Immediately, she checked her exposed skin and didn't find a single scratch. Once she realized that she wouldn't be turning into one of them—not imminently, at least—she began to shake. She'd almost died in her home.

Almost.

But she'd fought back and won. Her last safe sanctuary had been destroyed but she'd survived.

Later that night she left her house for the last time. Before she did, she packed two small bags. One held essential clothing and food; the other her weapons. The butcher knife. The corkscrew. And two pairs of strappy heels.

Spiced Wine

On cold nights, especially in the darkest part of winter, the guests at the Black Dragon Inn often like to sit close to the heart with a large mug of spiced wine. The warmth of the wine drives away the chill and the scent of the spices brightens the room.

  3 tsp. sugar
  1/4 tsp. cinnamon
  1 tsp. ginger
  1 tsp. pepper
  1/4 tsp. nutmeg

Place two cups of red wine, along with a teaspoon of the spice mix, into a saucepan and stir until well mixed. If a sweeter wine is desired, add two or three tablespoons of sugar. Heat until warm but do not let boil. Serve hot.

For a non-alcoholic version, use grape juice instead of wine and add one or two teaspoons of red wine vinegar for a bit of tartness. Depending on the sweetness of the grape juice, the amount of sugar may be reduced or eliminated entirely.

The Bard's Tale

74

SAUCE FOR THE GOOSE

Brian Pettera

"So there I was, on my back staring at an eight-foot greatsword with this enormous Rock Troll standing over me. He stops and sniffs and looks at me pack lying off to the side ... We became great friends after that, but before he met me he'd never even had barbecue before, don't you know!"

Faas Pitorum – Traveling Dwarven Tinker

Bravo Cragleaper lolled at his table, idly fingering his half-empty mug of ale. Feet on another chair, his seat tipped back into the corner, he gazed at the middling crowd congregating at the inn that night. He was young for a Dwarf, not yet reaching his first hundredth. His dark, brown hair hung in a short ponytail down the back of his neck. He was dressed in black leather breeches, black leather mountain boots and an ash colored tunic well hidden by the shirt of ring mail casually draped over his upper body. Its coif lay upon the back of his neck like a little hood.

Laughs, jeers and shouts drowned out the smattering of applause that echoed from the small stage set in the near corner near the main door of the Inn. The Last Home Inn didn't rate full time entertainment, but it had a standing policy of offering any traveler a free night's room and board (drinks not included) to anyone that showed enough guts and talent to entertain any of the nightly crowds, large or small. The final arbiter was Nebling Half-Hand, the Inn's proprietor and local talent judge. The squat, full girthed Dwarf was rumored to have lost a couple of fingers in a milling accident when he was younger. That was one of the stories, but he claimed it was a war wound received from an Orc Hunter-Seeker squad in the Grandmon Mountains a few decades ago. His claim was rarely challenged, as there is a definite relation to how one accepted the story, and the amount of drinks Nebling bought in one of his rare, good moods.

Bravo lounged, his short, massive frame showing its great strength by the rolling muscles of his neck and back. His ever-present beard was braided into many little rows and tied off with thin leather straps. Rich brown eyes peered out of furrowed brows tanned from frequent exposure to the elements and were occupied by the current entertainer for tonight. The swarthy youth on stage, who was trying his third song of the evening, went off-key once again, making Bravo cringe and chuckle at the same time. The gangly boy had apologized after his first two songs, claiming that if he'd only had a lute or sitar that he would have done a better job. Bravo doubted this; one had to carry a tune in order to sing, or at least *he* thought so. Not being an expert at singing himself, he had certainly *heard* enough singers in his short eighty-two years of life. After all, bars, taverns and inns were one of his best hobbies.

Raising his mug, he drained the goodly remnants and called for the serving wench to come to his table.

She sauntered over to his table. "And what can I do you out of Sir Dwarf?" she said with a twinkle in her hazel eyes.

Bravo appreciatively eyed the buxom blond serving wench. "Hmmmm, I'll have to think about that a little longer," he said looking her up and down in appraisal "but for now it'll be to bring me a couple more full mugs. What happened to Sally? She was here earlier; I'm kind of used to her after all."

At 5"4 she would have stood eye to eye with Bravo but still be dwarfed by his stocky frame. "She's got a little one now, doesn't work late nights anymore. You're just gonna have to deal with me now." She smiled and stuck out her hand. "I'm Madison, Madison Johns. I'm new in an older sort of way" she said laughing.

He took her firm grip in one of his massive hands. He knew right away she was a woman of substance. He could tell by the strength and the light roughness of her hands. You could always learn a lot from someone's hands. "Well a pleasure Madison, I be Bravo Cragleaper"

Her eyes widened slightly, "Ohhh, I've heard quite a bit about you sir." She grinned even wider, "Some of it even good."

Just then there was scattered applause and not a few hoots and laughs as the grim faced boy left the stage. After motioning him over to join him, Bravo paid Madison with a couple of silver pennies. He expertly flipped a third into the cleft of the serving girl's ample cleavage and gave her a friendly leer. She scooped up the pennies and exited with a smile and a flounce in her step.

The young man sat down at the other side of the table as the Dwarf pushed one of the mugs towards him. The boy's dark-brown eyes shielded a guarded look, which switched to a hesitant smile as he accepted the drink.

"Bravo," the Dwarf said as he unfolded his heavily muscled arms and extended one hand.

The young man took the proffered hand, seemingly impressed by the dwarf's strong, calloused grip. "Thanks, I did the best I could under the circumstances," he replied.

"No, my name is Bravo," he deadpanned. "Leave it to a chucklehead human stripling like you to assume I was cheering on *that* performance," he continued with mild derision.

"Umm, right." The boy coughed slightly into his hand clearing his throat. "I really can sing better than that. I'm just not used to this altitude, and I'm getting over a cold. I also made the mistake of using some new stuff I've been working on, which is really meant to be sung with a lute accompaniment not *a cappella*."

Bravo listened to the boy, sipping his beer while he idly cracked another pork rib with his teeth and sucked out the marrow. When he finished it, he dropped it onto the platter piled high on the table before him. "Right, if you say so boy."

The youth managed a long glance at the platterful of bones and motioned over to the busy Dwarf behind the bar. "He's probably not gonna stake me tonight is he?"

Bravo glanced over at Nebling and back to the young would-be troubadour before him, chuckling. "Him? Not on your life." He pulled a small bag out of one of his many belt pouches and fished out a large silver coin. "He won't, but I sure will." He smacked the coin down on the table in front of his guest. "I can't swear by your singing, but I haven't *laughed* that hard in a long time. As far as I'm concerned, you entertained me. Now, are you gonna tell me your name or do I have to call you 'boy' all night?"

"Alsigg, Alsigg Rabonn at your service sir, Troubadour, Bard and Entertainer." He whistled softly, picking up the silver kradorr off the table, carefully examining the

Dwarven coin. "Thank-you sir," he whispered, turning it over in his hand.

"Like I said earlier, my name is Bravo, Bravo Cragleaper. Now don't go a-gawking on me young mister, umm, Alsigg. Eat, drink, and get a room, not necessarily in that order."

"But sir, this would give food and lodging for a nobleman for a week!"

The Dwarf shook his head in disbelief. "Boy, if you want to be an entertainer, you're going to have to take remuneration in hand, not go off gawking again like someone gave you the crown jewels or something! Sheesh!"

"Alsigg, my name is Alsigg." He paused, looking even younger than the seventeen years he actually was. "Remuneration?"

Bravo rolled his eyes. "You're back to *boy* now. Yes, remuneration. You know, pay? Tips? Recompense?" He paused looking intently at the gangly youth. "Bard huh? Can you even read and write?"

Alsigg looked suddenly uncomfortable. "Well sir, yes and no. Can *you* even read and write?" he challenged.

Bravo laughed. "Elvish, Dwarvish, Common, Orc and eight or ten other human and non-human dialects. Nice try though, now what do you mean by 'yes and no'?"

"Well, I can't actually read and write Common well, but I can in um ..." he paused again, looking sheepishly at the dwarf, "Orcish."

"Orcish?"

"Yeah, Orcish."

"What kind of bard only reads and writes Orcish?"

Alsigg let out a big sigh. "It's a long story."

Bravo looked around mockingly. "I'm not that busy. Besides, you're a bard right? So tell me a story."

Alsigg sighed again, slumping in his chair. "What kind of bard only reads and writes Orcish? An Orcish bard? An

Orcish bard fostered me. He was a mixling. His mother was human and his father was a Great-Orc from the Reaches of Sagratt. I was born near Gilberts, where Groash, my foster father, lived. Down there, half-castes and mixlings, though not common, are more accepted. My parents owned a farm outside of the village. Raiders attacked us. It was a mixed group but mostly Targ. They burned our barns and house. I was only six at the time. Groash was returning from Huntley, another village a few miles away in the other direction from our farm and Gilberts. He had a regular route that he undertook every month, entertaining in about a half dozen local villages. He came when he saw the fire in the distance. As he approached, he heard the yelling of the raiders and saw the fire. Most of the raiders had left with our stock but a few remained, finishing up. My father had hidden me in the slop hole of the swine pen, but they had dogs and I was discovered. A Targ was about to cut my throat when he fell over me into the slop." Alsigg paused to take a breath, emotions stealing over him so strongly that he began to tremble.

Bravo leaned over and laid a hand on his shoulder. "Steady there, Alsigg." He caught the serving girl's attention again. "Madison my sweet! Two more rounds of ale, and bring me a bottle of your best Sgraack, two glasses please don't you know!" Bravo waited for the buxom blond human server to bring the drinks. He poured two glasses of the potent Dwarven whiskey and pushed one over to the distressed young man. "Try this; it'll steady you if anything will."

Alsigg gulped down the drink, coughing a little before wiping his mouth on his sleeve. He took a big breath before continuing. "Sorry, this isn't like telling a saga or ode. All right, so the Targ fell over me into the slop hole, and I couldn't get him off because he was too heavy. Like I said, I was only six, not to mention that he happened to be dead. I heard some grunts and a scream. At first, I thought maybe my Pa wasn't dead after all and that he was trying to save me until I saw Groash pulling the Targ off of me. It was dark and blood was all over him, so I just screamed at the top of my lungs in sheer panic. He wiped his face on the sleeve of his fine tunic, looked at me and said, "That's a fine kettle of slop you've gotten yourself into young Rabonn."

I stopped screaming and hugged him as hard as I could as he pulled me out of the slop hole. You see, I knew who he was. I had seen him many times before, performing for the kids in town. Once, Ma had even had him over for dinner. He loved gooseberry pie. Everyone around knew my Ma made the best gooseberry pie.

Groash took me home with him that night. I guess he didn't know what else to do with me. There were already people coming in from Gilberts. Someone had seen the glow of the fire and sounded an alarm. There had been other raids of late. It was too late though, everyone was dead, except me."

Alsigg looked up, his hooded eyes looking deep into the Dwarf's, whose own were focused on him with raptor like attention. "I didn't have any relatives that I knew of. The people of Gilberts were very kind and set up a fund to send me to the orphanage in Elgin. By then, I had been staying with Groash in town for almost two weeks. When I heard that they were sending me away, I started crying. I cried, I yelled, and I wailed. Finally, Groash covered his ears with his hands and roared, "Enough! With lungs, like that how can I let you go? I guess I'll have to keep you and foster you myself!"

That's how it started. I grew up with Groash; he taught me many things. I learned how to build and repair stringed instruments. I can whittle and build several reed instruments from scratch. I can sight read music and play almost a dozen instruments. I stretched my first hide drum when I was eight. I've read eight books, all Orcish or translated into Orc. I've learned several oral traditions, and he taught me my letters and numbers. Numbers are basically the same everywhere, but letters I learned in Orcish. He was going to teach me Common this spring, but then he died of the croup this past winter. He taught me basic dance, juggling, and how to sing, no matter what anyone thinks tonight!" His hard glance waited for a comment from the quick-tongued dwarf. "I can read a little common because I can speak it, but I really can't write it at all. Not to pry, Mister Bravo, I'm not an expert on Dwarves or anything, but it wasn't my understanding that they are exceptional scholars or linguists."

Bravo looked upon the complex Human before him and nodded slightly. "True, most of the Kruash only speak Kruasha, Common and Orcgrash. That's most, not all. I'm a professional guide who's been around, *and* has a knack for languages."

"Guide?"

"Yeah, I'm a mountain guide. Sort of like one of the rangers of the lowlands except that I work in the mountains. I've also led the occasional caravan, ran hunting groups, brought out prospectors, and done the occasional search and rescue. Once I even guided an expedition of wizards into The Sandarac Range to study," he scrunched up his face to make it all wrinkly, and adopted an old quavering voice, "indigenous species in their natural habitat." Bravo laughed. "Never expect brilliantly intelligent people to get along any better than children."

Alsigg laughed too. He was hungry, and after a little haggling with Madison, he managed to order a platter of ribs, arrange accommodations in a private room, and have someone take his luggage there for him.

A while later, Bravo looked back over at Alsigg, who was just finishing his second order, licking each dab of sauce from his fingers. Alsigg sat back with a beatific smile on his face. "Oh man, the stories about this inn were all the epitome of accuracy, and more. Even I can manage to cook a little, but there must be some magical components in this sauce, it's so incredible. How did this Nebling come by it?"

Bravo smiled. "Nebling? He didn't 'come by it'. This recipe is *his*. You short-lived humans sometimes forget that once a Dwarf starts a project close to his heart, he'll spend untold amounts of time perfecting it. That's what makes us such good craftsmen. He tried some similar sauce a long time ago on The Steppes. The original recipe wasn't too hard to make and the ingredients rather simple. The early product, though, was only pale ghost of the sauce he ended up with." Bravo leaned a little closer to the attentive young bard. "Only took him eighty years to perfect it! The Last Home's ribs are famous. There are a couple of caravans who schedule The Last Home on their route just because there are fools who would actually travel a week from the closest town of any size for a platterful or two of ribs. The pork ribs are bliss, and the barbecued chicken is heavenly, or wherever one's spirit ends up, but the beef baby back ribs," he whistled and smacked his lips, "they are legendary! There are only certain times of the year that Nebling will butcher an entire steer, and when he does, the Inn's rooms will start to sleep double, triple, and even quadruple. It's the sauce of course. Nebling could cook snake in it and it would still command respect. Could, and did!"

Alsigg looked surprised. "You're joking of course."

"Nope, but that's a story for another day."

"Hey Bravo, I'm not going to let you off that easy! Anyway, I'm a bard. Well, almost one, so I collect stories. Since I've already told you one, a personal one mind you, you owe me one now."

Alsigg continued to nag him for several minutes before the Dwarf raised both hands to ward off the insistent bard. "Alright, alright, you certainly have a glib enough tongue when you want one, so maybe there's hope for you yet. I'll save the snake story for another time though. Instead, I will tell you a little more about the Inn and how they got such good beer." Bravo glanced at his now empty mug, turning it over slowly in his hands. "Except that I'm kinda dry right now." He looked meaningfully at Alsigg. "Can't expect me to teach you a story with a dry throat can you?"

Alsigg rolled his eyes. "Dwarves!" He ordered another round, being pretty well set with the change from his kradorr. "Alright, give it up."

Bravo put his feet back up on another chair and leaned it back to the wall as he told the attentive young man a little about The Last Home Inn and its famous barbecue.

"Its recipe was a fairly well guarded secret, but was available to anyone who asked for it. The price? It's simple, only one year's labor at the Inn! The only people who thought the price was too steep had never eaten Nebling's ribs. Every spring a couple of dozen women and men showed up at the Last Home requesting work in exchange for the recipe. He'd choose the four or five most likely looking applicants that passed the withering barrage of questions that he would spring at them. He'd get innkeepers like himself, or their wives (always considered); lowland cooks looking to reap a profit (rarely considered); chefs of note who served royalty or men of great means (sometimes considered); and many others besides. Once, he'd spent the year with a late middle-aged human Brew Master of some note. The first month had been hell as their commanding (or rather, cranky, crotchety and downright stubborn) personalities were too much alike. Nebling had almost dismissed him except that his wife took a real liking to the guy. It wasn't for another couple of months until he found out why.

Nebling's wife, Grunhil, made all of their beer. Before then, their beers, all three of them, had been fair to good but not great. The next malt was outstanding! When he had questioned Grunhil on the great difference between this brewing and the last batch, she merely smiled with a twinkling of her eyes and nodded at The Brew Master. The Human—whose name was Olaf but everyone called him Brew Master—merely bowed at Nebling, beaming with a smile from ear to ear. Nebling had spent the next week questioning all of his customers on the quality of the new beer. The answers were predictable. Everyone loved the improvement on the old beer, and surprise! Grunhil had another new beer to introduce! Nebling declared that the Brew Master had fulfilled his tenure and could depart if he felt comfortable with making the barbecue recipe. It was the first time that anyone had ever been released early *with* the recipe. He was surprised when the Brew Master replied that he still had much to learn about the running of an inn, and if it was all right with Nebling, could he finish out his year. Humbled, Nebling immediately acceded. It was a huge party when the Brew Master finally left. Nebling had even wiped away a tear on his departure. He had learned just as much about life, beer, Humans and business from Olaf as the Brew Master had learned about life, Dwarves, barbecue and inn-keeping from Nebling.

Alsigg stared admiringly at Bravo. "Wow, you really do know quite a lot about the Inn.

Good story, now how much of it is true?"

The Dwarf feigned shock. "Truth? You impale me with the dagger of your suspicion." He snagged Madison as she was rushing by to serve another table. "Honey, Sweetie-Pie, Baby? Could you get me just two mugs of the good stuff? Please?"

It was the pretty, gold-tressed server's turn to feign horror. "Bravo! Don't Baby, Sweetie-Pie me you lecherous, old skunk! If you want a couple of Olaf's, you have to go through Nebling! You of all people should know the rules!" Away she went in a huff.

Alsigg grinned. "Quite a way you have with women there, Bravo. Every answer I get from you only brings up a lot more questions. What rules? And why should you of all people know them?"

"Well, the rules are that the Olaf, which is what the really good new beer is called, is only brought out on holidays and special occasions. The first couple of seasons they brewed it, almost everyone laid off the other beers until they drank up all the stores of the Olaf. So now it only comes out occasionally. They brew it in the fall because some of the ingredients are exceptionally hard to find except during the beginning of autumn. How come I of all people should know the rules?" The burly Dwarf shrugged his shoulders with a resounding *ring* of the layered mail armor he was wearing. "Well if you got to know," he paused, "I just had to get that recipe. So, a few years back I petitioned old Nebling and he let me slave for him for a year. I'd been a customer for a long time, and I can be a little gregarious at times, but I think he accepted me out of sheer meanness."

"Was it worth it?"

Bravo grinned and pointed at the two, now empty, platters in front of Alsigg. "Do you cook?"

"Some, as much as any bachelor who travels the land does, I suppose."

"Well, I cook a lot, and I commonly cook for others a lot too. Sometimes people even pay me to cook for them. Not only that, I like to eat, so yeah, it was worth it. Now, let's see if we can figure out how to get some of that Olaf." He gave a measured look at his new, young friend. "So you really think that you're a bard to-be, do you?"

Alsigg nodded.

"You want one more shot at this crowd?"

He nodded again. "Sure, but I'm not in good singing form right now and the only instrument I have handy is my flute. I didn't use it earlier because well, it didn't really look like a flute crowd."

"This isn't singing exactly. You said that you've learned several oral traditions, right?"

"Yeah, mostly Orcgrash though, but I'm picking up more all the time."

"Do you know the lay of 'Gurak's Folly'?"

"Sure, it was one of the first I ever learned. You're not suggesting that I perform *that* one here do you?" He swept his arm in a panorama of the room. There were Dwarven artifacts, like crossed battle-axes and broadswords, on the wall. There was also an Eldarr pennant, a couple of Kruash and Human chivalric shields, and even an Orcgrash war drum sitting in the corner. The artifacts were impressive, but what was more remarkable was that half of the patrons were Dwarves. There were a couple of Elves—a rare sight in these parts—and all the rest were Humans.

"Absolutely, and in the original form. Trust me, if you think that you have what it takes, then here's your chance. Remember, when you travel, you're not always going to have a positive crowd to start with. It's up to you to win them to your side." Bravo stood up and broad-jumped to the top of his table, barely missing the platters of denuded bones. Arms wide he addressed the suddenly interested crowd. "Friends, companions, and," he paused, flourishing towards Nebling, the erstwhile and half-amused owner "previous employers!" Several people chuckled at this. "I sense that not all were satisfied with the performance of my young friend Alsigg, Bard of Gilberts." There were a few 'ayes' and sniggers from the crowd. "Perhaps it is because you do not have the wit to understand this new comedic routine of lyric poetry that he was demonstrating for you." This time there were a few growls and mutterings to match the chuckles. "No, you say? Highbrow enough to understand anything, you're thinking? You didn't actually think that he was singing for your entertainment did you?" The crowd murmured getting caught up in Bravo's dialogue.

One stood up. "If he wasn't singing what was he doing?"

"Yeah!" said another.

"Right!" A couple more echoed.

Bravo waved his hands down to quiet his detractors. "Just part of the big setup my friends, just part of the big setup. Now, if you think that I'm just blowing hot air," There were some guffaws and loud hoots at *that* statement, "I said; IF you think that I'm just blowing hot air, I just might be willing to make a small wager."

"What kind of wager Bravo?" asked one face from the crowd.

"Yeah, what kind of wager and how much?" said another.

"The wager to you," he said sweeping his hand across the crowd. "Will be all the silver or lesser coin that you can muster."

Alsigg leaned over closer to Bravo and in a loud whisper asked. "Bravo? Are you sure about this? I don't really have the money or inclination to be wagering right now."

"Don't worry about it boy I'm staking you on this one." He raised his voice again, addressing the room. "I'm also willing to wager drinks for the house, for the night, versus one round of Olaf's from HIM!" Bravo grinned as he stabbed his finger directly at the VERY surprised and, now scowling, owner of The Last Home Inn. The crowd erupted into cheering, all turning to gauge Nebling's reaction.

Nebling stood with arms folded, glared at Bravo and slowly shook his head.

The crowd groaned and, as one, turned to look at the powerful Dwarf standing, arms akimbo, upon the table at the back of the room.

Another finger shot out to impale the figure of Nebling. "By Drilsagg's honor, I swear that this is an honest wager and I stand for it!"

The crowd of onlookers turned again as one to see the grim proprietor's reaction.

Nebling paused and stared hard for a second at Bravo, then almost imperceptibly, he nodded.

The crowd cheered and slapped Bravo's back as he jumped down from the table. They would win the wager, however it went.

"Also, win or lose, you will stake my young friend here after his next performance." Bravo leered at the ambushed innkeeper.

Again, there was an almost imperceptible nod from the glaring Dwarf.

The crowd cheered again.

"Well boy, it's showtime!"

Alsigg nodded as he slowly got up from the table. The room grew silent as he walked past the crowd and picked up the Orcgrah war drum from the corner where he had placed the tools of his trade upon entering earlier that eve. Grabbing an unoccupied stool, he stepped up onto the small stage. He placed the large drum between his knees and gave a couple of tentative thumps to test its tenor. Apparently satisfied, he took a deep breath and stared at a point above and beyond the crowd. In an eerie, harsh, guttural voice, he began:

Akgrook un Carsh Relch Gurokk Laarg
(The Lay of Gurak's Folly)

THUMP!

The room grew uncomfortably silent; a couple of humans muttering about not understanding were quickly shushed by some Dwarves, while others glared with open anger at Alsigg Rabonn, Orcish Bard. If Alsigg noticed the mild rage growing, or the open looks of resentment, he did not show it. He sat upon the tall, wooden bar stool, dark crimson tunic a little travel stained, but highly presentable, and a nice complement to his black breeches and black leather soft boots. He had long, black, mildly curly hair tied back into a horsetail. The dark hair highlighted his light skin, high cheekbones, pug nose and mysterious, gray-green eyes. His slight frame easily gripped the heavy Orcish drum, showing a wiry strength, and he stroked it with his long-fingered, strong hands. He began a simple, heavy beat that changed in cadence and strength as each verse progressed, his voice grunting and snarling out the harsh, guttural speech.

Gar malach ro tar org saleh
Gar malach ro ya fruk garrg
Gar malach ro shuush o hrah
Ro chaach a skrii, Ro shass galoo

We remember the march of death
We remember the endless fight,
We remember the blood and smoke
The clash of arms, The Long Good-bye

Gurak was a fearsome foe
A leader born of blood and might,
However, hidden was his heart of greed
Beneath his armor and long, drawn sight.

He scoffed at other leader's fears
As he presented his plan that day,
To raid the Stumps, The Kruash of gold
To reave their vaults through a secret way.

Angry voices marked that day
As Gurak stormed from the Orcgrah throne,
Many rallied to his rebel voice
Walking across their ancestor's bones.

We remember the march of death
We remember the endless fight,
We remember the blood and smoke
The clash of arms, The Long Good-bye

Gurak's Folly was the Stumps deep home
The Kruash's eyes as black as coal,
Their surprise to find the Foe
Axe and Blade fall to release their souls.

Deeper delved their raider force
Looking for the golden torrent,
Left behind was a silent cavern
Filled with wives and waifs forever silent.

The Drums began their tragic beating
The alarms sounded before the prize
The Stumps had found our soulless guilt
Their wrath and horror began to rise.

We remember the march of death
We remember the endless fight,
We remember the blood and smoke
The clash of arms, The Long Good-bye

Gurak tried to drive them on
As Stumps tore beard and hair in rage,
Drums spoke death and doom to all
Orcgrah caught like rats and cage.

As one, the People realized their madness
They turned and ran with souls affright,
Gurak stayed to find His Folly
The Kruash hunted, souls black as night.

The Kruash People as grim as Death
Began the hunt their drums like thunder
Their fury as likes an unending storm
Never to break nor bend nor sunder.

We remember the march of death
We remember the endless fight,
We remember the blood and smoke
The clash of arms, The Long Good-bye

Three Hundred entered the cursed mountain
Thirty escaped to spread the tale
Kruash hunted them one by one
Joined by Eldarr, Human, Fur and Scale.

The Orcgrah fight as they always had
But this time their foe will neither stop nor rest,
Old Nation scars and obstinacy rules
No truces asked only blood born quest.

Even Kruash allies quail at the cost
In death and lives lost like no other,
But nothing comes between these foes
Blood and hate like twins and brothers.

We remember the march of death
We remember the endless fight,
We remember the blood and smoke
The clash of arms, The Long Good-bye

At the last the Orcgrah King
Too late is he, who returns to reason,
He gathers up the best and youngest
And the oldest of all the seasons.

He sends them to parts unknown
With the help of hidden allies,
Hundreds, thousands slip away
Beyond all sight or quiet spies.

Gurak's Folly, Orcgrah's Doom
The People spread to the faint far lands,
For bloody gold and forgotten honor
The Nation broken into desperate bands.

We remember the march of death
We remember the endless fight,
We remember the blood and smoke
The clash of arms, The Long Good-bye

We remember the senseless blood
We remember our best and brightest,
We remember the brand of Unforgiven
We remember when we had Honor.

We remember the Long Good-bye,
We Remember.

THUMP!

The last drumbeat echoed off the rough-hewn rafters, and Alsigg closed his eyes and lowered his head. A man could hear the harsh breathing of repressed emotion, the crackling of the wood in the fireplace, and the minor creaking of one of the tall evergreens outside the inn swaying in the ever-present wind. There was little else, and the silence was deafening.

A squeal pierced the silence, from a chair pushing back, and Bravo stood for all to see. Tears shimmered in his eyes, and facing the stage, he forcefully slammed his mailed arm onto his own chest. WHAM! The ring of steel upon steel sounded like a resounding force across the silent room. Another Dwarf stood and slammed his chest, and then another, and another, until all the dwarves stood. WHAM! WHAM! WHAM! WHAM! Some were openly crying, a couple tore at their hair and beards in rage and shame. WHAM! WHAM! WHAM! WHAM! A couple of Humans, either understanding the harsh speech, or empathizing with their Dwarf companions, also stood and executed this harsh salute. WHAM! WHAM! WHAM! WHAM!

"STOP!" Alsigg's voice, loud and strong with a timbre far beyond his years roared out, bringing the room into silence again. "Please, please stop hurting yourselves. It's done. *They* forgive you! Now forgive yourselves. No more pain, not today, not here. Not from me."

One of the standing Humans looked around at the tears and stricken faces and began to clap. This was something the other Humans knew and took up the applause. The Dwarves looked around at the growing applause and the forlorn figure of Alsigg upon the stage. They started nodding at each other, and then, they too, began to clap. The staccato beat of hands and the drum of boots on the oaken floors grew giddily powerful until the Inn itself thrummed with the powerful waves of vibratory ovation. It grew until the applause was thunderous, glorious, and overwhelming. Like an irresistible fire, it consumed the hatred, shame, and fear leaving only the thin ash of spent emotions and introspection.

A battered, leather-brimmed hat spun upon the stage, top down, and a couple of silver coins quickly followed with almost unerring accuracy into the hat. More coins still followed until a virtual shower of copper, silver, and even a few gold, half filled the hat.

Alsigg picked up the heavy hat and executed a silent bow as he left the stage. He ambled back to his table fielding the many backslaps, high fives, and handshakes of his appreciative audience. He turned as he sat down to the slam of the cellar door opening behind the bar. The applause having already died down, most of the patrons turned at this new disturbance.

Nebling stood at the top of the stairs, a heavy cask on his shoulder. He set it heavily down on one of the cradles, grabbed a bung from under the bar and slammed it home with one stroke of a large mallet. "Olaf's on the house!" he roared.

The cheers were almost as loud as the applause for the latest performance.

Several mugful's later, Bravo leaned back again in his chair, a contented smile across his face. "My new friend, indeed you *are* a Bard. An Orcish Bard, but a bard all the same. You've got the gift of 'The Voice' for sure."

A surprised Alsigg looked across the table at his new Dwarven friend. "But how did you know to pick that piece? I wouldn't have thought it would be a Dwarven favorite."

"Indeed, not a favorite, but it sure does invoke a lot of emotion, don't ya know. Don't worry, I was ready to wade in if you did a crappy job and keep them from beating the hell out of you."

"Gee thanks"

"No trouble at all. Well, time to drain the dragon." Bravo stood up and stretched. "Water closets are the doors on either side of that hallway," he said pointing. "If you're a man, or reasonable image of one anyway, Piddler's Point is out the door at the end of the hallway, just follow the walkway." He grabbed his cloak and climbers stave and began to walk away.

"Bravo?"

"Yeah boy"

"One question, don't you ever take off that armor?"

"This armor? On occasion, rare occasions of course, but on occasion. This is my casual armor. You should see my formal armor." Bravo's hearty laughter was resounding as he walked toward the back door.

Barbecue Sauce for the Goose
(recipe by Brian Pettera)

On the autumn days when the cook sets a whole pig or quarter of beef to roast on a spit in the side yard, he also takes time to mix up a kettle of barbecue sauce. The origin of the recipe is a bit of a mystery—the cook won't say where he learned it, but only hints at short, bearded folk who love adventure, ale, and food. The inn is always packed for lunch and dinner on those days, as the smell of roasted meat and the sweet, spicy sauce are taken up by the wind and carried for dozens of miles around.

3/8 cup apple cider vinegar
1/2 cup white vinegar
(2) 6-ounce cans tomato paste
3/4 cups brown sugar
1 Tbsp. worchestire sauce
1-2 Tbsp. pepper sauce
1 Tbsp. honey
2 Tbsp. molasses
3 Tbsp. ground mustard
3 tsp. sea salt
1 tsp. black pepper
1/2 tsp. cumin
1 tsp. chili powder
2 tsp. smoked paprika
1 tsp. cayenne pepper
1 tsp. onion powder
1/4 tsp. garlic powder
1/4 tsp. allspice
1 1/2 cups water

Combine all ingredients in a medium saucepan over medium heat. Whisk until smooth. When mixture comes to a boil, reduce heat and simmer for 60 minutes, stirring

often. Cook until desired consistency is reached.
Remove pan from heat and cover until cool. Chill and store
in a covered container. The sauce can last 6-8 weeks
when refrigerated.

VOICE OF A SIREN

Tracy Chowdhury

Back pressed against the cold stone of the tunnel wall, I turn my face away from the man standing before me, his rank breath washing over my neck. My mind keeps telling me to push past him and run, but my body refuses to obey. My legs are heavy like a ship's anchor, holding me down to the floor and keeping me immobile. Luxor places a hand on each side of my head and leans in close. I fight to keep my breathing normal even though my heart feels like it's going to beat out of my chest. I squeeze my eyes tightly shut. If I wish hard enough, maybe he will disappear into the surrounding darkness and I will awaken and realize this is just a terrible dream.

"Your brother says I can have you. I've been waiting a long time for this moment."

I choose to remain silent, not surprised by this comment. Rigel always had a way of denigrating me as a young girl, and now that I am older it's taking a more twisted path. Sex is an obsession for him, and I imagine he would love to see me writhing beneath the men with whom he keeps close company.

Luxor places his nose against my neck and inhales deeply. "I have a feeling you will be the sweetest woman I've ever had the pleasure of taking." Despite my closed eyes, I sense his smile. "Rigel once said you wouldn't grow up very pretty. Hells, he was wrong! I suppose his sentiments were for the best. What man wants to hunger for his own sister?"

My breath shudders and catches for a moment. Truth be told, I wouldn't put it past Rigel to eventually have me for himself. The thought shakes me to the core, and suddenly I find the impetus to struggle. Hoping to catch him by surprise, I thrust myself away from the tunnel wall and into Luxor's chest. He grunts and falls back, allowing me the opportunity to rush past. I run, and just as I think I might be free, I feel an impact from behind.

I stumble to the floor. Luxor grabs me by the waist and hauls me back up to face him. I steel myself against a show of violence, very aware of how Rigel and his men tend to handle their victims. Hells, I'd seen it firsthand little over a fortnight ago when they left a girl to die in the streets of Ishkar.

If I hadn't been there, Mikayla certainly would have perished.

The assault never comes. Instead, I hear the voice of my brother from the shadows behind us. "Ahhh, I see you want to give Luxor a bit of a struggle," Rigel chuckles. "Very good, little sister. I never thought you had it in you."

I stiffen in Luxor's grip. I hate Rigel's voice, categorizing it with those things I consider most vile. I allow my gaze to seek him out, and after a moment, I find him standing a few foot-lengths away. With him are the other men in his company.

A dreadful feeling steals over me, one that makes me sick to my stomach. I renew my struggle against Luxor, knowing my welfare depends on being free of him. Time seems to slow as my brother leans within the shadows against the tunnel wall, his lips curving into a malicious grin. He then makes an offhand gesture ...

    I feel myself swung around and slammed into the wall. My next breath evacuates in a swift whoosh of air. I gasp as the rrrrip of tearing cloth fills my ears. I push ineffectually at my assailant, feel his hands at my backside and his mouth at my exposed breasts. My legs buckle and Luxor follows me down to the floor, pulling up my skirt and putting a hand between my legs. I inhale sharply with the intrusion and turn away, unwilling to look at Luxor's face. Instead, my gaze comes to rest on my brother.

    With an intense, predatory look, Rigel pulls away from the shadows. He strides over and lays a staying hand on Luxor's shoulder. The man reluctantly ceases his activity, pulls away and adjusts his trousers. Rigel crouches beside me on the ground, puts a hand to my chest and brings a pendant into view. It is the gift given to me by Mikayla, a gesture of friendship and appreciation for what I had done to save her from the terrible injuries she had sustained the night of her attack.

    Rigel's gaze hardens and it shifts to my face. "Where did you get this?" His expression is shuttered and I hear tension in his voice.

    "I ... I bought it from a street vendor just the other day."

    Rigel must have sensed the hesitancy in my demeanor, seen the falsehood reflecting in my eyes. His other hand closes around my throat, and he begins to squeeze. I struggle for breath, claw ineffectually at the vise-like grip. He leans over me, bringing his face close.

    "Where ... did ... you ... get ... this ..." He speaks the words slowly and succinctly, his blue eyes boring into mine. As I fight for my next breath, time seems to slow. My vision fades away at the periphery. Rigel's eyes are so

barren, so devoid of emotion. They are soulless eyes, ones that I might see belonging to something other than a human.

The grip finally eases from around my neck, yet Rigel keeps his hand there as he awaits my reply. With vivid clarity, I know it is useless to continue with the lie. Somehow, he is aware I have some kind of connection with the girl he and his men had raped and left for dead in the alleyway. If I remain along this path he might kill me via suffocation; but what will he do when I come out with the truth?

"A ... a girl gave it to me."

Rigel is taken aback by my sudden candor. For a moment there is stillness. He then releases my throat, grabs the tatters of my blouse in his fist, and roughly pulls me up into a sitting position. "What girl?" he growls, some of his brown hair falling over his forehead to cover one eye.

I swallow convulsively, wrapping an arm protectively over my bare breasts. "She was lying, beaten, in the side-streets."

"Was she dead?" he asks in a harsh tone, absently sweeping the errant hair out of his face. The action makes him seem vulnerable. I pause and consider telling him another lie. However, I choose against it. I am obviously not very good at that game, especially with Rigel.

I slowly shake my head. Rigel stares hard into my eyes. He scrutinizes me, wondering exactly how much I know. I can imagine his thoughts at that moment ... if he had the ability to hear what people were thinking, he would definitely be listening into my mind.

"Where is the girl now?" His voice is calmer, and has an almost predatory quality.

I don't need to lie this time, for I have no idea of the girl's whereabouts since she left the sanctuary of the apothecaries' residence to which I had taken her. "I don't know."

Abruptly releasing my blouse, Rigel rises from his crouch. I sense the tension emanating from him; see it in the rigidity of his back and shoulders. Silence reigns in the tunnel as he paces. I slowly rise from the floor, pulling the remains of the torn blouse around to cover myself.

He swings back around to face me. I see uncertainty reflecting in his maniacal expression. It scares me because I know what the indecision is all about. Should he kill me, or not?

My eyes snap open, and for a moment I wonder where I am. The pale rays of a newly rising sun filter through the wooden boards of the loft ceiling, and I scratch at an itchy place on my side where I lay against a himrony bale all night. In spite of the chilly morning air, sweat trickles down my back. Dreadful memories of the people I left behind have infiltrated my dreams no matter how hard I try to think pleasant thoughts before falling asleep.

I hastily vacate the barn and head into the city before anyone notices me. I walk the streets alone even though there are people all around. I am like a shadow, stopping at one vendor's booth before swiftly moving along to another, admiring the plethora of food but too afraid to take it. The scent of freshly baked bread assails my nostrils at one booth and the tantalizing aroma of roasting ptarmigan tempts me at another. Across the street I spy round, pink papas fruits being set out among bins of pale green cantalonas, deep red suplatas, and orange tangerinas. By the gods, never in all my years have I felt hunger like this.

However, Rigel's men aren't here, and I have my life.

I hear a roll of thunder in the distance and I wrap myself more tightly in my cloak. Regardless of its warmth, I shiver uncontrollably as my mind takes me to that dark place from which I barely escaped. I am lucky my brother didn't kill me before I found a way to leave Velmist.

With longing, I gaze at the bins of fruit. I have yet to eat since disembarking the ship that brought me here. My growling belly tells me to filch one of the delectable pink orbs, and my mind envisions the plumpest one. Sadly, I can't bring myself to do it for I have never stolen anything before. Growing up, I heard stories of the punishments meted to petty thieves. I like both my hands and fear for their continued attachment to my arms if I am caught.

My chest tightening with despair, I scuttle away from the temptation. I blink away the tears that threaten, and I am overwhelmed with emotion. A year ago I never would have imagined what my life has become, leaving my home under cover of the darkness with nothing but the clothes on my back and a few hundred gold that barely managed to procure my passage into Quartajena Cove and to the port of Yortec.

The sky rumbles ominously once more. Experience tells me that the air will get cooler when the storm passes. I really need to find a decent shelter this time, not the himrony loft I've been sneaking into the past three nights.

The sky slowly darkens as the storm clouds roll in. The people remaining in the streets hasten their steps, hurriedly completing their errands before the rains come. I hesitate when I hear a conversation taking place between two women outside of a nearby clothier's booth. Their dialect is a bit different than what I am accustomed, but I understand them well enough.

"I think we are going to the Silver Harp this eve. I've heard good things about the group of entertainers that have been performing there the past few nights."

"The Silver Harp ... I've always wanted to go there. Isn't that the place known for their exotically spiced foods?"

"The proprietor is from the distant realm of Nampir. When he settled here, he brought with him the spices used in the dishes on which he was raised. The fish patties are divine, and with them, he serves something called 'kitchori'. I've never tasted anything like it anywhere else."

I approach the women, courteously pulling down the hood of my cloak. They turn to me questioningly. "Excuse me. I don't mean to intrude, but I overheard you talking about a place called the Silver Harp. Could you please tell me where it is?"

"Certainly, dear. Just proceed up the main thoroughfare and to the right. You will go up a hill and it will be at the top. It's a large establishment with a veranda that wraps around the sides of the building. You can't miss it."

I nod and give a slight bow of appreciation. "Thank you so much for the directions."

The women nod and smile, returning to their conversation. I proceed up the road, an idea forming in my mind. It is one borne of desperation, but I would rather work for coin than steal. My thoughts turn inwards. Once, before he became sick, my father told me that I had the voice of a siren. In spite of the negative imagery, I took it as a compliment. It was one thing about me that made him proud, and he would sometimes ask me to sing for visitors he hoped to impress. Over the years he hired various instructors to build my gift, and each one taught me something useful. Maybe, just maybe I can use it to my advantage and finally reap some reward.

It isn't long before I see the establishment in the distance. The stone is colored a deep gray, and when I get closer, I notice that the sign outside is painted silver. As I approach, I spot three people out on the veranda along the side of the building. I walk up the steps and consider just going through the front door and asking the proprietor about the entertainers, but I hesitate. Instead, I walk around to the side. There are two young men and a woman who haven't moved from their places since my arrival. They all look despondent, and I hesitate again. *Should I question them about the entertainers?* I school my expression into the most pleasant one I can muster in my current circumstance. None of them seems very approachable, but I go up to the closest one. The woman leans against the wall with her arms folded at her waist.

"Excuse me, but could you possibly tell me where I might find the group of entertainers that is performing here tonight?"

The woman shrugs and nods towards the men, both of whom are looking in our direction. "To my knowledge we are the only ones working here right now. What can we do you for?"

My eyes widen as I can hardly believe my good fortune. I find myself at a loss for words, not expecting the object of my search to be so easily found. I take a bit too long in my reply, for her brow raises expectantly after a few moments. "Uh, well, I was hoping that maybe I could join you for a night or two."

Silence reigns. The woman casts a glance at her comrades and I sense her skepticism. She clears her throat and chooses to remain polite with me. "What skills do you feel you can bring to a group such as ours?"

I am suddenly awash with trepidation. My father was convinced I had the loveliest voice he'd ever heard, but that didn't really mean it was true. I mean, only a complete fool would have refuted him. I curse to myself for not thinking of this earlier. Here I am, presenting myself to some people who can help me out of my desperate situation. I have no food or lodging, and my approaching future looks bleak. In spite of my fears, I need to adhere to the belief that I have at least a passable singing voice.

Again though, I've taken too long in my reply, for the woman is wearing an expression of irritation. "I ... I can sing."

She glances again at her companions, then back to me. "Really? Show me."

My mind forms a blank. "What do you want me to sing?"

She shrugs again. "Anything you want."

I'm hoping my mind isn't playing tricks on me when I see her expression shift to one of hopefulness. I suggest the first thing that comes to mind. "The Ballad of Shinshinasa?"

She raises an eyebrow, obviously thinking I have chosen something complex and that I won't be able to deliver. I set my travel pack on the floor beside me. The two men continue to watch unobtrusively. I take a deep breath and begin to sing. It doesn't start out as well as I hoped, but that's because I hadn't the time to warm my voice first. It is a piece with irregular meter and difficult to perform, but it came to mind because it is one of my favorite ballads. I used to practice it assiduously, always wanting it to be just right. My father loved it too, and I wondered how much of that was because of me.

I imagine the beating of drums as I continue to sing, followed by the sweet, haunting melody of an accompanying lute. I delve deeper inside my mind and imagine the battle being fought, a battle that ended with so much death on both sides that no one walked away the victor. There were so many dead, and the survivors so paltry, the fallen remained where they lay. To this day, no one likes to cross the Plain of Antipithanee, the sun-bleached bones of those fallen men littering the 'scape.

The armies march over the endless savannah
Humans treading with great numbers,
Oroc mercenaries lured with promises of gold.
Fateful footfall as they lumber.

Faelin with unequaled wisdom,
Outstanding weapons and brilliant skill,

Silver lloryk and golden larian carrying riders
Wielding sword, and bow to the mornings chill.

The trumpet of bugle and the moan of Oberon
Hails as armies collide upon the vast plain,
Thundering of hooves and clang of steel
Cries of men dying in the name of truth and in vain.

And the vultures that circle see no difference
Not realizing that blood spilled is colored the·same
The armies lay upon the desolate battlefield
The scent of death prevails, and it needs no name.

The whisper of summer winds sweep over the plain
That the buzz of flies cannot curtail
Sightless orbs stare into a realm the living cannot see
Stiff hands grip sword, mace, and flail.

The company from Shinshinasa walks
Among comrades never met before,
Among men who fought for illusions of pride
       and nobility
Seeking to settle feeble slights and even scores.

They paid the heavy penalty for stark reality
And then, the enemy emerges from the East
They steel themselves for battle and wait
With the bridles of their valiant steeds.

I close my eyes and envision the girl, Analiza, about whom much of the ballad focuses. She was human, trained by her widower father alongside her brothers in the art of warfare. The call to arms requested only men, but she was determined to fight alongside those she held most dear. So she bound her breasts and donned men's clothes. She stole away from her grandmother's home and rode into battle with the reluctant, straggling forces from Shinshinasa.

Analiza stands before the approaching foe
With fear singing through her veins,
Foreboding twisting about her heart
Her dread holding her in chains.

When the faelin warriors are before them
Astride their huge canine beasts, eyes full of malice
She shouts in the deepest of her deep voices
Looking to break through their hearts so callous.

"Stop! Please, my brothers, and ask yourselves
Who are we fighting for? It cannot be for our
        children's sake,
Who will starve without their fathers to feed them,
Cold without their fathers to clothe and house them
        and not forsake.

Who are we fighting for? It cannot be our wives,
Who will feel loneliness without their men to warm
        them in their beds at night,
Desolate without a partner to share the responsibilities
Of raising a family and doing it right.

Who are we fighting for? It cannot be for our parents
Who will suffer the agony of losing their sons,
Vulnerable without him to care in their old age,
For time is marching on with nowhere to run.

Let us look at ourselves now! What do we see?
Only men who have the same things to lose if we
        perish this eve.
Is it really the answer and all we can do?
Because I find that so hard to believe.

Right now, here, at this time, are those things
worth dying for?
Why are we fighting? Is it for power or
glory or wealth?
What about the things that are worth living for?
Like your families, your faith, and your health."

I complete the last stanza and the veranda is silent. During my song, the men had come closer and stand on either side of their comrade. They all three stare and make me wonder if I've formed a blister on my face or if I've transformed in some way during the past several moments. My heart sinks, for I obviously chose the wrong piece to sing. Maybe I should have gone with something a bit simpler, or something more uplifting.

Finally one of the men speaks, the taller one with light brown hair. "So, you want to join us for a night or two, eh?" He offers his arm. I reach out to accept and we grip one another's forearms in the typical Ansalarian greeting.

I nod and offer my best smile. "Yes, I can really use the coin." I know it's not always the best route, but I chose to speak the truth.

"Well, I think the three of us agree you would be great accompaniment for a couple evenings. Your recitation was quite beautiful."

The woman raises an eyebrow. "Really? Just for a couple nights?" Her tone is exasperated. "Marissa just quit on us, and we were standing here wondering what the Hells we were going to do."

He gives a deep sigh. "I understand that, but we need to take one step at a time. So for now, a couple of nights is a start."

My heart soars and I clasp my hands together, much like a child, and hop in place. I am certain my smile is so big it looks ridiculous. "By the gods, thank you so much!"

"My name is Bowen." He points to the other man and the woman. "And they are Faisal and Candis. What should we call you?"

I hesitate. I don't want to give them my real name. I can't take the chance that Rigel's men will come looking for me. So I give them another, one that might sound good as a stage name. "Jewel. You can call me Jewel."

The audience falls into silence as my fingertips brush over the strings of the lyre. The sound of their recent applause still resounds in my ears, and I am pleased they enjoyed the Ballad of Shinshinasa just as much as they did the night before. Tonight Bowen gave me permission to sing anything else that suited my fancy. The first thing that comes to my mind is something I created myself. I wonder about the wisdom of this, but once it's there, I can't get it out of my mind. I'm a bit nervous, making it more of a challenge to play and sing at the same time, but I have done it before …

Hush, whisper the voice of a siren …
Don't look back, don't lose heart.

She was only a child
Walking the streets alone
Without someone to believe in
Without someone to care

She dreamed of fire
Prayed with all her might
To give her a voice that would not tire
She dreamed of rain
Waited for the day
When all her fears would be slain

Hush, whisper the voice of a siren ...
Don't look back, don't lose heart.

She was only a child
A precious girl, little pearl
Without someone to hold onto
Without someone to love

She dreamed of flame
Ran away to give herself more time
Her heart broken, so much shame
She dreamed of seas
Resisted the temptation of what eyes perceive
Not believing in everything they want to see

Hush, whisper the voice of a siren ...
Don't look back, don't lose heart.

She is still only a child
Surrounded by the evil of the night
Arcane lights shine into the shadows
But somewhere there is triumph

She dreams of love's desire
Her heart yearning for passion
Reaching out, higher, higher
She dreams of tempests,
That somewhere, somewhen
She will be found, unharmed again

Hush, whisper the voice of a siren ...
Don't look back, don't lose heart.

Later that night, we wait backstage as Bowen completes the final act. It's been a long day, and I can barely wait to take advantage of the bath the inn provides every evening after performances. Beyond the thick, burgundy curtain, I hear the sudden onset of thunderous applause. In all my life, I've never heard anything like it. I glance over at Candis to see her reaction. Her smile stretches from ear to ear, and her brown eyes are bright with excitement.

Bowen swiftly pulls aside the curtain. "They want us all to come out on stage!"

Faisal jumps up from his stool. "By the gods! I knew this was an awesome performance!"

Candis grabs my hand and the four of us return to the stage. My heart quickens, and I remind myself that I'm not out there to perform anymore this evening. Instead, I'm just there to smile and bow to the patrons of this fine establishment, people who have filled Bowen's lucky bowl to overflowing with copper, silver, and gold. Now, any coins tossed in its direction slide off the top of the pile and onto the floor to join a growing pool of others.

With Candis on one side, and Faisal on the other, I bow to the generous crowd that has gathered at the Silver Harp Inn, a crowd that has grown over the course of the evening. Bowen's good friend, Dangur the Druid, is also there. In spite of strict cultural norms, he has come to the inn both nights bearing fat pouches of gold donated by his Order. The pervading happiness in the air is infectious, and the obligatory smile comes easily to my lips. The adulation is inspiring, and I'm looking forward to the next performance.

It's then I remember ... my two evenings with the group are over.

Later that night, I sit in front of the fire in the common room. The inn is closed and those who are lodging there have retreated to their chambers. My belly is full of the inn's renowned spicy fish patties and rice and lentil combination called kitchori. Washing it down is a cold mug of sweet mead. The company is good, and I thank the gods for watching over me. Bowen and Faisal have imbibed their fair share of ale, but have managed to remain rather clear-headed. Their stories are funny, and I know why they are so good at their chosen profession.

The men's attention finally shifts my way. Bowen regards me with a raised brow. "So, how do you feel about joining us another few nights? Our performance tonight was a winner, and we would like to keep the coin flow coming. Not to mention, the proprietor is more than pleased, and he has given us bonuses." Bowen pulls four pouches from the inside of his silver-embroidered, royal blue vest and sets them on the table.

Faisal is the first to reach out and pick one up. He loosens the drawstrings and pours the contents into his hand. Ten gold coins reflect in the light of the lanterns and his smile widens. Candis takes hers in hand, and Bowen repossesses the third and places it in his vest. Only one pouch remains in the middle of the table. Of course it's meant for me. I slowly take it. The coin pouch at my hip is full, but this is extra.

Bowen sees my confusion and he grins. "Last night's wonderful performance brought an excess of patronage to the inn. Kelvyn made a lot of coin tonight, and being a generous man, he wanted to share it with us." Bowen nods. "Go ahead and take it, Jewel. It's yours."

My chest swells with pride. All the coin I have ever possessed was given to me by my father until now. This is the first time I've earned it.

Bowen regards me for a moment. "So, what is that piece you sang tonight? I've never heard it before."

The other two look at one another and shake their heads. "Indeed, we've never heard it either," says Candis.

A rush of anxiety sweeps through me but I keep calm. "Oh really? It's something I learned as a girl. I can't believe you have never heard it." *Damn, what was I thinking? Of course they have never heard it; I was the one who created it! I can't believe I didn't think far enough ahead to know they would ask me about it later. Why didn't I sing something everyone knows?*

Bowen continues to watch me, his gaze piercing. "Everyone has a story to tell. We want to know yours."

I regard him intently and shake my head, valiantly maintaining simplicity while my heart sinks. I even manage to chuckle. "No story. Only what I have told you already."

Bowen cocks his head. "You can't join the group until you tell us."

Silence reigns. Only the popping of the fire can be heard. I look over at Candis. Her wide eyes tell me she had nothing to do with this. Fear suffuses me, and my heart hammers against my ribs. I hate to lose the one good thing I have in my life right now, but ...

"I ... I can't tell you."

Faisal spreads his arms wide. "But why?"

I whisper my next words. "Because my life depends on my secrecy."

More silence. "We are your friends. We will keep your secret," says Candis.

I shake my head. "People will pay you gold to give me away."

"No, not us," says Bowen. "We will vow to keep your secret."

"They will offer a lot of money. It will be difficult to turn that down." I shake my head again. "I can't expect you to turn down the amount of gold they will offer."

Candis leans forward to place a hand on my arm. "Look at us, Dearie. We are not poor. We are good at what we do. We *earn* our gold. We don't get it for free, especially if we've made a promise."

I look Candis in the eye, then Bowen and Faisal. I want to believe them, but I'm afraid. Rigel's scouts aren't here now, but it doesn't mean that they won't come here looking for me in the future.

Faisal touches my cheek with his fingertips. "Hai, you tell me your story and you are my sister. I do not lie. I would never give you up. My honor is worth more than any amount of gold."

I smile and place my hand over his. I want to believe Faisal so much my chest aches. Bowen leans towards me and places a hand on my shoulder, then Candis with a hand on my arm. "Come," Bowen says gently, "tell us your story. Maybe start with your real name."

In spite of my fears, I give in. I always knew I would have to place my trust in somebody somewhere along my journey. I give a quavering deep breath. "My name is Joneselia Mondemer. After my brother, I am successor to the throne of Karlisle. Now I am weak and afraid. My prayer is to become strong and brave. Maybe then I can return home."

My new companions stare at me through wide eyes.

"Why do you need to be strong to return home?" asks Faisal.

"Because my brother wants to kill me."

Evening approaches. With my cloak wrapped securely around me, I walk quickly through the streets. Thunder rumbles and I hasten my step, hoping to make it back to the inn before the rains begin. It's been unusually stormy for the moon cycle of Cisceren, and I can't help feeling the gods have me in their favor. My hope is that the storms are making travel by sea more difficult, decreasing the chances that anyone sent from Karlisle to find me will meet success.

The sky suddenly darkens and the winds increase. Most people, recognizing the severity of the approaching storm, have already sought shelter. I pass the side street leading up to the Silver Harp Inn, making my way a few streets further to the one that will take me to a place called the Whistling Wayfarer. During the fortnight I've spent with Bowen and his group, we have taken our performance to another location. Soon we will leave the city of Yortec entirely and move on to another. Bowen says that, as a performer, it is best to never settle in one place for too long. Staying on the move provides a fresh audience, and new environments are a source for ideas to bring to the next performance.

I am inclined to agree with him, albeit for another reason. At some point, I will be discovered. It is dangerous for me to stay in Yortec any longer than what I have already.

Dangerous. I frown to myself. *Now why would that word come to mind?*

My eyes dart into the widening shadows, my nerves getting the better of me. Bowen will be upset about my being out this late, but I really wanted to get my skirt mended before tomorrow evening's performance. I would have taken it to the seamstress earlier, but didn't notice the tear until later in the day after I had washed it and hung it out to dry. I proceed past two more streets before I'm overcome with trepidation. The fine hairs on the nape of my neck rise, and I glance behind me. I blink when I think I see someone darting back into the shadows of the nearest building.

My breath catches in my throat, and I hasten my step even more. By the gods, is someone really there? Am I being followed? My heart beats a staccato rhythm in my chest. I'm not that far from the next street, the one that will take me to the Whistling Wayfarer. A light rain begins to fall. A few stragglers remain here and there, people who are rushing to their own destination. Maybe that's all it was, not someone following me, but someone who was also trying to seek shelter.

I gather my courage and chance another look behind me. I don't see anyone and I sigh with relief. The creepy feeling subsides and I chuckle to myself as I continue up the street. The dark stone of the establishment is visible not long after, and I see Bowen standing out on the veranda.

As I approach, he greets me with furrowed brows and pursed lips. "Silly girl, get yourself in here. You know I hate to worry."

I'm so relieved and happy to see him. I hurry up the stairs to get out of the rain, and without thinking, I rush up and wrap my arms around him. "Bowen, I am so glad you are out here waiting for me."

At first he may have been taken aback, but he must have felt me trembling because he holds me tight. "Jonesy, of course I am out here waiting for you. It's late and the storm is coming in. It's gonna be a bad one I hear."

I don't make a reply, and when he speaks again his voice is concerned. "Are you alright? Did something happen?"

I shake my head. "No, I'm fine. The storm just has me a little shaken is all."

He turns me towards the door with an arm around my shoulders. "Let's get inside then ..."

Later that night I sit in bed, brushing out my hair. Candis is beside me, the rhythmic rise and fall of her side telling me she is already asleep. The constant patter of rain against the window is lulling. I want to shut the lantern and find some rest myself, but my scare from earlier in the evening bids me hesitate. I have plenty of oil. Maybe I can keep the flame low throughout the night and the nightmares will stay away.

Bang, bang! The winds make a loose shutter hit against the building and I jump. Putting a hand to my chest, I breathe deeply to still my racing heart. A moment later, I roll my eyes in exasperation, hating myself for my fearfulness. Why can't I let go of the idea that someone is watching me? I rise from the bed and walk to the window. Pulling aside the curtain, I gaze down onto the street. Everything is darker than usual, the winds and rain having extinguished the street-lamp quite a while ago. Of course I see no one out there.

With a deep sigh I perch myself on the window casement and lean my head against the cool glass. It feels good, and after a while, the steady drone of the rainfall calms me again. I hear the loose shutter once more, but it doesn't startle me the way it did before. My eyelids get heavy and I feel myself starting to doze off …

There is a flash of lightning and my eyes snap open. My body is thrust into alertness and I stare out onto the street.

Thunder rumbles and I wait. My breath fogs the glass and my sweaty palm leaves a temporary imprint. I strain to see, but it's just too dark. I wait, and wait …

The lightning flashes again and my eyes widen. The man is still standing there beside the lamp-post, staring up at my window.

I scream …

"Jonesy, wake up! Jonesy!"

I open my eyes to find Candis standing beside me. Her eyes are wide with worry, her mouth pinched. She grips my arm, steadying me within the casement, otherwise I would have fallen already.

"Candis, there is a man down there!" I point out the window. "He's watching me."

She looks out the window and shakes her head. "No, there is no one out there, Dearie."

I steel myself and look back out the window. "Yes, he's right there. I …" My voice trails off. There is no one standing by the streetlamp. As a matter of fact, the storm has passed and all is quiet outside the window.

The door bursts open. Startled, Candis and I find Bowen and Faisal standing there at the entry, hastily clad in only their trousers. Each man has a dagger.

Bowen's voice is gruff. "We heard screaming. What happened?"

Candis put a hand on my shoulder. "Jonesy had a bad dream. Everything is fine."

Bowen looked at me intently. He sheathed his dagger and entered the chamber, Faisal following behind.

I wring my hands. "I'm sorry. I didn't mean to wake everyone. I … I thought I saw someone standing outside."

Bowen approaches and stands before me. He's so tall and I have to look up to maintain eye contact. Just like Candis, he looks out the window for a moment before turning back to me. "Tonight is our last performance. Tomorrow morning there is a caravan heading out to Xordrel. We will be in accompaniment. I've already spoken with the right people." He puts a hand on my shoulder. "Don't worry. Karlisle won't find you here because we will already be gone."

I give a wan smile and nod.

"We should get some rest," says Candis. "If we are leaving tomorrow, we need to spend the day preparing …"

With a smile I stand back to admire my new laundry skills, nodding to myself in appreciation. Since meeting Candis I have learned so much. I thank her every day, and now it has come to the point where she just rolls her eyes and walks away. Really, she has no idea how much the skills mean to me, and how she has endeared herself to my heart.

I proceed to hang the last few pieces of clothing on the line. It has been a long day and I'm getting tired. The performance originally scheduled for this evening has been postponed until tomorrow. When the proprietor realized how serious we were about leaving the city, and that it would be our final performance, he asked for one more day in order to give him the chance to create some excitement. We had become rather well-known, and his inn generated quite a bit of income during our performance nights. He went so far as to reveal his plan with us—that he would raise his fee to any who wished to enter his establishment on our last night.

Of course he was willing to share a percentage of the earnings.

After speaking with the caravan master, Bowen agreed. The master was willing to spend an extra day in Yortec with the promise of a percentage of the extra coin we earned from the performance. It was a winning situation for everyone involved.

Pleased with my laundering work, I think of the next thing I need to accomplish. I take a look up at the sky, and judging by the sun's position, I determine it's about time for me to go and collect my skirt from the seamstress. Before I leave, I need to go back up to my chamber and get the silver I need to pay her. I walk between the clothes lines back towards the rear of the establishment. Hanging on either side of me are most of the clothing items that Bowen, Faisal, Candis and I possess. Tunics, trousers, skirts, blouses, gowns, cloaks and smallclothes sway in a wind that is much more docile than the one from the evening before.

I've almost reached the back door, when an arm suddenly whips out from among the clothing. It snags me about the waist and pulls me against a warm, solid form. Before I can utter a protest, a big hand presses firmly against my mouth. I instinctively struggle, and my captor easily lifts me up and slams my back against the cool stone of the inn.

The rough stubble on his jaw rubs against my face and his voice is deep. "Hehehe, your brother is gonna be happy to hear from me."

My heart stutters and plummets into my knees. *No, this can't be happening!*

"I been after you for quite a while." He pulls away just enough for me to see his face. I don't recognize him, but Rigel has a host of loyal men that will do almost anything for him. He sees the question in my eyes and he grins. "Yeah, I been following you, been watching. You didn't really think you could escape him for long now, did you?"

He chuckles again as he lifts me up and drags me towards a horse I see standing in the distance among some trees. I struggle and attempt to scream, but the hand over my mouth muffles my efforts. I claw my fingernails ineffectually over his beefy knuckles and tears course down my cheeks. Thoughts of facing my brother suffuse my mind. *What will Rigel do with me first?*

My captor abruptly stops. His arms loosen, and his hand drops away from my mouth. I manage to stumble away before he topples. When I turn around, I see him lying in a heap on the ground, five daggers protruding from his back. Not far away, Faisal rises from a kneeling position and swiftly approaches. He walks past the fallen body and comes to my side.

"Jonesy, are you all right? That man didn't hurt you, did he?"

I shake my head and point a trembling finger towards my would-be captor. "Wh … whose daggers are those?"

Faisal regards me from dark brown eyes for a moment. He sucks at his bottom lip and finally turns away. He walks over to the body, placing his fingers at the thick neck before pulling the daggers out of the man's back, sheathing each one into an inconspicuous belt around his waist.

I simply stare with wide eyes.

Faisal walks back to my side. He looks down at me with a concerned expression. "Are you afraid of me?"

I shake my head. "No." I take a deep breath and then tell him the truth. "Well yes, maybe."

Faisal puts a finger beneath my chin and urges me to look up at him. "Please don't be afraid. Every group, no matter how small, needs a warrior. It is my duty to keep us safe. When you have the time to think about this, I hope you think I did my job well."

I feel overwhelmed. My body begins to tremble, and it's hard to breathe normally. I can't believe how close I came to being taken away. Faisal notices my reaction and his expression shifts to alarm. *Maybe he thinks I am still afraid of him!* To waylay his misconception, I do the first thing that enters my mind. I reach up to wrap my arms around his neck. I have only known Faisal, Bowen, and Candis for little more than a fortnight, but already I feel so close to them, *like they are my family.*

"I was so afraid! He was the one who was following me yesterday, and the one I saw standing beside the lamp-post last night. He told me so himself!" I sob uncontrollably and any more words I may have wanted to convey are lost. After a moment he reciprocates the embrace, and his arms envelop me in a swath of warmth and protection.

"It's alright. He can't hurt you now. I made certain of that."

I cry for several moments before I'm able to calm myself. Yet, I still hang on to Faisal. He seems to understand I need him and doesn't break away, giving me the best support he can offer. "Hai, you are my sister. For you I have done this thing, and for you I would do it again. No one may have you against your will, not under my watch … not if I can help it."

The following night, I take the stage one last time in the city of Yortec. I wear my mended skirt, along with the embroidered blouse that matches it. The audience is bigger than ever, with people crowding around the tables and standing against the walls. There are even some who stand at the entry with nowhere else to go. My fingertips skim over the strings of the lyre. I've been given license to sing whatever I choose, much like the first time I performed with the group. Unlike the last time, the song that comes to my mind is a happy one, a song full of hope and promise. I created most of it a few years ago during a short time in my life when I felt happy. This past fortnight I finally completed it with the help of Bowen and Faisal. They are with me on stage as accompaniment.

When the future is darkened by past fears,
When you spend the nights fighting your tears
When the skies are gloomy, and the winter worn
When the days are difficult and belief is torn
In life I hope you decide to take a chance
Instead of sitting it out, I hope you decide to dance

I hope you dance
I hope you dance

When the future is clouded with uncertainty
When your direction in life is difficult to see
When it is easy to fear the mountains in the distance
When you are tempted to choose
          the path of least resistance
In life I hope you decide to take a chance
Instead of sitting it out, I hope you decide to dance

I hope you dance
I hope you dance

When the future is shadowed with difficult choices
When everyone inundates you with well-meaning voices
When you still feel small standing before this ocean
When you hope the closing of one door
          will make another one open
In life I hope you decide to take a chance
Instead of sitting it out, I hope you decide to dance

I hope you dance
I hope you dance
Instead of sitting it out, I hope you dance.

I just finish the song when Candis rushes out onto the stage. Her arrival is unexpected, not part of the performance we discussed earlier today. She comes over to me, her eyes wide with fear. She puts a hand on my shoulder and leans in close to my ear. "Jonesy, you have to go! There are men looking for a girl fitting your description, and they are riding up to the establishment right now!"

I jump up from my seat, panic surging through me. Candis quickly takes my hand and grips it tightly for a moment before I abruptly leave the stage. By the gods, my father's men have tracked me down. Why didn't I realize there would be more where the first one came from? It doesn't matter that the man claimed to be working for my brother. In truth, my father's men and those loyal to my brother are one and the same. If I am taken by any force from Karlisle, my fate will be the same.

No matter what, Rigel will have me ...

I rush backstage and out the back door. I find myself at the rear of the establishment where I was almost abducted yesterday morning. A shroud of hopelessness envelopes me. *Is there any point in trying to hide? They have managed to track me this far and are obviously very good at what they do.*

I run along the back of the building, turn the corner, and stop to lean against the stone. I take a moment to collect myself and catch my breath. Hot tears run down the sides of my face and I struggle to come to grips with my reality. I sink down onto the grass and wrap my arms around my knees. My father's men will force me to return home to Karlisle. Once there, Rigel will have easy access to me. If I am lucky, he will simply kill me.

This time, Faisal won't be there to save me.

I startle when I hear someone approaching. I jump up when I see a young woman standing a few foot-lengths away. By her small stature, and the narrow shape of her tapered ears, I can tell she isn't human. Curling red hair frames a beautiful face, one that is strangely familiar. She continues to walk towards me, and I am about to flee, when she raises a hand.

"Wait!" she says in a low voice. "I can help you."

I quash my impulse to run and wait for her to get closer. "How? Those men are everywhere."

The woman places a finger to her lips. "Shhh. I will show you, but you mustn't be afraid."

I regard her skeptically for a moment, wondering what she is about. Finally I nod in agreement. What do I have to lose? The men are onto my trail, and it's only a matter of time before I'm caught.

A look of concentration sweeps over the woman's face. Her eyes get a faraway look and her fingers draw runic designs in the space before her. She whispers and I sense something stirring in the air, something I can't see. My flesh quivers. I've heard of spell-casters, but never met one before.

Brief moments later she takes my hand. Slowly, so as not to be noticed, we make our way to the stable. Once there, we pass by a series of stalls, many of which are occupied. At the back we climb up a ladder and into the loft. We crawl behind some bales of himrony and hide there. Neither of us says anything for a while, but finally the young woman turns to me.

"I know who you are." She regards me solemnly, her voice monotone.

My heart leaps in my chest. "Are you going to turn me in?"

She shakes her head. "No, I said I would help you." She frowns. "What are you running away from?"

"It's a long story," I reply shortly.

The woman raises an eyebrow and gestures into the space surrounding us. "So? I have some time to spare."

I don't reply.

She sighs. "What's your name?"

I frown. "I thought you said you know who I am."

She nods. "We met once, when we were younger. My grandfather was meeting with your father in the beginning of talk that would one day come to be a treatise between our people."

My eyes widen with enlightenment. "You are the Princess of Elvandahar, Damaeris Timberlyn."

She nods again. "You are the youngest daughter of King Zerxes of Karlisle. I'm sorry, I just don't recall your name."

"Jonesy, you can call me Jonesy."

Damaeris frowns. "It doesn't sound familiar."

"I don't like my given name so I go by this one."

She shrugs. "All right."

"I remember your name because my father told me I should strive to be more like you."

She cocks her head. "Why did he say that?"

"You were so prim and proper standing beside the King of Elvandahar, and you seemed the utmost of sophistication. You impressed him."

She grins. "Well, just so you know, it was all an act. I am neither prim, proper, nor sophisticated."

I give her a pointed look. "So what are you then?"

Damaeris hesitates and regards me intently. By the expression on her face, she knows that I am fishing for information about her spell-casting ability. "I thought I was asking the questions here."

I maintain silence.

"What are you running away from?" She asks the question again.

For some reason, I don't tell her about Rigel. Instead, I focus on the secondary reason for my leave-taking. "My father is very sick. His mind ... it ... it's not quite right anymore."

Damaeris seems quite taken aback. She hesitates, carefully formulating a reply that doesn't sound too harsh. "Jonesy, you can't just …"

I cut her off. "I'm so afraid. Please, don't try to tell me I should go back. You don't know …" I stop speaking mid-sentence, unwilling to speak of my brother. I lower my eyes to the himrony-laden floor.

Suddenly I feel a hand on my shoulder. I look up into deep brown eyes. "I said I would help you. You can trust me."

I nod and blink the tears out of my eyes. I'm about to say something when Damaeris' attention is diverted to the outside. Her body tenses, and within moments she is muttering another incantation. She finishes just as the men burst through the stable door.

Panic sets in as the commander gruffly shouts his orders. The warriors swiftly begin their search. Sensing my rising fear, Damaeris puts a finger to her lips and takes my hand. I huddle deep within the mounds of himrony beside the Princess of Elvandahar and pray to whatever benevolent gods are watching over me to continue doing so. I've come so far and overcome so many hurdles. To be taken now …

The men thoroughly conduct their search. Two of them climb the ladder and look around the loft. Damaeris grips my hand tighter as the men approach our hiding place. We remain motionless, listening to their whispered talk as they get close.

"Damnation, I hope we find her because the Commander will be a difficult bastard to live with otherwise."

"Pfft, the Commander is difficult to live with regardless."

Both men chuckle after this statement, but the first man speaks gain. "I'm serious, people are gonna pay for the leak that enabled the Princess to escape."

"Yes, I know. And if we go home without her, I'm afraid of what Prince Rigel might do."

"That man gives me the shudders. The way he talks, it's almost like he's obsessed …" He stops mid-sentence. "Ah, never mind. I talk too much. Forget I said that."

The second man pats the first on the back. "Eh, you're fine. Many of the other men have a similar sentiment, including myself." He looks around and gives the loft one last glance. "Come on, let's get back down. There is nothing up here."

I watch as the men leave, my breathing returning to normal only after they are gone from the stable. I can hardly believe they never saw us. I look over at Damaeris. Her abilities are strong if she can hide us so easily. She regards me thoughtfully from narrowed eyes.

"This isn't just about your father, is it?"

I swallow heavily. "My brother has become very corrupt, especially since our father's illness worsened. It wasn't until Rigel threatened me that I realized my life was endangered. I left Karlisle as soon as possible."

Damaeris gives a gusty exhale, her expression questioning. "But why does he wish to harm you? His claim to the throne is solid since he is your father's only son."

My expression is grave. "Maybe I'll tell you about it sometime."

Damaeris nods. "I'm heading home to Elvandahar. I know you would be back-tracking, but you would be safe with me and the men with whom I keep company. With the aid of my grandfather, I feel we can find a way to help you."

I think about her offer for a moment. Despite the joy I've experienced from working with Bowen and his group, I know that staying with them is not a long term solution for me. I finally nod my agreement. "All right, I'll come with you."

The following morning dawns crisp and clear. Everyone has gathered in my chamber at the Whistling Wayfarer Inn, a room I had shared with Damaeris this past night. Not even the innkeeper knows I'm still taking residence at his establishment, for he could be forced to divulge any information he might know to persons returning looking for me. In spite of being so bogged down by her own endeavors, it was Damaeris who took the time to tell Bowen, Faisal and Candis my whereabouts before leaving the inn early that morning to conduct some business in the city. Already I feel so indebted to someone I barely even know. I have already explained my reasons for parting company, and everyone supports my decision.

Candis is the first to step forward. She embraces me more heartily than I imagined she might. "You don't realize how much you became like a sister to me these past three weeks. I wish our time together could have been longer."

Bowen steps up beside us. He waits for a moment before wrapping his arms around us both. He squeezes, and Candis and I lose our breaths for a brief moment before he relaxes his grip. He gives me a crooked smile. "Never forget, this is what family feels like."

I nod as warm tears spring to my eyes. Candis and Bowen step aside and Faisal walks up to me. My heart threatens to burst from my chest as he wipes away my tears and takes my hands. "Hai, the gods have blessed me, and I have had the fortune of calling you my sister. Never forget the feel of Bowen's embrace or his words. We do not lie about family. You are one of us forever."

In spite of my overwhelming emotions, I manage to reply. "I want to see you again. How will I ever find you?"

Faisal is thoughtful for a moment and then he grins. He digs around in one of his travel pouches and finally finds what he is looking for. It is a medallion made of onyx, the first of its kind I've ever seen. He nods towards my chest where my pendant lays, the one given to me by Mikayla. I pull it out from under my blouse. Once taking it in hand, he places the onyx medallion behind it. He mutters something beneath his breath, and a brief glow envelops the two objects. A moment later he releases my pendant, but the medallion can no longer be seen.

Seeing the question in my eyes, Faisal smiles. "It's magic; with the properly spoken words, the medallion became a part of your pendant. Now, all you have to do is take your pendant in hand and think of us. Do it every day, and we will find you."

I raise a skeptical brow. "Really? All I have to do is think about you?"

Faisal smiles and gives me a wink. "I would not lie."

With a sigh of relief, I recognize the gift he has given me and I wrap my arms around his neck. "Faisal, thank you. You have given me so much. Already I can hardly wait until our next meeting."

Faisal squeezes me tightly. I can hear the smile in his voice when he speaks again. "When next we meet, you will have become the strong person you currently hope to be. You have rough times ahead, but you will persevere. Always remember the words of your song ...

Hush, whisper the voice of a siren ...
Don't look back, don't lose heart."

Khichori
(recipe by Tracy Chowdhury)

The cook at the Black Dragon Inn always asks travellers about their favorite recipes, and because the inn is located at a crossroads those recipes sometimes come from distant lands. The recipe for Khichori came with a caravan of spice traders, and while the combination of flavors wasn't quite what the locals were used to, it quickly became a mainstay at the inn.

Khichori
2 cup rice (basmati or jasmine preferable)
3/4 cup lentils
1/2 an onion, chopped
1 Tbsp. minced garlic
1/2 Tbsp. ginger paste
1/2 Tbsp. cumin
1 tsp. turmeric
4 cardamom pods
1 cinnamon stick
8-9 whole cloves
5 Tbsp. ghee
2 bay leaves

Cook rice and lentils and set aside. Meanwhile, heat ghee in a large pan and add remaining ingredients. Stir fry for several minutes to release flavors. Add cooked rice and lentils to the pan, mixing everything until consistent. Serve with spicy fish patties (see next page).

Spicy Fish Patties
14 oz. tuna or salmon, cooked (you can use canned)
2 large potatoes
2 eggs
1/2 an onion, chopped
1 Tbsp. minced garlic
1/2 tbsp. ginger paste
1 tsp. turmeric
green chili (to taste)
1 tsp. salt (or to taste)
1/4 tsp. red chili powder (optional)
handful fresh cilantro (chopped)

Boil potatoes until soft. Combine all ingredients in a large bowl. Using your hands, smash everything together until mixture is uniform. Shape into small patties and fry them in vegetable oil until brown (a deep fryer is helpful). Serve with plain rice or khichori.

VERTHANDI

Gabrielle Harbowy

The innkeeper's tiny daughter is curled upon herself in my chair, watching the fire. She pretends she doesn't see me, but is too young to hide her sly little grin. This is our game: she steals my seat, I pretend to be surprised. Some days I pretend I don't see her at all, and make as if to sit right atop her. The days I only thank her for warming the cushions for me, she seems disappointed.

Her innocence brings a tightness to my chest. That there are places where children can sweetly play, reminds me that there is some sweetness in the world. That it is a place worth nurturing and protecting.

Nurturing and protecting are a part of what I am here to do. They are tasks that take many forms. Not all of those forms are sweet.

Drawn by the sound of my lute strings, the innkeeper emerges from the kitchen with a mug of steaming broth. It is all she has ever seen me eat or drink.

The innkeeper's name is Aundria. She is like a peach: soft and sweet on the surface, but with a solid core of will and strength. Enough courage to break up a brawl, as I learned my first night here. I was unsure at first, but now I am certain that what is to come will not break her.

I take the mug in both my hands, bow my head over it in thanks, and then look up with a smile into doe-brown eyes. "You warm me, mistress," I say, as I do every day, and every day she laughs happily and turns to bustle about her work. The broth is rich, with floating slivers of onion and carrot and tiny shreds of beef. It is not watered down.

The innkeeper's husband, Iohan, is the cook. He manages the kitchen with compassion and iron that both equal and complement hers. Never have I seen two people fit together so seamlessly. He comes from a long line of smiths, but when he set out to woo the innkeeper he traded the heat of the forge for the heat of the cookfire. It is well. He has a finer touch for spices than he ever had for steel. Even this rustic broth is more a work of artistry than I have sampled at the finest palace banquets. Truth be told, I drink it every day because I know that once I move on from here, I will never taste its like again.

I drink half before setting it aside, hands nicely warmed and fingers limber. A few simple child's melodies to start. By the time the inn is full of weary diners and lively revelers, I will be long lost in music, unaware of my fingers on the strings and cognizant only of the heartbeats of inn and town and all who reside within or pass through. Their life pulse sets the meter of my song.

For now, the song of daybreak. It fills the inn with the hope of new beginnings. It can drive poison from the food and ill intent from any who hear it.

More important than it sounds, for I have seen how the threads of these lives may snarl if I do not keep them smooth. Yestereve, the visitor at the end of the upstairs hall offered the cook certain diversions, which he gently declined. He and his wife do dabble in the pleasure of others' company from time to time, but only together, and with a discerning eye. He judged this particular opportunity unstable, and so she is: in the small hours, she slipped into the kitchen and painted venomroot extract on every knife and spoon.

Two tendays hence, the traveler—who is not as common-born as she seems—shall seek company with another innkeeper in another town, and will there beget a child who will grow to become the trusted advisor to the greatest ruler this land will ever know.

Fate is often seen as a weaver of strands; this I have been, when times have called for it, but at this moment I am best suited as a weaver of melody and harmony, descants and counterpoints. Every life has its motif, and I am here now as I am anywhere when I am needed—to ensure that the disparate melodies align themselves into chords, when the timing of one player can tip the song toward dissonance.

The traveler must not already be with child when she arrives at that inn, and these good people and their patrons...Call them strings, or songs, or whatever you like, theirs are not meant to end today. That is not their fate.

It is...kinder than what must be.

Visitors come and go. Some seek only a meal, or a few hours by the fire. Some seek their fortune, but my song whispers to them that they will not find it here.

Toward evening I feel the tickle of prophecy along my spine. Yes. It comes soon.

The innkeeper sends her little daughter up to bed. I ruffle the child's hair before she goes, and take one last look into the depths of her eyes. I know I will never forget anything about her—it is not in the nature of the disir to have the luxury of lapses in memory—but of all the tableaux in which I see-have-seen-will-see her, I wish to remember this one most of all.

Two figures enter in a gust of chilled air. They stamp the snow from their boots but leave their faces in the shadow of their hoods. Now I must retire, for my very presence may distract these two gods, and draw this song out of tune.

"You resided with them," the Youngest pouts. "You didn't let me play with her *my* way. Now she will not grow to inherit the inn and fall in love with the handsome traveler."

I cannot be cross with her, for she is the Youngest and her thoughts are always on love.

"Sigyn will still find love, my dearest. But now she will have a Destiny, as well."

She leaves off from her spinning and crosses her arms. "Why must they all have grand Destinies, sister?" she demands of me.

"Not all of them, dearest. Just the ones who are marked for it. The ones who are strong enough to bear it. Have you seen how they all look to tales of greatness to nourish their souls?"

"Yes. So?"

"So, some of them must be great."

When the muses carry tales of the girl, they will say that her origin is unknown; that her life begins when she becomes a goddess. But I know where her story is born. It is here, in this inn, in this snowy hamlet.

Her mother weeps. Her father, who has never seen the innkeeper inconsolable, hides his own grief in anger; in mead. He blames the woman whose advances he refused, and calls it revenge. The innkeeper calls it a curse, and blames the gods for toying with their lives. She is nearer the truth, but I say nothing. I play my lute and duck my head, and try not to think of how empty my chair was this morning with no sly little one to warm it.

I could pacify their anguish with my song, but I do not. They have earned it, as have I. I have caused their grief; enduring it is my penance.

"My poor dear Verthandi," the Youngest whispers. My head rests upon her shoulder, my hair smoothed by her hand. "Do you not wish you'd let the girl have a simpler life?"

"No...I do not regret it, sister," I answer. "She is suited to this destiny. Weave it with me and you will see."

I attend her wedding. She is still quite young, but carries her mother's iron and her father's compassion, woven together into a quiet strength. Her unbound hair shines in a soft curtain over her shoulders. She loves the god, the trickster, to whom she is given as second wife. He loves her. They bring out the playfulness in each other.

And the loyalty.

I still my fingers on the lute. "Do you see?"

"All right. She has happiness. And handsome sons. And look how she adores him when he dramatizes the tales of his dalliances. Hers is truly the sweetest laugh."

It is not just the bond that they call love, the one that develops over many years of coexistence. A mighty passion exists between them, as exists between her parents.

Ah, her parents. They still run the inn. They still grieve. But their grief has brought them closer, so I take that scant consolation and hold it close to my heart. I have stopped looking in on them.

It is the way of tricksters to play at trickery, and it is the way of trickery to offend. Sigyn's husband has offended; he is complicit in the death of a son of Odin, and such things do not go unpunished. She has seen her two sons twisted and broken to punish their father's misdeed. Her beloved is chained in a cave, and a serpent brought to dwell above him. It is to drip its venom on his face unceasingly, until the twilight of the gods.

This trial is his alone to endure, but the girl—woman, now—attends him. With arms outstretched, she holds a wide bowl between the venom and her husband, protecting him from its sting. This she does unceasingly, devotedly, without complaint. Her mother's strength and her father's compassion gleam in eyes that only mist with tears when she chances to look upon the ropy entrails with which her love is bound. Like her parents, she too knows the pain of losing her children.

Sometimes she sings to her captive husband, sharing songs I played for her in her youth. When she does this, my heart swells to fill my chest with the sweetest of sorrows.

I travel the mortal realm with my lute once more. There are shrines to her now. Not many, but enough. She is a goddess of grieving as well as comfort. Women worship her three aspects: innocent child-bride, nurturing wife, and mourning mother.

Her own mother has dedicated a shrine to Sigyn the mourner—a twist in Fate's song to which even the trickster himself might bow. Yet I take no joy in it, and must look away.

"It is a brave and honorable thing you do," I tell her, while clasping her husband's hand warmly in mine.

"It is my Destiny," Sigyn answers. "I do it gladly." Black droplets make steady, percussive whispers as they splash into her bowl, marking time.

"There is another, a mother who lost her child long ago, who needs your comfort. Will you go to her? I will hold your bowl an hour, so that your beloved does not suffer for your absence."

Her lower lip finds its way between her teeth. She is torn between that shared pain and this one.

"Yes," she says, after a time. "I will go."

I shift the lute to my back and carefully replace her hands with mine, letting not a drop touch the bound and grateful trickster. Carrying her burden, even for a time, lightens my own.

Stewed Beef

Evening meals at the Black Dragon Inn tend to be smaller than lunch. Most folks ate their big meal at lunchtime, and at the end of the day they just want some bread and a simple bowl of stew. But the cook knows that simple doesn't mean bland. He keeps the balance of spices just right, and broth that was made from boiling the meat ends up so warm and rich that it is almost a meal in itself.

1 lb. beef, cut into small pieces
1/2 medium onion, chopped
1 cup water
2 cups red wine
1 Tbsp. parsley
1 tsp. hyssop
2 tsp. salt

3 slices bread
1 1/2 cups broth

1/2 tsp. cinnamon
1/8 tsp. cloves
1/8 tsp. mace
1/2 tsp. red sandalwood
1/8 cup red wine vinegar
1/8 cup currants

Place beef, onion, 1 cup water, wine, parsley, hyssop, and salt into a large pot. Bring to a boil, reduce heat, and allow to simmer.

Meanwhile, tear bread into large pieces and place in a bowl with broth. Let the bread soak for a few minutes, stirring occasionally, and strain into pot, discarding the solids. Cover and let simmer for one hour.

Measure out cinnamon, cloves, mace, and sandalwood into a small bowl. Stir in vinegar a little at a time to prevent clumping. Add spices to pot along with currants, stir, and simmer for another 15 to 20 minutes.

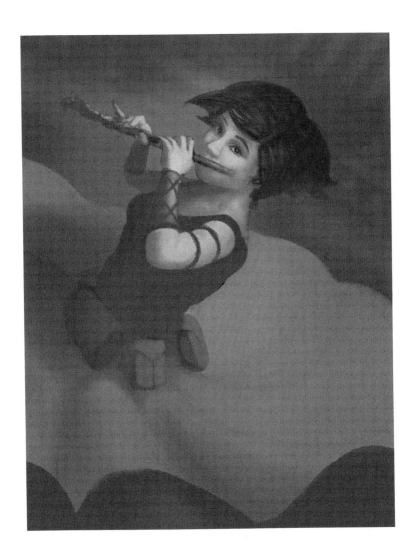

LEGENDARY

Dylan Birtolo

Cedric burst through the door to the inn and jumped down the three steps to splash in a puddle on the dirt road. Before the drops of water hit the ground, he was running to the Golden Chalice. The tavern was not his usual choice of respite, but he had just been informed that the fabled Yshara Tierflame was entertaining this evening. Ever since he had first heard her sing—some ten to twelve years ago— he had been obsessed with becoming a hero. Her ballads were singly responsible for a lifetime of plundering tombs, battling orcs, and wandering the countryside.

Yshara was widely regarded as the best performer in the world by all who were lucky enough to hear her sing. While others copied her music, none could enrapture a crowd with the same level of skill. More than one person suggested that magic may be involved, but all such rumors were quickly dismissed. Even if there was a mystical element, no harm was caused and people left feeling inspired and motivated.

He swerved around a corner, his feet sliding in the mud as he took the corner too fast. He only managed to stay upright by reaching out to a nearby wall and pushing off. The Golden Chalice was just across the street. Cedric could see through the open door and make out the shadows dancing in response to the flickering fireplace. The entire audience sat enraptured, staring at the small raised stage that was at the far end of the main room. He slowed his pace, not wanting to disrupt the performance as he approached.

When he was still several strides away from the entrance, he was overwhelmed by the rich and savory aroma of succulent meat. His mouth started to salivate in response to the appetizing odor. That was empirical evidence about the importance of the event. Philip Hoster, the tavern owner, would not sacrifice one of his prize swine for just anyone. Cedric was sure Philip had opened the best casks of ale as well. Nothing but the best would serve for the arrival of Yshara.

When he got to the door, Cedric stood still, staring at the scene in front of him. It was as he expected—everyone was still as they watched her perform. It was as if they were frozen in ice, afraid to move or breathe lest they disrupt the moment. Yshara stood on the small platform that was one step above the floor. She played a few final notes on her flute as she danced and spun around the stage. When she stopped, she swung the flute with a flourish, tucking it up her sleeve in a blur of movement so it looked like it disappeared. She gave a deep bow and the spell was broken as the crowd began to applaud.

He took the moment to filter into the room and lean against a wall. All of the seats were filled, and there were many other standing patrons enjoying the show. He requested a drink from a passing wench and stayed for three of Yshara's songs, barely noticing the beverages he consumed. By the time she finished her last ballad, the hour was quite late and several of the patrons filed home immediately. Yshara took a table in the corner where people left her alone so she could eat and drink.

As she enjoyed her evening meal, Cedric couldn't help but frequently glace her direction. When he did, he noticed that more often than not, she was looking at him. It caused him to squirm and look away, feeling a rush of blood to his cheeks. After the third glance, she raised two fingers and gestured for him to come join her. He took in a deep breath and steeled himself before walking over to meet a legend he had known of most of his life.

"Good evening," he said as he stood on the opposite side of the table from her. "Your singing was beautiful, as always."

"You've heard me before?"

She gestured for him to sit down and Cedric obliged. He pulled out the chair, dragging it across the wooden floor and aware of the attention it generated. He could feel the stares of several people boring into his back and was sure of their envy. It made the back of his neck red and warm.

"Yes. I've heard you ever since I was little. You're the one who made me want to be an adventurer!" As soon as he blurted it out, he realized how childish it sounded. "You're songs are very inspirational. I'm sure that's something you hear all the time."

Yshara nodded gently and kept her eyes focused on the young man across from her. "And have you been successful?"

"I have. I've traveled to the Eastern Sea and passed through the Deathfang Forest to visit the mountain tribes. I may not be a Politus the Giant, but there are quite a few people who know my name and my deeds."

Yshara picked up her mug and eased it to her lips, taking a long sip. He could see her throat move several times as she quaffed the beverage. Judging by the smell, it was a very rich mead that probably tasted more like honey than alcohol. Throughout it all, she kept her eyes focused on him in a way that made him feel uncomfortable, like she was measuring his worth. He resisted the urge to squirm.

"My dear sir, I am not here simply to pass on tales of times long past. I seek to compose a new ballad. Perhaps, if we were to journey together for a while, you might serve as the inspiration for such a tale. Would you be interested?"

It had been one week since they had last seen a town, three weeks since he had seen his home. Yshara had assured him that she knew where a demon had decided to terrorize the populace. The traveling had been void of danger but not uneventful. Each evening, She told him tales of heroes long since past or never existed. The tales continued in his dreams until he felt as if he were taking part in their trials himself.

Now as they neared the top of the Ridgeback Mountains, he found himself excited at the prospect of the combat to come. He knew demons were dangerous only by reputation; he had never fought or hunted one before. Yshara's presence helped to assuage his fears and he knew that he would be successful with every core of his being.

Even before they crested the top, Cedric saw the plume of smoke. It was too dark and thick to be a normal production from the village. When they clambered over the top, his suspicions were confirmed. They could see the ruins of a village. Roofs were burned, and walls of the small buildings crumbled until they were no more than piles of rubble. If it weren't for the obvious lines of stones where the homes used to stand, He would be hard pressed to recognize it as a village.

"The demon lord would have moved on, but some of his minions may remain. We should investigate."

Cedric agreed with her and they made their way down to the ruins. He walked slowly down what used to be the main street, glancing from one side to the other. Yshara walked behind him, her chin held high and staring straight ahead. He drew his sword and axe, holding the sword in his right hand. He usually didn't fight with both weapons at once, but she convinced him it would be more suited for the epic ballad she was composing.

A small avalanche of rocks sounded off to their left. Cedric whipped around to face that direction, squaring his shoulders to face the sound. He sniffed. Sulfur was heavy on the air, pervasive enough to pierce through the stench of smoke and ash. There was a blur of movement out of the corner of his eye, and he turned to face it, but it was long gone. He felt a chill run down his spine from the base of his skull to end in the depths of his stomach.

"Be careful," he whispered, glancing over his shoulder behind him. "There are…"

A howl cut through the air as four small imps rushed out of their hiding places and charged him. They were only half his size, but they showed no fear as they bore down on him in rage. They reached out with sharp red claws trailing streams of fire. When they opened their mouths to howl it looked as if one was staring into a gateway to the swirling pits of hell.

He swiped with his sword at one of the demons before it reached him. The creature easily jumped back out of range, evading his strike. Cedric turned from it to face the next beast approaching him and brought his axe down in a powerful blow. The weapon struck the creature in the skull with a series of quick cracks before the demon collapsed to the ground. He yanked on his axe, but it stuck and the effort nearly knocked him over. He let go before it pulled him completely off balance.

One of the creatures sprang forward, swiping at the back of his unarmored leg. The claws bit deep and pain shot through his entire body with a heat that drove the wind from his lungs. The imp jumped backwards as he turned awkwardly, trying to hit the creature with his sword. It taunted him with a cackle once it was out of range.

He didn't have time to respond as once again he was assaulted. He saw this imp coming and managed to twist out of the path of the blow. As the claws swiped past his chest, he could feel the heat against his neck and bottom of his chin. He swung awkwardly, without much power behind the blow. The sword bounced off the imp's hide, knocking it back but not drawing blood. The imp let out a sound somewhere between a cackle and a hiss as it lunged at him, forcing him to backpedal as he recovered from the swipe.

Pin pricks sized points of searing pain burned through his armor on his shoulders as one of the beasts leapt onto his back. Its claws passed through the steel plates protecting him and soon bit into the tender skin underneath. Cedric screamed and dropped to one knee, reaching up over his shoulder to grab the imp. His hand closed around thick flesh, so he tightened his grip and hurled the creature over his shoulder. He staggered to his feet just in time to back up and keep the other two at bay with a wild swing of his sword.

His breath was coming in ragged gasps and every inhale burned his lungs. This was not how it was supposed to end! He was supposed to be a hero!

"Yshara!" he called out.

He tried to find her while keeping his eyes on the demonic creatures. They circled around him, taunting as they dance in and out. Yshara stood several strides away from the circling imps. To his surprise, they didn't even glance in her direction. Her long dark hair began to fan out away from her body, strands floating out to either side of her head. Her skin gave off a subtle glow and she looked straight ahead as if lost in focus and seeing nothing. She raised her flute up to her lips and began to play.

The notes that streamed from her instrument were discordant and made almost every muscle in his body seize up. He dropped to the ground on his hands and knees, fingers clenched tight around the hilt of his sword. Each note sounded more unearthly than the last and felt like it stabbed through his ears into his brain. The pain subsided to a gentle throbbing, and he was able to raise his head. What he saw amazed him.

While Yshara played, the three imps stood enraptured. They stared in her direction, slowing swaying back and forth. She continued to play, and Cedric eased himself to a standing position. He walked over to one of the imps, keeping his sword in front of him, but the creature never reacted. He gently poked it with the tip of his blade, but the imp continued to sway and stare. Not wanting to waste the advantage while he had it, he slaughtered the creatures while they seemed oblivious to his presence.

When he finished, Yshara stopped playing, lowering the flute from her lips. Her hair dropped back down to rest against her shoulders once again. She blinked, and her eyes refocused on Cedric and the carnage of slaughtered corpses around him. He let his sword hang loosely from his fingers, barely held up.

"What was that?" he whispered.

"A way that I can help."

"How did you do that?"

"It does not matter. It is not a skill you can learn. Come, we must continue to search for the demon lord."

The next couple of days, they followed the trail of devastation left through the mountainous wilderness. Even without Yshara's assistance, the trail would have been easy to follow. It gave him the impression that the demon lord did not care if it was found. Confident in its own power, it was willing to face anyone foolish enough to follow the path it carved through the mountains. How long ago had it been since Cedric shared that level of confidence?

They were camped for the evening, and Cedric was rooting through his pack looking for the last of his rations. Yshara sat across from him, watching him through the faint flames of their meager fire. She chewed on her own dried food, mouth moving slowly as she ate.

"Tomorrow we will catch up to the demon lord," Yshara said. A chill ran down Cedric's spine in response. She tilted her head, as if she could see his body's involuntary reaction. "You seem concerned by this."

He swallowed a large piece of dried meat and coughed on it a few times to clear his throat. "With how much trouble I had with the imps, can you blame me? I used to think that I had a chance, but this is a demon lord! This feels like insanity. I'm not a hero worth singing about."

"Do not doubt yourself, Cedric. All great heroes have their trials and you are no different. You are the object of my next ballad. You will be victorious."

"Only if you help me like you did with the imps. I wasn't much of a hero then."

"When I finish the tale, you will be the great hero I know that you can be. No one will even know of my involvement beyond anything more than chronicler."

Cedric sighed and leaned back to rest on his arms. He turned away to look in the direction of the demon's trail. Somewhere out there, his future waited. For better or worse, it would come to an end tomorrow. At least if he died, it would be quick at the hands of a demon lord. He heard a rustle of clothing as Yshara stood and walked to stand just behind him. She placed a hand lightly on his shoulder.

"When you slay the demon lord, which you will, think what it will mean. I will pen the tale of your journey and your triumph, and it will be heard all through the five kingdoms. Every court will want to hear the latest legend, Cedric the demon slayer."

He couldn't help but smile as she spoke and a warmth filled him as if brought about by her touch. It was a euphoria more heady than that brought by alcohol to think that someday soon, other children might be inspired by his story and his victories. His name would be heard in lands where he had never been. Of course, many people would probably want to hear the tale from his own lips, the lips of the man who killed a demon.

It was about an hour before midday when they found the cave where the demon lord had taken shelter from the sun. It was a large opening in a sheer rock wall with deep gouges in the stone from the monster's claws as it scrambled into the shelter. The lip of the cave was singed and blackened, and the odor of sulfur was once again heavy in the air. In the village the odor had been merely present, but here it was oppressing.

They climbed to the edge of the cave and Cedric drew both of his weapons. Yshara stood calmly behind him, her flute dangling in her right hand. He glanced back at her and she gave him a nod, gesturing forward with her chin. He took a deep breath and crossed the threshold of the cave. He could feel her close behind him and hear her feet as they scuffed across stone.

Up ahead there was a deep rumbling that he could feel in his torso as much as he could hear it. It sounded like a small avalanche, with rocks rolling and cracking against each other. He tightened his grip on his sword and axe, shrugging his shoulders to loosen up the tension. A faint light illuminated a sharp corner up ahead, and it sounded like the rumbling was coming from just around it.

Cedric crept up to the corner and peeked around it. He could see the demon lord lounging on the rocks and feel the heat emanating from the beast. It had a faint red glow outlining every muscle and ridged bone under its hide. The beast was monstrous, taller than he was even when it was sitting and propped against the wall. The demon's chest heaved as it snored, oblivious to the intruders.

He crept forward, hoping to use the surprise to his advantage. He had taken two steps when Yshara put a hand on his shoulder and pulled him back. She looked at him and shook her head. He raised an eyebrow and she leaned forward to whisper in his ear.

"A hero would not sneak up on the demon. A hero must charge forward heroically." He opened his mouth to object, but shut it when she glared at him. "You will be immortal."

Those words steeled his nerves and he stood up straighter. He smiled in anticipation of the coming battle. With a scream of rage that echoed through the narrow cave, he charged with his weapons high over his head. The demon's eyes snapped open and glared at this unwelcome intrusion. As it struggled to its feet, it took a deep breath and spat fire in his direction.

Cedric dodged to the side, rolling out of the way of the flames but feeling their heat as it licked at the stone behind him. The rocks under his body got uncomfortably warm just being this close to the inferno. He continued to rush forward, closing the distance just as the demon was getting to his feet. With a shout, he swung both weapons forward over his head, trying to sink them deep into the demon's leg.

The sword bounced off the rubbery hide with such force that felt like his arm was going to be torn off, but he managed to hold onto the blade. The axe fared a little better—carving a small cut and making the demon bleed. Its blood was hot and lit up the room. When he yanked his axe back, drops of blood flew through the air. They smoked and hissed where they hit and pockmarked the stone.

The demon swiped with his claws, attempting to end the fight quickly. Cedric saw the attack coming and ducked, the talons slicing through the air close enough for him to feel the wind from the blow. The demon raised his other hand and slammed his fist into the ground, attempting to squash the human. Cedric scrambled forward, staying just ahead of the lethal blows.

He picked up his weapons again, swinging them both in a fierce arc at the demon's wrist. He let the axe lead the way with the sword close behind. This time the axe carved a chunk through the flesh and the sword sank deeply into the wound. The demon howled in rage, yanking its hand back with enough force to drag Cedric off his feet. He fell onto his knees with a crack.

Unfortunately, the demon was faster than he was. It kicked out, knocking him up and off the ground and sent him flying through the air until he collided against the stone wall. He heard a couple of his ribs crack and all of the wind was knocked out of his body. As he attempted to draw breath, the pressure in his lungs increased and he was filled with an intense pain that sent him into a coughing fit. He struggled to get to one knee. The demon charged.

Cedric brought his axe over his head and dropped it down, using the weight to his advantage. The demon swatted it aside as if it was a toy, sending it far to the back of the cavern. His shoulder burned, and his left arm hung limply at his side. He tried to bring his right arm up and use the sword, but the demon swiped at him, gouging several lines through his armor, cutting deep into his flesh, and sending him sprawling.

The entire cave shook as the demon bellowed its rage and charged again. He barely had the energy to lift his head and watch his doom approach. His sword was several feet away from his outstretched hand, and even if he had it, he did not have the strength to wield it. He closed his eyes as the demon lunged forward, claws extended.

Several seconds passed.

Cedric cracked open his eyes and saw the demon frozen, his arm completely extended. Yshara stood between them, playing her flute. The tune was soft, something that he could barely hear. Small wisps of smoke flowed from the instrument and the tendrils reached out to coil around the demon, holding it in place. The only movement that betrayed the demon's consciousness was its eyes. They focused on her with the rage of a burning star.

She stopped playing and lowered her flute by her side. Cedric's eyes went wide with fear, but to his surprise, the tendrils of smoke remained coiled around the creature from another plane. Yshara watched the demon, but spoke to Cedric without breaking her concentration.

"Pick up your sword. You must kill the demon lord."

He crawled towards his weapon, beholden to her command. When he reached it and coiled his fingers around the hilt, he felt a surge of strength that momentarily overcame his pain. He struggled to his feet on legs that visibly shook. The tip of the sword scraped against the rock floor as he advanced on the demon. It continued to stare at Yshara, transfixed.

Lifting the weapon over his head, he grabbed it in both hands and let out a scream. He brought the weapon down as hard as he could on the paralyzed creature's neck. To his surprise, the steel ripped right through flesh and bone, decapitating the creature. He felt a rush of heat as the creature's blood spilled forth, warming the entire cavern.

The rush of energy he felt before drained out of him as the demon fell. The sword felt three times as heavy in his hands and he let it drop to the ground with a clatter. Cedric let his body fall as well, collapsing to his knees and letting his knuckles drag on the ground as he stared at the body.

"I did it," he whispered.

"Yes, you did. You are truly a hero." Yshara walked to stand behind him as she spoke. She rested the palm of her hand on his right shoulder.

"It was you. You didn't need me. You could have done it on your own."

"You had to deliver the killing blow."

"Why?"

"To power the magic and guarantee your place in history."

She bent forward and tightened her grip on his shoulder. Her right hand shot forward, sinking a dagger up to the hilt in his side and piercing his lung. He tried to gasp, but gurgled instead. She yanked the weapon free and red runes danced along the length of the blade, bright enough to be seen through the blood. She used her finger to transfer a significant amount of the red fluid from the weapon to her flute. She let the weapon fall to the ground and began to play.

Kyler rushed through the streets, dodging around the foot traffic as he made his way to the Gilded Peacock. He had heard that Yshara had come to play and would be gracing the town with her presence for one night only. The rumors spread faster than her travels, and he had heard that her latest composition was even better than the last.

When he got to the tavern, it was crowded to the point of bursting with patrons standing in the doorway and sitting on window sills. He used his small size and youth to worm his way to the front as much as he could. When he could press forward no more, he found the nearest table and climbed on top of it for a view of the fabled singer. He watched as she stepped forward in her livery, her flute held gently at her side. When she opened her eyes, the entire tavern fell into complete silence, all enraptured by her gaze. When she spoke, many patrons held their breath to better listen, including Kyler.

"This night I will sing you a tale the likes of which have never graced your ears. This is the story of Cedric Demonsbane."

Eggs and Apples

Sometimes in the late evening, a customer comes into the Black Dragon Inn looking for a bite to eat, only to find that the regular customers have already managed to eat everything the cook had prepared. There are usually eggs in the larder and apples in the cellar though, and the cook has found that the dish his mother used to make for when he was feeling off is a perfect for keeping weary travelers happy.

1 apple
2 to 3 eggs
2 Tbsp. butter
1/4 tsp. sugar
1/8 tsp. ginger
1/8 tsp. salt
pinch cloves
pinch cinnamon
pinch pepper
pinch saffron

Peel, core, and slice apples, and parboil them in water until just tender. Drain off the water, put the apples into a frying pan with butter, and fry them until soft and golden. Remove the apples from the pan and set aside. Beat the eggs in a bowl and then fry in butter, adding apples just before the eggs finished. Sprinkle with spices and serve hot.

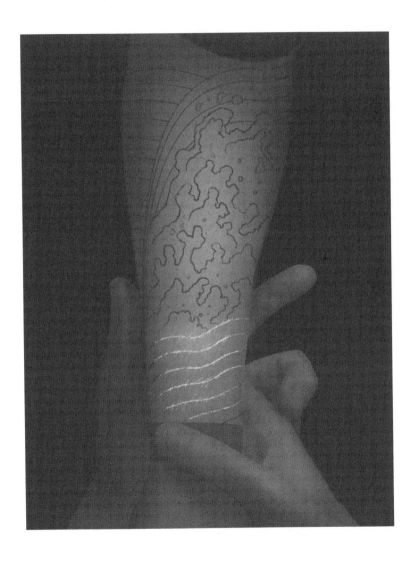

THE ARTISAN

C. S. Marks

My real name is Clovis, but I have been known as "Nightingale" for many years. I have played and sung songs both glorious and tragic, accompanied by my trusty lambalain, in the courts of kings and in the homes of the wealthiest men. I have eaten the finest food and drunk of the best wine, as befits my status—bearer of tidings, bringer of news, he whose voice rivals the nightingale's. It's just not right that I should be required to trudge through driving rain, sliding and floundering in mud up to my shins, to take refuge in as lowly an establishment as *The Skulking Raven.*

Please don't misunderstand ... I love the *Raven.* It looks decrepit and smells worse, but, then, so does the majority of its clientele. When I play there, I leave my finery behind. Tonight I'm wishing I had worn at least one of my silken undershirts, though, as it's a rare cold night in Castalan. But it will be worth it, as I do love the old tavern, where I can truly be myself.

It's such a relief to finally catch sight of it. The old, weathered sign swings and creaks ... I can hear it despite the rain. One can barely read the legend anymore, but the image is unmistakable—a disheveled, disreputable-looking black bird with a rather formidable beak. It appears to be lurking and smiling as though it has a great secret which could bring about the downfall of many. Yes, I said *smiling*. Difficult to do with a beak, I know, but it's there just the same. The warm orange-gold light filtering through the soot-filmed windows beckons me inside, and I know I will be welcome.

As always happens in bad weather, the place is filled with people. Still, everyone knows me here, and they have been expecting to be entertained. I soon find myself in the best seat—near the fire but not too near—and the proprietor, Urich, has brought me a vessel of wine already. I won't need to pay.

The smell of the place takes some getting used to, being a mixture of wonderful roast meats and fragrant pipe-leaf together with unwashed men who smell even worse than usual due to the rain. There's always a bluish haze in the air; you can see the underside of a thick layer of smoke near the blackened oaken ceiling. Whenever the door opens, a gust of air from outside makes it ripple and swirl like water. The sawdust on the floor ... I don't even want to think of what it's mixed with, but it smells of vomited liquor and barnyard boots.

I love the sound the wind makes when it rattles the ancient glass panes in the filthy windows. I recall asking Urich about the windows once. "Why do you not clean them? There are layers of soot from the First Reckoning, I'm thinking."

"That's one of the stupidest questions I ever heard," said Urich with a curl of his lip. "Think about my customers. Do they want people to be able to look through the windows and see who's here without actually coming inside? Of course they don't." He smiled beneath hard, humorless black eyes. "Fool ..."

I suppose, in a way, I am a fool. I thought my fame would last forever. Now I'm here, and not in the King's court. No longer the bearer of news, as I am privy to far less than I used to be, but the people here aren't looking for news, anyway. They just want a good story. I'm getting to be an old man, and I have pains in my body now that won't go away, but I can still give them that. It's a good thing I rarely try to sing anymore, as my voice is not what it once was. I recall my singing-master's comment that only wine improves with age. I think that's mostly right.

I have unwrapped my lambalain from the waxed canvas casing, making sure it's good and dry before I try to play it. The warm, mellow hedgewood neck and spruce top beckon like an old friend—my fingers have worn grooves and struck many scratches in the wood over the years—and I check to see if it is in tune, throwing the worn leather strap back over my head. It's a fine instrument, and needs almost no attention even after days in the damp.

"A tale, Nightingale! Let's have your best tonight!" yelled a half-drunken man with the hands of a dock worker. *Only half-drunk? Must not have been here long,* I thought.

"Yes! A tale!" shouted another, and soon the entire great room had taken up the chant. "Tale! Tale! Nightingale! Tale! Tale!"

I held up my hand, and they quieted. "A tale?" I said, punctuating my words with chords on the lambalain. "A tale of triumph, or a tale of woe? Of where we've been, or where we may go? Words that inspire, or fate that's dire? What would you have from the Nightingale's lyre?"

Through the general muttering, I heard several requests, but none appealed. Then I saw the design on the back of one man's hand—the name of a woman, pierced by a blade—and I knew.

"Tonight I will tell the Tale of the Artisan," I said. "Draw near, if you would hear."

Naturally, everyone in the room quieted and drew a little closer; what else was there to do on a dank, rainy night? The Artisan's tale wasn't known to many, for he was very mysterious, but I knew I could enthrall my audience, for I had actually met him. I knew why he had come to dwell in the sutherlands, and I had a fair idea of who and what he truly was, though I didn't even pretend to understand him. He was perhaps the most gifted skin-artist that has ever been.

Most people are familiar with the practice of using needles and multicolored ink to engrave permanent designs on the skin. Some men, in fact, go to great lengths to cover themselves with pictures, letters, and runes. They may think it makes them seem fierce, or it may serve as a reminder of memorable events, or of loved ones, living and dead. The artists who craft those designs, naturally, vary in ability, and men soon learn that good ones are worth the price, for the designs will endure for a lifetime whether they are pleasing or not.

I have seen some that made me cringe, and I wondered whether the offending "artist" lived to offend another day. I know this much: drunken men should never patronize a skin artist. I'm sure there's little to compare with the feeling of sobering up to find some hideous image permanently affixed in the skin of one's arm. Or chest. Or place best left covered. If you were a less-than-masterful skin artist, you would most likely have a price on your head from someone, hence the tendency to move from one settlement to the next. If you were masterful, you could command a very high price for your work.

The Artisan came from the far northern lands. I remember the first time I saw him—in the King's Court in Dûn Bennas. I had recently finished with my part of the evening's entertainment when I noticed him sitting alone beside one of the tall windows. The evening breeze stirred the greyish-green fabric of the hood he wore, revealing a few strands of very long, silvery hair underneath. The eyes didn't seem to go with the hair ... they were old eyes, and dark, but the skin around them was smooth and youthful. At first I wondered whether he was a man or a woman.

"Who is that?" I whispered to one of the court musicians, who sat near me.

"Some kind of skin-artist. Kind of makes your skin crawl, eh?"

I knew then that the Artisan was male, as women are not permitted to be skin-artists. "What's he doing here?" I asked.

"Who knows? I just wish he would leave. His presence unsettles me. I've heard he just likes to watch people, but whatever it is he's looking for, I have no interest in." He took a long swallow of spirits from a flask he had concealed under his tunic. "They say the King is trying to employ him, but I haven't heard anything more." Another swallow from the flask. "I can tell you this much ... I wouldn't let him *touch* me, let alone decorate my flesh."

"Have you ever seen the designs he renders?"

"A few of them, and they are undeniably beautiful. But he likes to engrave runes as well ... no design is ever plain. The runes say things in tongues I don't understand."

I would later come to learn of the significance of those runes, and why people feared the Artisan. Now, in the *Skulking Raven*, I would tell as much of the story as I had managed to piece together. Bards are trained by Loremasters, and I had acquired enough knowledge to tell the Artisan's tale with a minimum of ... creative embellishments, though I was always free to embellish as much as I liked. This was one of my very best offerings, one I knew would set the *Raven's* patrons talking for some time to come. Plucking a few rather ominous notes on the lambalain, I began.

* * *

The Elf named Finayn glared down at the work he had just completed, frowning in disgust. When a shadow fell across the pig-skin he had been practicing on, he tried to hide it, but to no avail. His Master's hand fell upon it before he could whisk it away.

"Don't look at it, please, Master," said Finayn. "It's not good enough … I just can't seem to make the fine lines I've been striving for."

Léiras, the Far-sighted, shook his pale head, his light blue eyes roaming over the pig-skin, appraising each image on it. "You're too hard on yourself. This is a fine job; I've rarely seen better." He looked down at his apprentice, smiling his usual chilly smile.

Finayn sighed. "But you *have* seen better."

"Only a very few, and the artisans were much older than you are. By the time you've had as much practice as they have had, you'll surpass them."

"Then I must work harder," said Finayn. "It is my intention to become the best skin-artist this world has ever known, and I must not stop working." He looked up at Léiras with worried eyes. "Do you think I'll ever get there?"

"You will … that's what worries me. I fear you may gain more than the skills you crave if you do not temper your passions a little bit. You may gain some things you will regret."

Finayn, who was used to his Master's mysterious pronouncements, was less concerned than he should have been. He waited patiently for Léiras to continue.

"I think it's time you went forth into the wide world, working in real flesh. Your work is of the highest quality, and many will desire it. You will be able to provide well for yourself. Our friends in Tuathas, as with all mortal men, will make great use of your talents, I'm sure. When you get to the Citadel, look for a man named Campos. Actually, he calls himself 'The Blue Mage,' though I'm not sure what sort of magic he performs. He will arrange accommodations. Just give him this—he'll be very glad to have it." Léiras drew a small phial of greenish-blue liquid from the sleeve of his robe and handed it to Finayn.

"But I'm not ready! My work is too far from perfect," said Finayn, his face going almost as pale as his silver-white hair.

"I think you had better get ready," said Léiras. "I cannot teach you anything more. The lessons you require cannot be learned here, alas. Go and find Campos, and then your real education will begin."

Finayn didn't want to leave home, and he managed to put Léiras off until the onset of winter. He put all efforts into his work, promising to leave the Elven-realm at the coming of spring, to which, of course, Léiras had to agree. In the meantime, Finayn practiced on his own flesh in places usually hidden by clothing. Elves did not employ skin-artists, preferring to remain unmarked. However, they had taken to framing the pig-skins he had decorated, even stitching them into bags and boots. The designs, injected deep into the leather, would never fade.

At last spring came and Finayn had run out of excuses. He packed his belongings, said farewell to his Master and his few friends, and set out for Tuathas, the far western realm of men. The Tuathar were quite friendly with the Elves, especially those of Finayn's realm, and he was not worried. He resolved to continue perfecting his craft, no matter where he found himself.

As expected, the Tuathar welcomed him with open arms, and he soon found himself at the center of a fairly brisk trade. He did, indeed, find the Blue Mage, whose eyes lit up the moment he beheld the blue-green phial. Finayn never did learn what the liquid was, but it was obviously of great value.

Campos, who insisted that Finayn call him "Mac," soon installed the artisan in a comely little workshop in the heart of the Citadel's trade district. There was an apartment above, providing all the necessary comforts. Mac, an affable fellow, quickly learned that Finayn would give no trouble, and left him alone to practice his craft.

Elvish skin-artists were always assumed to be superior, and Finayn's work did nothing to dispel that assumption. At first he merely did as his clients requested, but then, one summer day, everything changed. He was looking at the right arm of a young tradesman, running his elegant fingers over the fine-veined brown skin, looking deeply into the flesh, when his mind strayed into a kind of trance. The rhythmic caress of his fingers on the young man's arm stopped, and his eyes glazed over for a moment. When they cleared, he saw a line of words wavering into view on the underside of the forearm. Translated, they said "I am a warrior."

Finayn blinked in surprise, and the words vanished. But he had seen them, and they were "right."

"I know what I should engrave here," he said to the young man. With your permission, we'll begin today." When Finayn had finished the work a week later, the young man was very pleased. The runes swirled gracefully around his forearm, together with elaborate tracings that looked like blue steel wire.

"It's beautiful. What does it mean?"

"It means that, though you be a tradesman, you have a warrior's heart," said Finayn, looking levelly into the young man's eyes. "Wear it well, and may your life be blessed."

He took the coins the young man offered, and thought little more of it. Later he would learn that the man had forsaken life as a tradesman, deciding instead to join the ranks of the King's guard. Finayn smiled, pleased that he had been so perceptive. Still, he wondered. *How did I know he was better suited to life as a warrior? It must be that he gave me some clue—perhaps his bearing, or the look in his eye?*

When his next chance came, he tried again, searching the flesh with his eyes and his fingers, waiting for the right message. It came without even trying, to his dismay. *Faithless and false, soon undone.* He looked up into the man's eyes and saw nothing of honor, only greed and selfishness. *This man takes what he wants, and gives nothing back,* he thought. *His fortune was built on false promises and deception.* Finayn swallowed hard. Obviously, such words would not do. "I am at your service," he said. "What designs do you desire?"

Before the next full moon, the man had been murdered. Someone had cut his throat and left him naked in a dark alleyway. The news did not come as a surprise to Finayn, but he wondered. *Were the words I saw on his arm prophetic? Did they influence his fate, or merely foresee it? What would have happened if I had actually engraved them there? Could I have chosen other words and changed his stars for the better?* He sighed, remembering the beautiful eagle he had graven on the back of the dead man's hand. "All that work wasted ..."

Finayn had wanted his works to be extraordinary, but he was only beginning to understand how truly extraordinary they could be. His designs were so beautiful that many desired them, and most who came to see him already knew what they wanted of him. He marked them with the names of their wives, husbands, children, and favorite horses. He made likenesses of beloved pets, birds of prey, gentle doves, snarling wolves, and dragons--plenty of those.

But sometimes they asked for his insight, and he would search for the right words. "Tell me what you would put on my arm," they would say. Usually the insights would come, and, if he revealed them, people were pleased. They began to refer to him as "The Artisan," and his heart swelled with pride. But the words of Léiras came back to him as he sat alone in the dark. *I fear you may gain more than the skills you crave if you do not temper your passions a little bit. You may gain some things you will regret.* He told himself it wouldn't matter ... that he didn't care. Then he met Miriam.

She came into his shop on a chilly, rainy afternoon. At first Finayn thought her ordinary—just another wealthy woman wanting his attentions. When he saw the deep melancholy in her beautiful eyes, he knew differently.

"I have brought the message my husband desires. He wishes it engraved across my right hand ... as a reminder," she said, placing a bit of paper on the table.

Finayn examined the paper, frowning slightly. "He wants me to engrave the name 'Halvaar,' together with the image of a sea-eagle, and the words 'All that I am is his.' Is that right?" The woman nodded, but he could see the hurt in her eyes. She didn't want to belong to anyone. Finayn had rarely seen such resignation in a young woman. "What's your name?" he asked.

"I am Halvaar's wife. That is all you ever need know," she said. "Now, will you do the work, or shall I go elsewhere? I should probably warn you that my husband is accustomed to getting what he wants."

Yes, I'm sure he is. "Let's have a look at your hand."

As he examined her smooth, white skin, Finayn saw many words forming there. *Trapped ... a flower that cannot bloom ... crushed by the weight of another's doubt ...* He drew a deep breath. "I will do my best," he said.

The woman would have to come in for a number of sessions, as the design was elaborate and working on the back of the hand was painful. He had a special mixture that he rubbed on the skin to dampen the discomfort, but he could not remove it entirely.

People talk to hairdressers, tavern-keepers, and skin-artists. Miriam told Finayn her name during the third session, and by the fourth he had learned quite a lot about her. Promised in marriage before she could walk, she had been allowed few choices in her life. She had been married for only two years. Her husband, a wealthy merchant more than twice her age, had spent his life acquiring things. She was his third wife.

"He keeps me well," she said wistfully. "That's something."

Finayn did not look up from his work, but his grip tightened on her hand. *No one should suffer the loss of freedom,* he thought. *People are not property.* He looked at the sea-eagle forming on Miriam's wrist. "I have been thinking," he said. "This could use a spray of sea-foam and a cascade of waves and rivulets flowing around to the back and spiraling into your forearm. That would look most appealing, don't you agree?"

"Halvaar already thinks your work is too costly," she said. "I don't know that he would pay for it."

Finayn thought for a moment. "Then tell him I had planned it from the beginning, and it is included in the cost already. It can be our secret." He looked into her soft brown eyes. "I would rather people notice the eagle and the water, not Halvaar's declaration that he owns you." He took his own small piece of paper and wrote a message to Halvaar, but he wrote it in his own tongue. "Here. Give him this. It explains there will be no additional cost."

She smiled. "He cannot read this. For that matter, neither can I, but don't bother re-doing it. If he thinks he is getting a bargain, he won't be able to resist." When she left him that day, Finayn saw gratitude in her eyes, but there was something else. For the first time since he had met her, he saw her spirit kindle, and he knew what he would do.

That night he sat quietly in the lamp-light, looking at one of the few remaining bare spots on his left arm. There he began the work of engraving the name "Miriam" in very tiny Elvish script, using deep sepia ink. *Warm brown ... like her eyes ...*

She came for twenty more sessions. The cascade of ocean waves took quite a bit of doing—had he actually been charging for them, they would have cost a fortune. But Finayn had his reasons. The extra sessions allowed him to spend more time with Miriam, but more than that, the convoluted, swirling lines of the water allowed him to place Elvish script all along her wrist and forearm. One would have to be sharp-eyed to see them, would need to be looking for them to find them, and would have to be far more learned than Halvaar to understand them.

I belong to no one, and I will be free. No man owns my spirit. Those who try will fall.

He wondered what would happen. He had not actually read those words on her flesh—they were *his* words. Could he influence her fate with them? Halvaar would never know they were there, and neither would Miriam. It would be a good test.

He saw bruises on her sometimes, though she had hidden them fairly well. Such brutality toward one's wife was rare in Tuathas, and unknown among Elves. Finayn would not ask her about it, but he guessed Halvaar had a long, abusive history.

Finayn's efforts redoubled. Here, in a bit of cresting foam, a tiny inscription: *Pain given me comes back tenfold.* Each night he ran his fingertips across his left arm, caressing Miriam's name, hoping he could help her.

He never got the chance to finish the work. Miriam came to the shop, a dark red hood hiding her face. She stepped inside as Finayn rose to greet her, but she did not speak. She merely placed a small velvet pouch on the table, turned, and ran back out into the rain.

He knew better than to call after her, but his heart smoldered with anger. Why had she hidden her face? Was it because she didn't want to look at him, or was it because Halvaar had finally decided he didn't care if people saw the bruises? The tiny sepia letters on his left arm burned as he picked up the pouch, reaching inside to find a few gold coins and a message, which he read aloud.

"Here is the gold you were promised. My wife is forbidden to see you henceforward. You will cease meddling in my affairs, on pain of death."

Finayn's anger burst into flame. *Me? You threaten me with death? You're the one who deserves to die!* He nurtured his anger for several hours, plotting and planning what he would do to Halvaar if given the opportunity, all the while knowing he would do none of it. He was a passionate soul, but not violent. Still, he imagined freeing Miriam and torturing Halvaar, until he was weary from his dark thoughts. Then came the fear ... fear that his actions had been discovered. *The beast can't have found the secret inscriptions. He would not understand them even if he had. But what if he employed a translator? What if Miriam herself discovered them and guessed their meaning? What if she tried to defy him and suffered his wrath?*

Finayn's rage and dread had exhausted him, and he actually slept for a while. He awoke to a burning pain in his arm and Miriam's voice screaming in his ears: *No ... no ... please don't ... I belong only to you. There is no one else— I belong to you! Please don't!*

The pain seared into his flesh, spreading up his arm, and he doubled over in agony. Then, to his horror, both the pain and the voice grew silent. Heart pounding, hair damp with sweat, Finayn pulled back his left sleeve. Miriam's name was gone! The flesh where it had been was seared, the edges charred as though from a branding iron, but the arm was otherwise unmarked. He knew what had happened to her, and that it was his fault. The secret inscription had not saved her … it had doomed her. *My arrogance destroyed her. I played with her life, and she has lost it.* He ran outside into the night. The clouds had cleared, and the stars shone as brightly as they ever did through the haze of the City. Finayn turned his eyes heavenward, but the stars held no comfort. There was no remedy for the pain and guilt he bore.

The *Raven* was unusually quiet. No one slammed his tankard down on the table, and any conversation was kept to a low muttering. *I'm in fine story-telling fettle tonight,* I thought, though my accounting of the Artisan's tale had been somewhat altered to suit my present audience. The Artisan, an Elf of the Old Realm, had set his lustful eyes on the wife of a wealthy merchant. She, naturally, had responded to his Elvish charms, a comment which elicited quite a few groans and expressions of disgust from my patrons, many of whom didn't care for Elves in general. The adulterous pair had committed all sorts of unseemly acts in the back room of his shop.

Of course, everyone wanted descriptions of those unseemly acts. "Use your imaginations!" I said, to which they laughed and replied, "We have you, so we don't have to!"

"Ah. Well, let's just say there are many things a pair of talented Artisan's hands can do."

I knew the truth would not do at all—the *Raven's* regulars would have little sympathy for Finayn and even less for Miriam—many of them probably beat their own wives, if they ever had them. The idea that a wife is the property of her husband, while not particularly enlightened in my opinion, is widespread in the lands around Castalan.

The next part of the story, however, was mostly true. Finayn had avenged Miriam—they found Halvaar's charred remains chained to a chair in what was left of his opulent house. No one mourned him, for he had beaten his wife to death after setting her on fire, but they suspected Finayn immediately. Though he had covered his tracks well, it wasn't long before he was imprisoned and brought to trial.

After hearing all evidence, the Magistrate handed down his decision. "You stand accused of a terrible crime, but we have heard no direct proof that the victim fell by your hand. Therefore, we cannot convict you of so dark a crime. However, circumstances point so strongly toward your guilt that I'm afraid I must banish you from the realm of Tuathas. You may not set foot upon our soil again, or you will be executed. That is my decision."

"Banished for killing a merchant? Seems like a public service to me," yelled one of the patrons. "Depending on what he's selling, of course."

"Killing a merchant is the worst sort of crime," said another, who, naturally, was a merchant.

About twenty voices shouted in unison: "Be *quiet,* or I'll ..." The rest varied from "thump your skulls" to "break your miserable necks." Yes, indeed—I had them enthralled tonight.

I continued the tale, describing Finayn as he wandered from settlement to settlement, quietly plying his trade, for untold years. The great realm of Tuathas fell to an eruption of fire-mountains, but there were settlements of men everywhere, and Finayn could provide for himself. He earned only enough to supply his own necessities and he would not render any design of his own volition—only what the customer ordered. Still, he saw the words forming sometimes. He vowed not to pay attention to them.

Despite his efforts to remain relatively unnoticed, his reputation spread. He could not hide his ability, and eventually he was called to stand before the King in Dûn Bennas. When the King beheld the beauty of the work, he ordered that Finayn be employed as part of the Royal Court. Soon all the fashionable ladies and men of high standing could sport designs done by the Artisan. Finayn saw words on some of them, but they were neither sinister nor melancholy. He broke his vow, engraving the words *Deep and Abiding Love* on one young lady's shoulder, together with a rose so realistic it looked as though one could pluck it and feel the dew on his hands.

Another customer, a stalwart fellow, received a fine rendition of a scarlet-winged dragon with the legend *Courage Burns Within.* People paid fabulous amounts for the Artisan's work, which soon became a symbol of status. Therefore, it did not surprise Finayn when King Roland, the seventh ruler of the realm, called for private counsel.

"It is said that whatever you write comes to pass," said Roland. "I would have you engrave words of power on me, for there is a matter which concerns me greatly, and I fear I will be forced to deal with it soon. I have had ... bad dreams." Finayn saw momentary, faraway dread in Roland's eyes before they filled with resolve again. "If your words are powerful enough, I will prevail."

Finayn had kept his ears open, and he had heard rumblings of unrest and discord within the City, but he didn't know much more than that.

"Who threatens you, my lord?"

"I cannot tell you ... better that you not know. But from this day forward, you must not engrave words of power upon any man other than me. I will provide well for you ... you needn't fear any loss of income or reputation. I trust you will agree?"

Finayn looked into Roland's eyes, searching his thoughts. He had always tried to stay out of men's affairs— it seemed they spent much of their short lives bickering and squabbling over things like rank and territory—but now he would be forced to deal with Roland's affairs, at least. The King's eyes beseeched, but with an undercurrent of menace. *He believes I can solve all his problems just by drawing the right words in his flesh. And if I don't ... I sense he will blame me. I will have to convince him that I do not wield such influence.* He touched the scar on his left arm, searching for the right words to say.

"My King, I'm afraid the rumors you have heard are exaggerated. I am ancient by your standards, and I am very perceptive, but the words I paint are not prophecies. I cannot make things happen. It seems I can look into men's hearts sometimes and find what it is that drives them; if so, the words are revealed. But I cannot alter the future. I would be most pleased and honored to decorate you, but I cannot claim to be able to protect you. The words I see come to me unbidden, and I have little control over them. What I see might not please you."

"Is that so?" said Roland, clearly unconvinced. "Well, I think you had better have a look, then. Tell me what words you read." He extended his strong right arm, pulling the sleeve back. "When you are in my realm, you must acknowledge my authority," he said. "Take my arm and tell me what you see."

Finayn stood still for a moment. *I dare not refuse him ... I know that. But what if I see something he doesn't like? What if I don't see anything at all? That might be worse, actually. And even if he does like what I see, I know it won't protect him from whatever it is he fears.*

At last he stepped forward and gently took the King's arm. He felt Roland tense as he did so. *He's putting on a brave face, but he fears me ... he fears what I will reveal.* He began running his long fingers over the skin, as he always did, hoping nothing would happen. *No matter what is revealed, I cannot afford to react to it. I must pretend to see nothing.*

"My skin ... it's so *warm*" Roland muttered. "Why is it so warm?"

"Please, my lord, I need to concentrate," said Finayn, closing his eyes. He could feel the warmth of the emerging letters beneath his fingertips. *What will they say? What will they mean?* He opened his eyes again. The letters wavered in and out of focus, and, as Finayn finally read them, his eyes widened just a little. *I must pretend to see nothing ... I have seen nothing.*

But he *had* seen it. He had seen it, and the King would not like it at all.

* * *

"Well? What was it? What did he see?" The atmosphere in the *Skulking Raven* had reached a palpable level of tension. I would have to tell them something.

"I don't know, and neither does anyone else," I said.

"What?"

"What did he say?"

"He's not going to *tell* us?"

"Half a moment," I said. "I need to catch my breath." *I had no idea I was so ... exhausted. I usually fare better than this ... my heart is racing like a jackrabbit's.*

"Oh, you're not getting off that easily," said a rough-looking but intelligent man seated on my left. "I have learned enough of history to know this didn't end well. Roland came to a bad death, as I recall."

"Yes, he did," I said. "Finayn told the King he had seen nothing, but I think we all know better. Certainly, if the words predicted Roland's gruesome fate, they would have been most disturbing and certainly not something one wishes engraved in one's arm. Roland died horribly of a slow poison, but not before he had thrown the Artisan into prison first. It was said that the King died screaming, with blood oozing from every orifice, even the pores in his skin. One accounting I read described him as a 'raving, bloody scarecrow.'"

"So you're telling me you aren't going to tell us what the Artisan saw?" said the man on my left.

"Yes, that's what I'm telling you. Would you like me to invent something?"

The man smiled one of the most predatory smiles I've seen in a while. "Why not? And make it good."

"Very well. It said: 'You are hopelessly doomed to die of a slow poison given you by order of your enemies. You will soon resemble a raving, bloody scarecrow. Your throne will be taken over by your dimwitted younger brother, who will be easily controlled.'" I tried not to let my voice drip with too much sarcasm. In fact, the younger brother, Olaf, *was* something of a dimwit according to the records.

"That works," said the man on my left. "I can imagine the King would not care for that pronouncement at all. What happened to the Artisan?"

"In the confusion and turmoil surrounding Roland's death and Olaf's assuming the throne, some kindly soul released him from prison, and he left the City by dark of night. Everyone suspected the Lore-master, but, as he had several people to vouch for him, it was never proven. As far as I know, Finayn is still alive. He likes to roam the sutherlands, still practicing his art. He's an interesting fellow, that's for certain. But for now, my tale ends." *I feel truly wretched. I hope I can get up to my room soon. A good night's sleep is what I need.*

I looked around the room at the disappointed, disgruntled faces glaring in my direction. "I know it's not much of a climax, but there you are. Still, I have one more trick quite literally up my sleeve."

I rolled back the sleeves of my tunic with a flourish. "I not only met the Artisan, I am an example of his finest work! I offer it for your general amazement."

I lifted my arms high in the air, turning them this way and that, to a chorus of approval from the crowd. They edged forward for a better look, muttering about how beautiful the designs were. The Artisan was a breed apart—no other skin-artist would ever match him.

"The letters look like they're floating!"

"Look, there ... that horse might just gallop right off into the air."

"I do believe that's the most life-like image of a dragon I've ever seen."

I had grown so accustomed to the images that I rarely stopped to admire them anymore, but now I took a long, appraising look. Yes, they were magnificent! But ... *There's something wrong, there ... on my left forearm. It didn't look that way before.*

I looked harder. *I need to go up to my room at once.*

I rose, bowed, and took my leave. The patrons let me go without an argument—apparently, my pale face and shaking hands convinced them—and I beckoned the tavern-keeper, asking for the key to "my" room. It was the same one I always stayed in at the *Raven,* and I looked forward to my bed and a long drink of water.

By the time I had climbed the steep, winding stairway, I was utterly winded. My vision had narrowed to a black tunnel, and blood roared in my ears. *Only a little farther now ... where's that blasted key!*

I don't remember opening the door. I'm lying on my bed now, and my head has cleared a little. I'm looking at my arm, trying to focus my eyes—I can't see anything out of the left one. The rain sounds wonderful ... peaceful ... I could go with it, wherever it's going. Someone had lit the lamp in the window to tell others that the room is not available. I can see the rivulets of water sheeting down the glass—how they sparkle and glow in the lamplight!

"Beautiful ..."

Now I'm looking at my arm again. Here, nestled beneath the wing of the dragon, the image of a nightingale. It's fading ... I can barely see it now. The words, done in such elegant Elvish script, are fading, too. The nightingale is dying, and night is coming. I'm smiling now. *It's not so bad ...*

I have told the tale of the Artisan, and he has finished mine.

Grand Meat Pies

On the mornings the day after roasting a whole pig, the cook at the Black Dragon Inn often finds himself with a lot of leftover pork. He knows it's good for now, but won't be by the end of the day. The customers won't buy cold pork, and if he puts it back on the spit to roast it would get too dry. His solution is to cut it up and make it into pies with spices and sometimes a bit of chicken. These pies go into the oven after the bread is done cooking, and when the customers start coming in for lunch the pies are hot and ready to eat.

1 pound roasted pork
2 Tbsp. lard
1/2 pound chicken, boiled
1/4 cup ground pine nuts
1/4 cup currants
2 tsp. sugar
1/2 tsp. ginger
1/4 tsp. cinnamon
1/4 tsp. cloves
1/2 tsp. salt
1/4 tsp. pepper
pinch saffron

pastry for a double-crust pie

Cut pork into small pieces, about 1/2 inch cubed, and pan fry in lard. Add to remaining ingredients, mix well, and place in pie crust. Cover with top crust and bake until golden. Serve hot, breaking the top crust and dishing out the meat as desired.

THE POWER OF WORDS

Aaron Rosenberg

Lamar smiled. "Don't worry," he said softly, his words as careful and precise as always. "I've got this."

His friends turned and stared at him. As usual, Berrywright was the first to regain the power of speech. "What do you mean?" she demanded, stepping in close and jabbing him in the chest with one slender, pointy finger. "You've got this? Don't be ridiculous." He tried not to smile down at her, but that was as challenging as ever. She was just so adorable when she got angry, which was often. Being told so would only anger her further, though.

"Our diminutive friend is correct," Yanog Reist agreed, long fingers curling and uncurling around the smooth lines of his staff. "On the face of it, such an assertion on your part seems foolhardy at best and dangerously unrealistic at worst." His face and voice were as devoid of emotion as always, his features all pushing the boundary between perfectly blank and mildly disapproving, but his eyes sparkled with emerald amusement. Lamar had learned over the years that by watching his friend's eyes he could see just how robust a sense of humor the mage actually possessed. He just didn't care to reveal that to most people.

"All you'll do is get your head chopped off." Nissa was as blunt as ever. "There's too many of 'em for us to beat. We need to draw some of them out, split them into smaller groups and take those out one at a time until we've thinned the herd enough to let us finish the job." Her big hands tightened around the haft of her massive axe as it were one of the bandits and she was already strangling him.

The others nodded their agreement of Nissa's assessment. She was the warrior in the group, after all. She was the one with the sense of strategy, which is why she was usually the one calling the shots.

But not this time.

"I'll be fine," Lamar assured the other three—his friends, companions, and partners on many an adventure. "Don't worry." And he kicked his horse into a gentle lope down the winding path before them and toward the town that lay below. "I'll meet you over where the river forks," he called back over his shoulder, knowing they'd be able to hear him. "After I'm done."

"How would we know you were done?" Berrywright shouted down. At least it didn't sound like she was going to follow him. He'd hate to have to knock her out again.

Lamar smiled. "Oh, you'll know," he promised.

The path took an hour or so to wend its way down to the village. Lamar passed the time by going back over everything he'd heard or learned about the town, and the people who now occupied it.

"Thugs, cutthroats, bullies and sneak thieves—the worst of the worst, lowest of the low." That didn't sound like something any of his friends would say. It was what that ranger had told them, however, after he'd staggered into the tavern and demanded "ale, man, and now!" Lamar had been quick to buy the man a full flagon, in exchange for which the stranger had recounted his latest exploits. "It's those bandits 'at've been holding the highway from here to the capital," the ranger had explained. "I tracked 'em to a small village beside the lake, 'bout half a day's ride from here." He'd paused to take a long swig of his ale, clutching his bloody side in obvious pain as his chest raggedly rose and feel. "I'd've taken 'em out myself," he'd warned when he'd recovered enough to speak again. "But there's too many of 'em."

Lamar knew he and his friends were all seasoned adventurers, and together they were a tight-knit party that could easily handle most situations. Not this, though. They'd been expecting a bandit pack about the size of their own group, perfect for lightning attacks up and down the highway. What they'd found instead had been closer to a small army.

"There's at least two dozen of 'em!" Nissa had said just that morning, after they'd seen the bandits pour out of the village like enraged ants, armed and irate and ready to swarm. "That puts them at six times our number," she'd added. "We might need to let this one go, at least for a little while."

But Lamar had been watching the bandits below, seeing the way they moved and talked and responded to each other, their breath frosting in the cold. That's when he had realized what needed to be done. There was a way for them to take on a banditry that large and not only survive but win. It didn't take their whole group, either. In fact, it worked better if he was alone.

The way he was now.

"Here's hoping this works," Lamar muttered, his hands gently strumming his lute to lend power to his words.

Here was hoping, indeed.

They had sentries, of course—a group that size that had survived this long, there was no way they didn't. Lamar didn't see them or hear them but he knew they'd done their job when a handful of bandits emerged from various huts and houses and assembled near the front of the town, directly in his path. Lamar slowed his horse, controlling it with pressure from his legs as his hands continued playing the lute. He came to a stop only a few feet from the men, who glared up at him, weapons already in their hands.

"Good morrow!" he called down in his biggest, cheeriest voice. His performing voice. "Am I speaking to the man in charge?"

"You're speaking to the men as is gonna cut you down," one of the men snarled back, hefting a large axe in one big, scarred hand, his muscled arms evident beneath the sleeveless leather vest he wore. If the cold bothered him, he gave no sign of it. "Don't worry who's in charge of that. We'll take turns." He grinned up at Lamar, showing several missing teeth.

The men laughed, then looked confused when Lamar laughed along with them. "Oh, very good," he complimented, still gently strumming. "I'll have to remember that one. Seriously, though, a band this well organized—you've got to have someone in charge. Could you call him out here for me?"

There were murmurs among the men. They clearly did not know what to make of this. Finally one of them, a lanky fellow with limp brown hair and watery green eyes, ducked away. He headed for the largest building in town, a squared two-story stone structure Lamar guessed was the one inn or perhaps the town hall or even both. A few minutes later he reemerged, followed by a man Lamar knew right away had to be the bandit chief. He was tall and lean, with strong features and surprisingly glossy black hair that fell in two thick braids down his back. His beard was also braided, and his eyes were dark and glittered with intelligence. He studied Lamar in return as he approached, one hand resting casually on the hilt of the longsword at his side.

"What have we here?" the man asked as he reached them. He squinted up at Lamar. "If you've come to join us, I'm afraid we're full up at the moment. Try again next summer. I'm sure we'll have lost a few by then." His men chuckled, evidently not realizing that they could just as easily be in that number as not.

Lamar laughed as well. "Thank you, no," he replied, "I'm not looking for a job. Just you. Clearly you're in charge here. What do they call you?"

"Boss, mostly," the man answered. He reached out and caught the horse's reins, not tugging on them but just holding them. "You're awfully calm for a man surrounded by bloodthirsty bandits," he pointed out.

Lamar shrugged. "I've been in worse places." Which was true, actually, though usually he had his friends there beside him. "Besides, if you want to win you've got to take risks. Right?"

The bandit chief—Lamar was trying hard not to think of him as Boss but fighting a losing battle there—frowned. "All right, enough games. Who are you and what do you want?"

"Oh, sorry!" Lamar pretended to be surprised at his own bad manners. He swept into a bow while still in the saddle, something he'd practiced many times just so that he could pull it off when he needed it. Like now. "Leroy the Golden Lutist, at your service." He held up his lute so they could all see it, and tossed his head so that his long golden hair floated behind him like a cloud of sunshine. "I've come to sing about you."

"To sing about us?" That was one of the other men. "You mean to us? Don't care much for music, meself."

"No, not to you," Lamar corrected him as gently as he would a small child, albeit one with a studded mace the size of his head. "Though I can do that as well, if you'd like. But about you." He faced Boss again. "There are stories of your daring attacks spreading far and wide, but right now they're just talk. Nobody knows much other than that you've been working this section of the royal highway and that you've never been caught or even stopped." He grinned. "Nobody's done a song about you yet, but that day's coming. I figured I'd get there first."

He had kept right on playing this whole time, a pleasant little melody that eased minds and smoothed tempers, and now he saw Boss smile, releasing his sword hilt to stroke his beard. "A song about us?" he repeated, staring off across the lake. "I like that."

Some of the other men were nodding and grinning as well. "We're gonna be famous!" The one with the axe said happily, and slapped one of his cohorts on the back hard enough to send him staggering a step. "Wait until me ma hears!"

"Everyone will hear," Lamar promised. "I will play this song all across the kingdom, and each time I play it, your fame will spread. Everyone will remember you and what you've done—which is why it's important I get all the details right."

The bandits were still laughing and cheering and congratulating one another on their impending notoriety— all except Boss. The smile had slipped from his face, and his eyes had gone cold. "What do you mean, 'everyone will remember you'?" he asked. "We're right here, and we plan on being here a long, long time."

Lamar gulped. "Oh, uh, I didn't mean anything by it," he said quickly, stammering a little. The more anxious he became, however, the bigger the smile that had returned to Boss's face. Only this smile was not a friendly one, or a happy one. It was more the look a fox might give a chicken it had cornered outside the henhouse, or a wolf might give a rabbit caught out in the open among the trees.

"For an accomplished performer, you are a terrible liar," he told Lamar softly. His hand that was still on the reins tugged downward, pulling the horse forward a step so that Boss was now right beside Lamar, who leaned down as the bandit chief spoke, his voice low. "What do you know that I don't?"

"Um, well …" Lamar glanced around desperately. The other bandits had started to realize all was no longer right in their world, and were beginning to cluster around him and his horse and Boss again. They didn't look angry yet, but they weren't looking as happy all of a sudden, either. "Look," he said desperately, "I hear things, all right? That's my job. I carry news to people sometimes, messages and gossip and so on, so I pay attention to what people say wherever I go. And I, I heard something a day or two ago, at a tavern in one of the nearest towns."

Boss nodded. "Go on."

"It was …" Lamar gulped again. "It's the king's men. There was a soldier there, he was telling the barmaid how his troop was getting ready for a big assault but he'd be back after to see her again. She asked if it was war somewhere and he said 'no, nothing like that, just cleaning out a bandit nest. Shouldn't take more than a few days, and most of that's travel.'" Lamar looked down at his hands, watching the one picking out chords while the other strummed. "That's why I want to get your story now, while I still can."

"So the army's coming for us?" Boss smiled that predatory smile again, lips pulling back to show his teeth. "I suppose that was bound to happen eventually. Did you hear him say anything about when?"

Lamar shook his head. "They were still there when I left," he answered, "but it looked like they were gearing up to move out soon. I'd wager they're only a day behind."

"They'll block off the road first," the lanky man from before pointed out. There were more bandits out in the street now, and whispers as those who'd heard him filled newcomers in on what he'd said. "Then they'll come in through the woods, pinning us down so they can take us out, archers first and then swords." He glanced behind them, out at where the lakeshore came almost up to the edge of the outermost houses. "With the lake behind us, we're boxed in tight."

Some of the others grumbled and cursed and even moaned. Not Boss, though. He actually laughed as he clapped the lanky bandit on the shoulder. "Aye, you'd be right, Wresh," he agreed, pitching his voice louder so all the others could hear him, "if not for one thing." He paused, making sure they were all listening, then exhaled slowly, creating a great big plume of frosty air in front of him. "What do you see?" he asked.

No one answered for a second. Then someone shouted, "Your breath!"

There were laughs and jeers, but Boss nodded. "That's right. And you know what that means?"

It was the lanky man, Wresh, who got there first. "It's freezing out," he announced, shivering despite a leather jacket and fur-lined cloak. He turned and looked out behind them. "The lake! The lake's frozen over!"

"That's right," Boss agreed. "If they'd come for us even yesterday, we'd have been sunk. But now we can just ride out across the lake, right out of their little trap." He grinned. "Grab your gear and get ready to move!" As the bandits scattered, Boss peered up at Lamar. "I thank you for the warning, bard," he said. "I'm in your debt."

Lamar bowed again. "Then let me sing about you," he pleaded. "It will only spread your legend, which will be good for you, and it will win me fame, which will be good for me as well."

Boss laughed. "Fine. But you're not coming with us. You can write about what you see here, and if you find us again somewhere down the road I might let you sup with us so you can learn more."

Lamar let some of his disappointment show, but nodded. "Thank you." He gently tugged his reins free of

Boss's hand, and turned the horse toward the side of the road. "I'll stay out of the way, I promise."

Boss nodded once more, then turned and began organizing his men's hasty departure. As promised Lamar stayed off to the side, softly playing his lute as the bandits packed up and prepared to leave the town, possibly for good. They came and went, buckling on armor and sheathing weapons and lugging bedrolls and waterskins and sacks of food and other sacks that clinked and rattled as they swayed. There were only a few pack mules, which were heavily laden with sacks of both kinds. It seemed the bandits did all of their work on foot.

Finally they were all out in the open and all packed up, and Boss nodded. "Let's go," was all he said, but that was enough. He turned and led the way out past the houses, over the edge of the shore, and onto the lake itself. His foot slipped once, the slick ice treacherous even for a skilled thief, but then he caught himself and began to walk, slowly but surely, across the frozen water. His men all followed, though a few of them didn't look terribly happy about it.

Lamar waited until the last of the bandits was on the ice before approaching the water's edge himself. "I forgot to ask," he called out, loud enough for Boss to hear him and turn. His hands stilled on the lute, letting its last few notes float away into the crisp winter air. "What do all of you call yourself? Do you have a name other than 'bandits'?"

Out near the middle of the lake, Boss laughed and shook his head. "No," he shouted back. "Never saw the point! Now if you'll excuse me—" He gestured at his men, and the ice, and the road behind Lamar.

"Oh, of course." Lamar started playing again, only this time the music was very different. Gone were the soothing tones from before. Now the sounds emanating from the lute were louder, faster, harsher, more energetic, more angry. They jangled into the cold air, vibrating through the chill and setting everything else into shuddering along with them. "There was one thing, though."

He could hear Boss's sigh from here, back on the shore. "What now?"

Lamar shrugged, and increased both tempo and volume. Beneath his music he could hear another sound, faint but growing stronger, but his playing helped mask it. "It's just that," he began, "you really should know—" The lute let loose with a series of sharp-edged, angry notes, and now the cracking was audible to all of them. "When water freezes like this, you want to be careful," Lamar continued. "Give it at least a few days, and don't put too much weight on it. Otherwise—"

He hit a particularly sharp note, which was rewarded with a thundering crack as the thin sheet of ice coating the lake shattered. Boss disappeared instantly, plummeting into the icy lake that had suddenly yawed open beneath his feet. Most of the bandits around him suffered the same fate, the ice fragmenting too fast for anyone to react or try getting to safety. Given how cold the water was, Lamar knew those heavily armed and armored men wouldn't last more a few seconds, the weight of their own gear dragging them down to the lake bottom even as the cold sapped their strength. Even if they managed to fight their way back to the surface, the cold would have seeped into them by then, and dragging themselves back to the shore soaking wet would be just as much of a death sentence. They'd all die of drowning or freezing or both, and there was no reason to worry about any of them any longer.

The two or three to the rear with the baggage-laden donkeys, on the other hand, had enough warning to turn and race back toward the shore, weapons tossed aside in their desperate attempt to outrace the fissures springing up at their feet. Lamar tensed but continued playing. He could draw his sword, of course, but he wasn't entirely sure he'd be a match for any of these hard, angry men, especially in their current panicked state. Fortunately, the bandits in question were still several feet from dry land when they suddenly sprouted arrows. They tripped and slid the rest of the way, landing in heaps up against the very shore they'd sought. None of them stirred again.

Nissa.

Lamar had known his friends would be watching, and had figured they would step in when they saw those bandits trying to flee. He was glad he'd been right.

Changing his tune now that the damage was done, Lamar whistled cheerfully to the donkeys even as the music from his lute called to them as well. The poor beasts were starting to panic just like their owners, so when they heard the music they turned about and ran back to shore and to Lamar, who petted their trembling sides and soothed them until they were calm again. Meanwhile, he studied the end of the scene out on the water.

A few of the bandits had managed to leap to larger, more stable chunks of ice. They didn't get beyond that, however, because arrows kept picking them off. Then there was the one who jumped from shard to shard until he was almost back on dry land—right before a quartet of glowing little lights darted toward him and slammed into his chest, knocking him off his feet and sending him tumbling into the dark, icy lake, which instantly swallowed him up. "Thank you, Yanog Reist," Lamar whispered into the wind. He suspected the mage might even have heard him.

At last it was all over. All of the bandits were gone, either plunged to their death in the ice-cold lake or riddled with Nissa's arrows or felled by Yanog Reist's magic. Lamar was completely unscathed, and he had the bandits' donkeys and all the loot the bandits had tied to the poor pack animals. He led the donkeys away from the carnage, back up the road, toward where the river that fed the lake forked. And there, as promised, were his friends.

"All right," Berrywright conceded grumpily as he reached them and reined in. "I suppose that did work out all right." Lamar suspected some of her current irritation stemmed from the fact that she hadn't gotten to kill any of the bandits herself. Her eyes brightened when he handed her the donkeys' reins, however, and she smiled, all grudges forgotten, as she zeroed in on the animals' heavily laden packs.

"I know not how you succeeded in luring them out upon the lake," Yanog Reist commented, his eyes alight as ever, "but I am impressed that you did so. It was a well-wrought plan indeed."

Nissa just grunted. "Good thing we were here to back you up," she muttered, but the slap she administered to Lamar's back was a friendly one, and there was almost a smile tugging at the edges of her lips.

"I knew you would be," Lamar told her, smiling himself. And to Yanog Reist he added, "I just talked to them. There's power in words, you know."

And he strummed his lute, the melody adding resonance to that simple statement. Simple, but true. There was power in words.

As long as you had the skill to usher it forth.

And that was one thing Lamar certainly had.

Roasted Turnips

Turnips aren't served up much at taverns. They're seen as common food, and folks don't much like to pay for things they can easily make at home. They do buy them at the Black Dragon Inn though. That's partly due to cheese and cinnamon the cook uses on them, but it's mostly because of a trick he learned from a tinker who was passing through last year. He roasts the turnips before adding in the other ingredients, and that takes out some of their bitterness and makes them sweet and mellow.

> 5 medium turnips
> 1 cup soft cheese, grated
> 3 eggs
> 4 Tbsp. butter, melted
> 1 Tbsp. sugar
> 1/2 tsp. cinnamon
> 1/4 tsp. salt

Trim and wash the turnips. Bake in a covered dish (or wrapped in foil) until soft - about an hour at 350°F. Let cool and then peel and cut into small strips. Add cheese and set aside.

Beat eggs, sugar, cinnamon, and salt. Pour over turnips and cheese. Add melted butter and mix well. Put into greased pan and bake at 350°F until set - about 35 minutes.

THE VOICE OF THE HARP

Rosemary Jones

The harp that sings of itself. That's the prize that all bards whisper about, that wizards crave, and that kings fear.

Well, one king, once.

Let's begin again.

Admire the harp. Note the gentle curve of the wood. The pale bone pegs. The runes of story and song picked out in the painted circles and spirals of green and red. The shimmering gold of the strings.

Ah, yes, those strings. A breath, a touch, and the music will swell to fill the loftiest hall and stir the hearts of the listeners. Or, with equal ease, its chords can whisper a babe to sleep.

Once heard, the harp's voice haunts all who hear it. More perhaps than its maker intended.

Or perhaps not.

Almost any village maid can sing the harp's history now. All of them tell it wrong. They sing of sisters, one fair and one dark. Of a river running swift beneath a miller's wheel. Of jealousy and revenge. But they have the story all twisted up and tangled, like a broken string, except for the part about the sisters and the part about revenge.

Let us start with the sisters. One fair and full of music, one dark and cunning with spells. The elder, the one with hair as golden as summer, was called Lark. The younger, she with the dark braids cascading below her knees, was named Lily.

Each learned her craft with care. Their father was a bard, a singer prized by princes. He married late and his wife died young, leaving him with two girls to ease a grieving heart. That ended his wandering, for he took all the wealth gifted to him by grateful lords to buy a manor. There he housed his greatest treasures.

Messengers came riding to the door from time to time, begging the old man to return where once he played. They asked him to celebrate a wedding or lead a funeral march. They offered gold, and titles, and great acclaim from the most powerful in the land. He refused them all.

But he sent messages of his own, tied to the legs of birds or let loose in little bark boats placed upon the rushing river. Those he called arrived in grand trains like wealthy courtiers or came knocking quietly at the kitchen door. Once the old man had played in both high courts and hidden ones. Now those enchanted by his music served as tutors to Lark and Lily.

Each learned her lessons well. In time, the elder became enamored of songs and the younger of spells, but both took care to understand the other's art.

Lark wandered the hills, collecting bird songs and the whispering of the wind, twisting them into new melodies. Her singing called the children into the meadows, and down to the river, to play games throughout the summer. In winter, her songs warmed the elderly, recalling heroic battles and great romances.

Lily cultivated herbs. She distilled potions under waning moons and brewed bitter drafts at dawn. She spent her days reading dusty manuscripts and teasing ancient secrets out of their faded script.

So they grew. Tales spread of their beauty. More messengers came riding hard from castles and great halls. Now they bore invitations to the great halls for all the family. Still the old man refused. Perhaps a shadow touched his heart. Perhaps he heard something in the wind. He was a bard after all, and they often foresee death.

Finally a request came from a dying queen, not from ruler to subject, but from old friend to old friend. A prince needed training to become a king who could rule his people as he should.

The old man sat and thought, watching the flames flickering on the hearth for many long hours. Then he sent the messenger back again with an invitation for the prince.

When the young man arrived, he found himself studying with two of the prettiest scholars that he ever met. He fell in love with Lark and then with Lily. He declared himself unable to choose between the sun and the moon, the day and the night, the fair and the dark. He sang songs, he composed poems, he swore great deeds, and he made promises that he shouldn't have.

But for all of his fine ways and manners, neither sister gave him her heart.

It left him stunned.

No one had ever refused him the smallest treat or withheld a single favor. The only son of a great king, he was used to plucking maidens like flowers.

He redoubled his efforts.

The sisters only laughed at him.

So his promises became grander.

They shook their heads at him.

Then anger crept into his heart. His words took a sharper edge. The fury of kings or kings-to-be can burn fields and leave an old man dead in a ditch.

Lily and Lark stopped speaking to him. They should have spoken to their father. But they stayed silent. And they paid for that silence.

In the hour between sunset and complete darkness, Lark went down to the river. She was listening for swans, for she had spent a summer trying to catch their songs and turn them into something for the harp and the human voice.

The prince came hunting along the river too. But he was not looking for swans.

Lark never came home.

The next morning, the prince rode away even as search parties were organized to find the missing sister.

That evening, they found Lark drowned, her golden hair entangled in the reeds. The servants could not bring the body out of the water until Lily waded into the river and cut her hair free.

The bard's heart cracked that day. He took to his room. He would not eat or drink. The servants despaired, certain the master would follow his fair daughter into the grave.

But Lily begged him for one last gift. She asked him to make her a harp, so her sister's songs could live again.

Once, twice, three times, he refused her. For he knew very well what she truly sought.

Still she pleaded. Still she sighed. Still she sat by his side, twisting the long golden hair of her dead sister into a single shining skein.

Finally he rose from his bed and called for wood to carve, and bone to peg the harp, and paint to decorate it.

His daughter fetched all that he asked for. If Lily took the bone from the graveyard and mixed her own blood into the paint, the old man kept silent.

When it was done, she took the unstrung harp into her arms like a baby, cradling it and whispering to it. The bard placed his own hand on it too. Like a father blessing a child, he sang to it all the songs of his long life. So together, they breathed music and magic into the harp.

Lily sent the servants running to fetch her bay mare. She placed the unstrung harp before her on the saddlebow. One last time, she bent down and kissed her father, whispering promises into his ears that no one else heard. Then she took to the North Sea road, following the tracks of a prince to a castle all decked out for a wedding.

They were feasting in the hall when she arrived. On his throne, the newly crowned king looked at her and laughed. He took the hand of his bride and kissed her fingers.

"If you are looking for this ring," he said to Lily, "you have come too late. For once I might have crowned you to sit by my side. But you and your sister laughed at me."

Lily knelt then, and offered the unstrung harp in her outstretched arms. "A gift," she said, "music for your wedding, as befits your grace."

Foolish, proud, and far too forgetful of the lessons learned in the bard's house when he was a prince, the just wedded king never questioned her as he should have. Instead he asked, "How can you play an unstrung harp?"

"The harp will sing its own songs, your Majesty," she answered.

Then she took out a golden skein of thread and strung the harp before him. When the last strand was tightened with the last bone peg, she blew softly across the strings.

"Sing, my sister, sing," she commanded.

Then, and only then, the king grew afraid. He almost called for his guard to smash the harp and hang the witch.

Except the harp began to play.

The music flooded through the hall. The song wrapped itself around each listener like a golden rope of melody. Entranced they sat and listened. The voice of the harp swelled until all other sounds, all other memories, whirled away.

The song drifted through the castle, catching all who heard it. They laid down their burdens, they stopped their chores, and they listened.

Then the witch laid her hand upon the harp. "Let them go," she whispered.

The harp changed its tune. Its song shifted. All who heard it grew afraid. The bride and all her maids ran crying from the room. The guards tumbled out the doors as if chased by armed enemies. Lords and ladies fled down the castle road to shelter shaking in the houses of bewildered villagers.

All ran except Lily and the king.

He sat frozen upon his throne. Captured by a song. Drowning in it as a girl once drowned amid the reeds.

When the castle was empty, Lily walked to his throne. "Listen," she breathed into his ear. Then she walked away.

And the harp played on.

Years later, a clever bard crept back into the castle, his ears stuffed with wax against the enchantment of the harp. But the harp was silent and the king merely a pile of bones upon his throne.

The bard carried the harp away. For a long time, he kept it wrapped in wool and silent in his house.

But finally, he could bear it no longer. He unwrapped the harp and set his hands upon the golden strings. The harp began to sing. Out came its story and the fate of all those entangled in its music.

It played on and on. People came to wonder. The bard tried to leave it. To take up his own instruments again, but the golden song of the harp's voice drew him back and held him as surely as it had captured the king.

When he died, another took it, and another, and then another. Each listened until they died, unable to sing their own songs, and unable to bear any silence after hearing the harp's voice, my voice.

Until I came to rest in this lonely cavern.

Until you touched the strings.

Until I began to sing again.

Potage of Rice

The patrons of the Black Dragon Inn often like something sweet after supper, especially on the colder nights around the winter solstice. That's when the cook will take some of the rice he'd put by over the summer and cook it up with milk and sugar until it's nice and thick. On the really cold nights he can charge a whole penny for a single bowl, but that's not too surprising given the cost of the saffron he adds to it.

4 cups milk
1/2 cup sugar
1 to 2 cups rice, fully cooked
1/4 cup almonds, sliced
2 Tbsp. butter
pinch saffron, ground

Bring milk to a low boil, stirring constantly. Keep stirring and simmer until the milk is reduced to half or three quarters of original volume. Add rice, sugar and saffron. Toast almonds in a frying pan with butter to use as a garnish. Serve warm.

TEMPTING FATE

Stephanie Drummonds

The taproom was nearly full the first time the bard came to my tavern. That in itself was a surprise. I'd been expecting a slow evening's trade. The weather had been wet all the day, alternating between downpours and a chill, clinging mist. No, I had resigned myself to a night of staring at empty tables, listening only to the pop of the logs and the steady drum beat of rain on the thatch—anyone with a snug roof and a hearth to call his own was like to stay there.

Then, just as dusk was starting to fall, a party of seven or eight dwarves stumped their way through the door. Water streaming from their heavy boots and felted wool hoods onto the rushes covering the rough plank floor, they claimed one of the low tables near the hearth and called for ale. Smiling to myself, I sent my nephew Oswin scurrying for mugs, while I pulled two pitchers of stout from a recently tapped keg.

"Welcome to the Black Horse Tavern, my bearded friends," I said with a broad, welcoming smile and setting the pitchers on the table in front of the group's obvious leader. "What else can I bring you?"

Whilst I was seeing to the doughty warriors' calls for bread, sausage and the bitterest ale I had in house, several more groups came in. I heard the wind whistling around the eaves each time the heavy oak door opened, caught glimpses of the swirling rain and rising mist and smelt the sharp, sheepy tang of wet wool, but I was soon too busy to note aught else.

The patrons who filled my taproom, gathering in small groups around the trestle tables, were nearly all strangers to me. That was the blessing and the curse of owning the only inn at a busy crossroads—not many regulars to keep happy, but also none to pull me through when travel was difficult and times were lean. Aside from the first bunch, the customers who came through my door that night were mostly men, long-limbed and rugged, dressed in wool and leather and armed for living in the wild.

I've no idea when or with whom the bard first arrived. In fact, I did not notice him at all until he spoke.

"It was on a night much like this one," he began.

At the rolling, sonorous tone of his voice, clear and deep as a well-cast bell, an expectant hush fell over the room. For a moment, there was nothing except the rustling of cloth, the muted scrape of wood on wood as the inhabitants, myself included, turned toward the sound.

The man stood on the wide flagstones next to the hearth. Like most of his sort in the taproom he was dressed in rough, unremarkable clothes—breeches and jerkin, tall boots, all well worn and in hues of brown and green to blend into any landscape. Though the hood of his cloak was thrown back, his features were indistinct in the shadowed light from the fire. All I noted for certain were deep set eyes and a sharp-bridged nose when I saw him in profile.

"It was on a night such as this," he repeated, "dark and fell, that I first heard of the Tree of Fate. Have any of you heard the legend?"

There was a general murmur among the patrons, mostly negative in nature. None, it seemed, knew the story. It was not one I had heard, and owning a tavern, I have heard many a tale, tall or otherwise. Yet the mention of it struck an odd chord in my mind, as though I ought to know it.

"Tell it then, lore master." The dwarf I had noted as the leader of the band spoke up from the end of the table closest to the bard. "A yarn would go down well with this excellent brew." He lifted the tankard as though in salute.

Nodding gravely, the bard began.

"All who have heard of this tree agree that it is old. That it stands majestic and alone in a wide clearing in an ancient wood. But the details have grown blurred by the mists of time. Some claim it is an oak, gnarled and weathered, the trunk battered by the elements. Some even claim that it grew from an acorn planted to replace the tree cut down to fashion the loom for the weavers of destiny."

I saw the heads of some of the dwarves nodding sagely at this description. I could picture such a tree, in full leaf, the green leaves just hinting at the colors of autumn to come, its branches heavy with acorns.

"Others have described it as a mighty maple, tall and straight, its bark glinting silver in the light of a hunter's moon."

This time, the nods and murmurs of agreement came from the men.

"Now and then," the bard went on, "I have even heard it called an apple tree, wide and curving, its sweeping limbs bearing both fruit and flower."

"I'd like to see that!"

I turned to see who had spoken and saw the small party of Halflings, one of the last groups to arrive, who had taken a low table in the corner furthest from the door.

They smiled amongst themselves, obviously envisioning such a tree.

"What do you think it is, master bard?" one of the men queried, his tone more condescending than I would have liked. The man was one I had not much noted before. He leaned on the far end of the bar, dirty fingers wrapped around a pewter tankard. There was little to recommend him. Greasy, dark hair was pulled back from a sallow face into a rough queue at the base of his neck; even darker eyes narrowed as he watched the man by the hearth and waited for an answer.

I was about to step in. I wasn't keen to let any patron, no matter how much coin he had, annoy someone who was giving my guests free entertainment. Word of that getting around would keep my kegs full and my tables empty. The bard, though, appeared unfazed.

"Any of them would be impressive, would they not?" At the general hum of agreement, his gaze swept around the room, passing over the man at the bar as though he did not exist.

My attention was drawn away at that point, by a tug at my sleeve. The last bottle of cider had just been served, my nephew informed me, and one of the tables was calling for more. Leaving him to pull another pitcher of Porter for the Halflings, I slid out of the taproom to get more. As I went through the store room and down the narrow stairs to the cellar, I could hear the bard's rich tones continuing, though I could not make out the words.

As long as I was there, I made several trips to the cellar, bringing up a variety of foodstuffs and spirits. Each time I came into the store room, I would catch a few words of the tale—the description of a deep, primordial wood, how each of the peoples came to learn about the tree, and what it meant to search for it.

When I returned to the inn's main room, carrying a basket filled with earthenware bottles of cider and a few more loaves of bread I'd laid by, I was able to pick up the thread of his narrative.

"Maidens looking to make a successful match and new wives hoping for healthy babes are among those who have sought this tree," the bard stated.

"Warriors?" asked one of the dwarves.

"Aye," the bard replied. "It is said that one who touches his blade to the tree's mighty trunk will never miss a stroke."

"Hunters?" asked a man.

"Of game and foe both," the bard affirmed. "A touch of the bow to one of the curving branches, and the shafts will ever fly true."

After setting the basket on the floor behind the bar, and handing Oswin a brace of bottles for the table he was serving, I looked about the room to see if any other customers needed attention. Few, if any, were looking in my direction; their eyes were fixed on the man who stood in the shadow of the hearth, spinning his tale. None of the patrons looked inclined to leave anytime soon. Well and good, this might be a successful night after all. Once his story was done, I thought with a smile, the bard was welcome to any spirits I had on hand.

"Where might such a treasure be found?" It was the man at the bar again, his voice still scornful.

"A treasure?" The bard's voice lifted in a subtle question. "Well you might call it so. And like most treasures, it is not likely to be found on a simple map, its location marked like some child's drawing."

This time, the bard spoke directly to the man at the bar. Though I could see that his gaze was fixed on the unkempt man, even now I could not determine the color of his eyes. In fact, I could still see very little of the storyteller's features. He stood where he had before, at the shadowed end of the hearth. That struck me as a little strange. Usually bards would move about the room, stopping at each of the tables, making the listeners feel, at least for a moment, as though he was speaking directly to them.

Unless it had been when I was in the cellar, this man had not moved. Still, given the rapt attention of nearly every person in the room, I could not fault him. He held them in thrall simply with the sound of his voice and the eloquence of his tale.

"Let the man talk, Henrik, unless you've a better story to tell."

As I listened to the roll of laughter and general agreement which ran through the room, I saw the man at the end of the bar bristle. Still, he fell silent, narrow shoulders hunching within his jerkin, face sullen. I looked about, trying to determine who had spoken the gently chiding words. From my perspective, directly behind him there was a small table near the far wall, where three men sat. Any of them could have spoken, but one, a broad-shouldered man with olive skin and close-cropped dark hair caught my eye. He raised one dark eyebrow, wordlessly questioning whether I disagreed.

I gave a brief shake of my head and looked away, trying to be a good host by asking Henrik whether he needed another ale.

As I was pulling a fresh tankard for the chastened man, I felt another furtive tap at my elbow. Oswin again, both hands grasping pitchers that needed to be refilled. Once more, I lost the train of the narrative as I bustled about my work, filling platters with cold sausages, bread and mustard.

The pouch at my belt was growing heavy with coin. This night was turning into my best in weeks. True, I'd be hard pressed over the next several days to replace the stores of food and spirits the dwarves and Halflings were tearing through, but in the long run, it would be worth it. An evening's trade like this could make up for many a slow day. Whoever this bard was, and wherever he had come from, I had to be glad of his arrival.

When I finally had a moment to draw breath, all my guests seeming content for the moment, I leaned wearily on the bar. I became aware of a certain heaviness in the room. Though the bard continued his tale, and most of the folks in the room were paying close attention, I felt ... what? Anxious? Uneasy? It was hard to put my finger on. Perhaps it was the steam filling the air from all the damp wool? Perhaps the logs on the fire were wet, so they smoked more, making it more difficult to see the whole taproom in its usual detail. Whatever it was, the heaviness wrapped around my chest, making it hard to breathe. I needed a moment.

With a mumbled excuse to Oswin about the necessary, I slid quietly out of the crowded room and through the storeroom. I opened the tavern's back door and stepped out into the night. I could not go far; the rain still fell in steady sheets, so I stood on the wide flagstone set outside the door. I was protected from the worst of the wet by the overhanging eaves of thatch, but I could feel the chill of the night seeping from the stone through the soles of my shoes.

The pressure in my chest had eased as soon as I stepped outside. I took a deep breath, the air redolent with rain, pine and moist earth. Logically, there was no reason I should feel uneasy—my inn was full of customers, all paying good coin. Given the continued rain, most would likely stay through the night, rolling up in their cloaks to sleep on whatever patch of floor they could find.

Why then, did I feel so strange? It was almost like the buzzing in my head I got from drinking too much of my own stores, though with the evening as busy as it was, I'd not had time for more than a mouthful here and there. Maybe it was something in the wind, which blew in fitful gusts around the posts and thatch of the inn.

I stayed outside a few minutes more, one ear cocked for the sounds from the taproom that would indicate my presence was required. I heard the steady drone of voices, responding to the bard's tale, but no calls for my services. Still, I thought it best not to stay away over long—young Oswin was an excellent helper, but he didn't have enough experience to handle a crowd if things got out of hand.

Things seemed calm enough as I made my way back behind the bar, feeling lighter of heart. Everyone, Oswin included, was still deeply engrossed in the bard's story. The atmosphere in the taproom was less oppressive, less thick. Now, it had been replaced by an aura of excitement, almost anticipation. Something was about to happen, but what?

"Have you seen the Tree of Fate, lore master?" one of the dwarves asked.

"Not yet, but I have committed my life, my heart, my very soul to the search for this wonder," the bard said dramatically. "Are there any among you who will take up the quest with me?"

The deep set eyes swept the room, lingering here and there. I found myself holding my breath. Would anyone accept the challenge? Was there anyone brave enough, or foolhardy enough? Not I, of course. He told a fine tale to be sure, but I couldn't see leaving everything I had behind to search for something that was likely no more than a myth.

For a few long moments, there was no response. I heard the sharp crack of a log splitting in the hearth and the pattering of rain against the heavy glass panes of the room's only window. There was a rustling, as my customers shifted in their seats, and a low murmur of voices as they conferred among themselves. I looked about the room, wondering.

Was I surprised when the dwarves' evident leader, the one sitting closest to the bard, rose from his seat on the bench? No, it was he who had been encouraging the story-teller all evening. He was taller than the others, wide and sturdy, with a hooked nose and long brown beard braided in two thick plaits. He wore a dark blue cloak and a red hood, and a broad-bladed axe hung from his studded leather belt.

"I, Caldor Shieldsmith, will take up this quest." He spoke in ringing tones, his voice quieting the whispered conversations at the tables, filling the room again with quiet expectation. He took a step forward, hooking his thumbs into his belt, elbows spread wide.

"I too will join the search," another voice echoed. This was one of the men who had passed the evening alone at a small table in the far shadowed corner of the taproom. When he stood, pulling himself to his full, rangy height, I could see he would tower over not only the dwarf, but nearly everyone in the room.

"Is there any other with heart enough to join these brave souls?" the bard challenged.

I felt a stirring beside me. Glancing aside, I saw Oswin straining forward. I laid a hand on his sleeve, and then gave a firm shake of my head when I caught his gaze. If I could not afford to go, I could as surely not afford to lose my assistant. Besides, my sister would never forgive me if I let her son go gallivanting off on some harebrained adventure.

"I will go."

I'm sure mine was not the only face to register surprise when I realized it was Henrik who had spoken. After voicing such doubt about the bard's tale, I would never have thought he would take up such a journey.

"Are you certain?" the first man who had volunteered queried, giving Henrik a skeptical look.

"Do you think me less courageous than you?"

"No, but doubt is hardly the way to begin."

The tension I had been feeling in the room kicked up another notch. The men faced each other across the room, drawing themselves to their full height. An uneasy silence spread around the room. Would there be a confrontation? Blows?

"Let him come," the bard's resonant voice cut through the charged air. "Whatever his reasons, the quest may bring him more than he ever expected."

"I hope so," Henrik said quietly, no hint of his earlier condescension in his tone. "I could stand to change my fate." The last was said so softly, I wasn't sure whether anyone heard aside from me.

"Join me then, all of you," the bard said, reaching out one long-fingered hand. "Let us clasp hands to seal our company."

The dwarf and the men who had committed to search for the tree moved forward, stepping onto the wide flagstones of the hearth. Toasts and shouts of encouragement rang through the room as the three approached the bard. "Good journey," came the shout from the table of Halflings. A glance showed them all on their feet, tankards raised.

As I looked back to the hearth, the three would-be travelers converged. The feeling I'd had before I stepped outside came back. The air in the taproom was thick with it; there was almost a color, a texture to the atmosphere. Something was about to happen.

Just then, the three surrounded the bard, eyes intent upon him. They reached out their hands, placing them on top of the bard's outstretched fingers.

There was pop, a shower of sparks and a smell of pine tar. Swirls of smoke curled from the wide hearth, and then suddenly, inexplicably, they were gone.

Pale, watery light streamed across my face, waking me from a fitful sleep. I came out of bed in a rush, worried without any particular cause. It had been a long night, and I was certain the moon had long set before I was finally able to seek my bed.

There had been cheers and applause when the bard and his fellow travelers first disappeared. It was an excellent trick, everyone agreed, and there was much speculation, even a few good natured wagers, as to how it had been accomplished. Where would they reappear? Some turned to the taproom's front door, others to the less accessible door of the storeroom. A few even fixed their attention on the deep shadows around the hearth, wondering whether the four could be hidden in the dark corners.

Long moments passed, time stretched. Nothing happened. Neither the front door, nor the storeroom door opened. Nothing moved in the shadows. Gradually, the ebullient reverie began to fade and falter. When another log popped in the hearth, splitting and settling in a cascade of sparks, I felt the mood turn.

I knew I had to act quickly. I could hear the questions being murmured around the room. "Where did they go then?" "Where are you hiding them?" Before long they would be turning on me, demanding who the bard was, where he had come from, and what he had done with their friends—all questions to which I had no answers.

Before the situation got out of hand, I did the only thing I could.

"Drinks on the house!" I called in a ringing voice. Thanks the gods, it had worked. The drinking and speculation had gone on long into the night. There had been a few pointed comments about the way I entertained my guests, but nothing had exploded.

Now, as I made my way through the dimly lit storeroom, I listened intently, hoping that had not changed. I could hear Oswin's whistling snores from the loft where he slept when it was too late to find his way home, but little else.

Quietly, I opened the door into the main taproom.

The room was even dimmer than the storeroom. Though banked for the night, the fire had burned low, and little of the weak sunlight filtered through the thick glass of the bull's eye panes in the taproom's one window. Still, it was bright enough for me to see something I had not really expected to see again. Among the group of dwarves sleeping near the hearth, I caught the flash of red.

Squinting, I tiptoed further into the room, not wanting to disturb the quiet cacophony of snores, heavy breathing, and the shift of sleeping bodies over the wood of tables, benches and floor. I had to be sure my eyes weren't playing tricks on me, that it was not just the reflected glow of the fire. No, I really was seeing the warm glow of a bright red hood mixed in among the more sober greens and blues.

I let out a slow breath, not even aware I had been holding it. Caldor Shieldsmith was back. He was sprawled on his back, arms crossed on his chest, his snores resonant.

I heard a rustling movement off to my right, and turned slowly. In the shadows, I saw the first man who had volunteered to join the quest. His long legs were stretched out on a bench, his back propped against the wall. At first, I thought he slept as well; then he turned his head toward me. Catching my gaze, he raised one hand in a quiet greeting. I lifted a tankard, cocking my head to one side, questioning. He shook his head, apparently as unwilling as I to disturb the room's peace.

I scanned the room again in the gradually increasing light. The corner by the hearth was still dim, but clearly empty. His companions might be here, but the bard had not returned. Somehow, I had not really expected him to. Then I realized there was someone else I did not see among the slumped and sleeping bodies.

Turning back to my right, I once again caught the gaze of the man propped against the wall. With raised eyebrows, I gave a significant nod toward the end of bar where Henrik had spent his evening clasping a tankard as though it were his only friend. The man's head moved side to side, gravely. The third traveler, it seemed, would not be back.

A coldness gripped me, and all of my usually keen curiosity drained away. What trick had caused their disappearance and where did they go? I had no idea. Had they found what they sought? What had happened to them, and why had Henrik been left behind? Again, I hadn't the slightest notion, and for once, no desire to ask.

Over the past year, the bard has returned thrice more to my tavern. In all that time, I have never managed to learn his name, or any of his history. He is merely, 'the bard', and likely always will be. In fact, I am still not truly certain what he looks like. I could pass the man on the street in bright sunshine and not know it.

I can never predict when he will come. Only that it is always on nights like the first, dark and wild, that he materializes like a ghost to tell his tale.

Tales of the bard himself seem to have spread on the winds throughout the surrounding country, for my business has prospered greatly since the first time he appeared in my taproom. Travelers who once only crossed my threshold when they could journey no further, now seek out my door. It is as though they hope the bard will come. On the odd night that business is slow, I find myself hoping the same.

Hoping, or perhaps dreading. I know the tale he tells will always be the essentially the same, though each time it has grown in the telling. Now it contains details of the exploits of Caldor Shieldsmith, with his red hood and broad axe. Also included are the bravery of Theron Half-Elven and the sword craft of Dark Ewan, among others who chose to accompany the bard on his search.

There are always some who are willing to take up the challenge, to join him on his quest. Like the first time, they will vanish the moment they have joined hands to seal their commitment. By morning, when the storm outside has passed, they are back, all but one, and the next time the bard returns their names and deeds will be added to the mythos of the tree.

Strange though, the exploits of Henrik, and all those who fail to return, go unmentioned. Not even their names will pass the bard's lips. I can only assume they lie dead somewhere; but surely even a glorious death would add to the story's allure.

Now, I know what you're thinking. I should keep the bard away from my tavern, not let him spin his tale, now that I know what he's up to. Except I don't know. It could be that he takes them to some barn outside the village and keeps them there until one wanders off. Perhaps he's actually in league with those who join him and it's all a good joke.

All I do know is that the bard is good for business. Since he first came to my door, I've fared well enough that I'll be expanding the tavern come spring, even hiring another boy or two to help Oswin behind the taps. You think me greedy? Well, maybe I am, but a man's got to make a living after all.

Should I warn them? Now, there's a question. Perhaps I ought to, at least tell them they're as like to never come back as they are to become part of the legend. But then, I worry. What if no one steps up to go? Will the bard take me, or Oswin? That's not a chance I am willing to take.

No, travelers come from all over now, hoping to find the bard and hear his tale. I'm not sure that any warning I give them would be taken to heart. They always have the choice—go or stay. In the end, I am only responsible for my own fate. They must look to their own.

Apple Spice Bread

Apples are cheap at harvest time and they keep very well in barrels, so it's no surprise that Nashal, the owner of the Black Dragon Inn, stocks up on them every year. Because of this, the cook can make his favorite apple spice bread all winter long. The warm spices and the sweet fruit keep the inn bright and inviting on even the coldest of days.

2 eggs
1/4 cup vegetable oil
2 tsp. vanilla
3/8 cup water
1 1/2 cup flour
1 cup sugar
1 tsp. cinnamon
1/2 tsp. cloves
1/2 tsp. salt
1/2 tsp. baking soda
1/4 tsp. baking powder
1 apple, peeled, cored, and cut into small pieces

Combine eggs, oil, vanilla, and water, and set aside. Mix dry ingredients together in a large bowl. Add egg mixture and mix well. Stir in apple pieces and pour into greased loaf pan. Bake at 325°F for 1 hour. Cool for 10 minutes and remove from pan.

A STAR FELL FROM THE SKY

Muffy Morrigan

The world ended as it began more than a thousand years ago. The Songs tell of a great pulse that lit the sky on fire and blanketed our world in ash. So, too, do the Songs tell of how we arose from the empty land and built our lives, our cities, our world.

At first we were nothing more than small groups, huddled together against the terrors of the night. Keeping a fearful watch beside the small flames of communal fires, we listened to the terrible sounds of the forbidding night, until we could breathe a sigh of relief with the first touch of the morning's light. And thus the world crept on—a cycle of light and dark, of bright days and laughter, of nights full of fear and watching.

The world was forever changed one dark autumn night when a star fell to earth.

The Songs tell of a man, an outcast living forever in the shadows cast by the flames, who ventured beyond the fires into the dark unknown. Terrible cries drifted on the air, the predators calling out, looking for prey. The people waited for his screams, they waited for the animals to howl in the triumph of a kill, but the sound never came. A different sound came instead, a simple melody hummed in a deep voice. Patrick the Lame had returned and in his hand he held a stone unlike any other. For it was not really a stone at all but the very star they had seen cross the sky. The Star Stone, though small, was heavy. Soon it would be weighted down with the burden bestowed on a leader. The outcast was redeemed. Patrick the Lame became the first Lord.

The Star Stone, first worn by Patrick, would be passed from Lord to Lord for nine generations. They organized the land. They brought communities together to raise the great walls that would protect the people from the terrible and fearsome predators that hunted in the night. Small huts were replaced by larger houses, mud giving way to stone. It was the Lords who founded the Singers. Teachers appointed to pass on the stories of the people, their language, their history and the Laws that held the society together.

The Singers civilized the world, they wrote Laws that brought peace and comfort to those who dwelled in the cities and towns. Slowly, though, despite the Lords' ever-watchful eyes, the Singers began to claim power. As a tiny drop will become a raging torrent, the Singers began to compose for their ascendency. They were simple Songs with deeper meanings. Songs of the Star Stone and its rightful keepers, Songs that were meant to undercut the power of the Lords—and they did. On the glorious First Day of Song, the people cried out for the Star Stone to be given to the Singers—they replaced the Lords when the Singers put on the long robes of the rulers of our world.

When we are children we are taught the first Songs, melodies of the daily passage of life. The Song of Planting, of knowing when the land is ripe and ready for seed. The Song of Building, of creating places we live and work. All learn the Songs, no matter what their calling, they learn of farm and commerce, war and peace. The Songs are the foundation of our lives. We are also taught with those first Songs celebrating life that there is a darker side to the world. In a minor key, the Chorus of the Damned sounds through the land seven times each year. It is the Song that tells of the horrors of those who stray, the dark fate that falls upon them, body and soul. The Singers use this to keep their power supreme and the world in check.

As days became months, months became years and years became centuries, the Singers wielded the Star Stone and ruled over the world. The world as it is now is the world the Singers, not the Lords, created. Through long centuries they have enforced the Law, and each year added a new stanza to the repertoire of Songs. With each new stanza, the control that holds the people in place is tightened until none dare stray across the line. Justice—or what the Singers called Justice—is swift, punishment final and reprieve not even a whispered hope.

Great cities of crystal have risen on the banks of the deep blue oceans, glistening like beacons of hope. Within their sparkling walls, the Singers sing the Songs. Those they have chosen to lead sit at the feet of the Great Singer, the Elder of All, Holder of the Star Stone. They repeat the Songs until they become nothing more than a reflection of the music of the Law that plays throughout the world. The Songs remain, the Singers in control—or so they Sing, but it is not the truth.

The first notes of dissent were singing a soft melody in the outlands.

The music began with an outcast, making a living moving from one small town to another. He was a singer of a different sort, creating music about the daily lives of the people he met—songs of love and loss, of life and death. His pay was food, a bed for the night, or shelter from the rain. He never asked for more, and took pride in his life and art.

I remember the day when first he came to town, a tall man with dark hair and eyes the color of the sky. He pushed a small cart that held all the parts of his life, small gifts and instruments. As he walked into town he smiled, humming a soft song that seemed to spring from the land and the wind whispered a counterpoint in the chorus. Until the day he walked through the gate into town, I believed that he was a myth. A cautious Song sung to children, to amuse them and warn them against straying from the laws of the Singers.

Yes, I did say warn, for this was no simple traveling man, despite his appearance. He was not merely a wandering outcast with labor for hire. No, this was Arthur Herald and he was the outcast, the Founder, the one who remembered and knew when words and music meet, magic is created.

Arthur Herald was the first Bard.

Though he walked alone at first, he soon had followers. Secret meetings were held in the deep dark of night, gatherings beyond the walls and fences, where the terrible predators roamed the world. Yet he was unafraid. Magic brings many gifts, and singing songs of the world, of the animals, trees and rocks brings life to things. The predators did not hunt him. It was whispered they came and sat with him as he sang the songs of magic.

My family was poor and our small farm even poorer, and one dark year the crops failed and my parents could not pay the Singers their share of the yield. I became the payment for the debt and destined for the great university in the city where the ocean is deep blue. Where crystal towers rise and knowledge is given, but always for a price. Sign your soul over to the Singers and they hand the world to you. Or so they Sing. Words used to lure parents into sending their young to the far off city, creating loyalty not to the people but to the Singers and their Songs.

Thus I was destined, but things are not always as fate may seem.

Two decades ago, I was preparing to go to university. Two decades ago, I was leaving my family and friends and the simple comfort of the outlands for the wilds of the great crystal city. Two decades ago, I walked out of the house to escape the weeping of my family, and I saw him.

The Bard had come, pushing his cart, singing with the wind. He was smiling as he walked down the dusty road, his eyes roaming over the houses and gardens and finally coming to rest on me. I remember how his smile brightened as he walked towards me.

"A Singer?" he asked in a deep bass.

"Destined by debt, I am to become a Singer."

"Destiny is fickle and the path is not always the road."

"It is not the road I seek, but the one I must walk."

"No."

The word echoed through me, the music in the single syllable filling me with hope. The dark journey to the city was replaced by the call of the world beyond the walls. A world I crept to in the evening, before the sun dropped from the sky. I knew the trees by name, and sometimes I believed, they answered when I hummed to them.

"I must pay the debt."

"I have come searching for you. I have heard of your songs," he said.

"My songs are only simple melodies."

"In simplicity there is power. Never doubt."

"The debt must be paid."

"The debt has already been paid. Your life is your choice. No one owns you, not family, town or Singer. You are free to walk away, should you choose."

I was held breathless, motionless by his words. To refuse the Singers was an act of rebellion—the punishment death. Even considering his words was daring. How could he know the debt and know it was paid?

"I paid the debt," he said, answering the unspoken question.

"Why?" asked I, not trusting to hope.

"I told you, I have heard of your songs."

"How?"

"The wind spoke to me. It was whispered in the trees. They said there is one who sings to us as you have, one who knows the songs we sing." He smiled, his blue eyes twinkling.

"I want to learn more." The words poured from me before I could stop them. "I want to sing the songs from the time before the world began." I stopped, horror coursing through my body. Those songs were forbidden.

"And you will. You will learn the songs of the land, the songs of the sky and the songs of the time when we flew through the air with the ease of a bird and raced through the land faster than a thousand horses can run. All of this you will learn and more."

He stepped to the porch, his eyes holding mine. "Our time is coming. The time for the Old Songs to be sung; the melodies of Patrick the Lame, and the world before the fire, need to be heard again. Will you answer the call?"

The final question was asked, it was a formal request, one that would bind both of us. Looking away from him, at the buildings around me and the trees that rose beyond the wall, I let my heart lead me.

"I will answer the call."

He waited while I gathered my small bundle of things. Clothes, one flask for water and one for mead, and the harp I had made. I saw his eyes light when he saw the small harp. I was proud of it. I had constructed it from a huge branch of a fallen tree. In my heart I believed the tree was proud that I had crafted a part of it to create music. I repaid the gift with my music and sang to it many a day—even a fallen tree has life.

We turned and walked away from the town, away from the life I had known, and stepped into the wide world outside the walls. Others walked with us, some for a few days, others for months and others longer. Each had a story, each had a song, and each, when they left, held a place in a world that was changing. We were Bards, singing simple songs, creating magic—entertaining and teaching a quiet lesson, a soft dissent.

Fifteen years I walked beside Arthur Herald. I learned, I listened and I sang. I watched the stars bright over our heads as we slept beneath the giant trees or in the great desert of the West. As the years rolled by, we gathered more people to sing with us. Some were timid and wished only to know the songs; others were bold and strode into the great cities to sing in the city square.

It was the bold that proved our greatest enemy.

We had long worked for change, but it had to come like the trickle of water under the ice of winter, not in a great boom of thunder before a storm. The Singers, who had long ignored our existence, lashed out. Some Bards turned traitor and led the Singers to us. Others remained and took Arthur Herald's name as our own to show our solidarity, our pride in what we were.

Bard became outlaw, and still we carried our title proudly.

We had to run for our lives, our group broke apart and each left in a different direction. It was as if we tore the hearts from our chests and left them behind on a dry, dusty road in the middle of the empty outlands. Those of us made family not of blood but song. Those of us torn asunder, left wondering if we would see the others again.

Grim days followed. We were hunted like beasts, pursued through every town, every village, every small stop we made. The first few were captured two years after we were branded outlaws, the next a month after that. We knew where they were imprisoned, in deep wells untouched by light, hard concrete walls that denied the touch of the living stone.

We risked gathering one night in the autumn, the scents of the season filling the air. Overripe berries mixed with the fallen leaves and created a tangible presence, as if the land joined us there beneath the stars. Arthur Herald was bereft. We spoke of hope, of loss, of love and regret. We wondered if we dared chance a rescue. As we debated, our answer came.

A Second Star fell from the sky.

The Singers were quick to Sing of the star—Songs about the bright light that streaked across the vault of the heavens, and about what it meant to the world. Words and music of the power of the Singers, and how the coming of the second Star Stone proves their power supreme.

Hope was born again for those of us who remained. We set out on a desperate course to free those taken. As we struggled, more of us fell. The Singers sing the Song of our defeat, how they found the Stone, how it is kept in their greatest tower.

But their Songs are a lie.

How, you may ask, do I know? How can I speak of the First Song, the Long Dark and the Song of the Damned? How can I know about the darkness of the prison and the dead walls in the deep? How can I know the Songs are a lie? How, indeed, can I know of those rescued and those who still wait—hope ever in their heart—even in the lifeless dark of prison? How can I know of those waiting for the faintest sound like the scratching of a mouse on the wall, the sound of rescue and light again?

The answer, like the True Songs, is simple.

I was taken by the Singers and thrown into the deepest pit. I wait in the lifeless dark. The prison walls cold around me, but I know there is hope. I wait patiently for rescue. I know it will come. And when it does, the Singers will fall. For you see, the Singers do not have that second star, it does not honor them or bear their name.

My name is Timothy Herald. I am a Bard.

And there is more. A thing the Singers do not know—
and yet should fear.

I hold the second star, the Bards' Stone, in my hand.

The Bard's Tale

Spinach Tart

In the summer's riotous green growth, the cook at the Black Dragon Inn likes to make spinach tarts to have on hand for lunch and supper. They're good to eat cold, so that means less cooking in the noonday heat. The only trouble is they tend to sell out quickly, so he has to remember to set one aside for himself.

1/2 pound spinach, washed and chopped
1/2 cup chopped mint
2 eggs
1/2 cup grated parmesan
4 Tbsp. butter
1 Tbsp. sugar
2 Tbsp. currants
1/4 tsp. cinnamon
1/8 tsp. nutmeg

Mix all ingredients together in a large bowl. Pour into a single crust pie shell and bake at 350°F until the top of the tart turns dark brown and a knife inserted into the center comes out clean - about 45 minutes.

THE SILENT SINGER

Richard Lee Byers

I hadn't wanted to go to Kreelan's Plaint, not to listen to the bards and would-be bards of the southlands compete and not to keep the peace. I was busy running my fencing academy. "What are they going to do if they do get rowdy," I'd asked, "sing at one another?"

Apparently it could get more serious than that.

Pivor, half a dozen of his retainers, and I had just ridden into the town square, which was jammed with folk who'd come to enjoy the festival and vendors of beer, sausages, and trinkets eager to separate the customers from their coin. My aristocratically slim and elegantly attired patron was flying the Snow Lynx banner that identified him as the lord, albeit, mostly in absentia, of "the Plaint," but even so, the press was such that the commoners couldn't make way quickly even if they recognized him.

On the far side of the square, a redheaded woman backed out of a tavern's open door. Cloaked in gray, a soft cap sporting a pheasant feather on her head, she held a gnarled staff poised for defense.

An angry-looking man with a black snake embroidered on his jerkin followed her. The staff flicked out and clouted him on the temple.

He clutched his forehead and stumbled back with the fight knocked out of him. But two more men wearing the same emblem came through the doorway. When they saw what had befallen their fellow, they snatched for the daggers on their belts.

By then, I was already trying to push my horse through the crowd. But it was still slow going, and the appearance of sharp steel made the matter urgent.

Beside me was an elevated stage. I scrambled from the saddle onto the platform and sprinted across it.

Which didn't get me all the way up to the tavern. But beyond the stage was a row of vendors' stalls. Some had roofs. Others at least had uprights framing the counter with a signboard crosspiece connecting the top of one to the other. With a silent curse for my own recklessness, I sprang to the first.

Never intended to support a person's weight, the rickety temporary structures swayed and bounced, cracked and crunched, beneath me. But I kept moving, never obliging any one spot to hold me for more than an instant, and although I was no tumbler or ropewalker, I possessed a swordsman's sense of balance. That sufficed to see me safely to the last stall in line, from which I gratefully jumped to the ground.

The dagger men had spread out to flank the woman with the coppery hair. She shifted the staff back and forth in an effort to fend off both of them.

"Stop!" I bellowed. Startled, the three combatants looked in my direction. "I order you, and I'm Lord Pivor's agent!"

I was wearing the silver and ivory medallion he'd given me to prove it, too. But the nearer of the dagger men, a horse-faced fellow with a mustache in need of trimming, sneered and retorted, "And we're Lord Amseroth's men! Stay out of this, or we'll slice you, too!"

Under other circumstances, that would have made me draw my broadsword. But from the clench-fingered, inexpert way he gripped the knife, I was willing to gamble I could subdue him without it. I stepped in, inviting a stab, and when it came, I twisted aside and hit him in the jaw with the heel of my palm. That staggered him long enough for a kick in the knee. Bone cracked, and he cried out and fell.

Confident he was done, I glanced around just in time to see the redhead incapacitate the remaining black snake with a jab to the groin. As I winced in masculine sympathy, she shot me a grin. "Thanks!" she called.

"Don't thank me yet," I replied. "Not until I find out who started this."

"I can tell you that," said a voice from the doorway.

I turned. The speaker was a plump fellow who also wore the serpent badge, but embroidered on finer clothing. Like his chestnut hair bobbed at the bottom of the ears, the caffa doublet would have been in fashion in Balathex, where Pivor and I hailed from, a year or two previously.

The staff fighter started toward him.

"No!" I snapped.

With a scowl, she stopped short.

"That lunatic accused me of murder," said the pudgy man. "My friends took offense on my behalf."

"You are a murderer!" the woman said.

"If someone's been killed," I said, "the culprit will answer for it. But I need to hear the facts, starting with your names."

"I'm Dyllonna," said the woman. "A bard."

"A *wandering* bard," said the plump man, putting her in her place, not that the distinction meant much to me. I'd grown up far to the east, spent much of my adulthood as a traveling mercenary, and the citified nobles of Balathex didn't keep household bards anymore. They left that to their country cousins.

"And you?" I asked.

He raised an eyebrow as though surprised I didn't know. "Rogros. Bard to…well, you already heard which lord. Also, reigning champion in the ballad competition."

"Because you killed the better singer!" Dyllonna said.

"Hold on," I said. "I thought the contests hadn't started yet."

"At the last festival!" she said. Three years past.

"A robber slit Evdel's throat in an alley," Rogros said. "I had nothing to do with it."

Dyllonna glowered at me. "You said you'd make the murderer pay."

"When I said that, I assumed the death had just happened. I'd need some sort of evidence to look into it at this late date even if the enquiry fell within the scope of my duties."

Rogros smiled.

Dyllonna snarled, "You're afraid of crossing his master just like all the rest!"

"I'm working for Lord Pivor," I reiterated. "I'm not afraid—"

"Evdel *will* have justice." She turned and stalked away through the crowd, the nearer of whom had turned into gawking spectators.

"If that bitch keeps slandering me," Rogros said, "I'll expect you to deal with it."

"Collect your friends and go back inside," I said, "or you'll wish you had."

Something in my manner convinced him to heed me. As the last of his cronies limped back into the tavern, Pivor and his retinue rode up. The blond patrician was leading my abandoned mare.

"What was all that about?" he asked.

I swung myself back onto my steed. "I'll tell you on the way."

It wasn't a long story, but the house he kept here in town was only a block away. I had to suspend the telling while the butler, groom, maid, cook, and gardener lined up to welcome him, and I reflected that it must be soft work serving an employer who only turned up once a year.

I finished my account lounging in a leather chair with a glass of a tart white local vintage in hand, which certainly made the task more congenial. At the end, Pivor arched a barber-sculpted eyebrow. It was apparently my day for it.

"*Are* you going to look into it?" he asked.

"No. Why would I?"

"You're Selden. Solver of problems and mysteries."

"Only when being paid for it." I hesitated. "Am I? Obviously, if *you* want me to..."

He waved his hand, and the diamonds in his rings flashed in the sunlight shining through the window. "No, no. From our perspective, the festival isn't about the bards, murdered or otherwise. It's about backwater lords gathering to negotiate dowries, trade agreements, and ends to any feuds that have broken out since the last one. And as the master of Kreelan's Plaint, it's my responsibility to provide a peaceful, pleasant atmosphere for the dickering. Focus on that."

I did. With the aid, actual or hypothetical, of the men-at-arms Pivor put under my direction and the doddering old town constable, I collared cutpurses and cardsharps and averted brawls among hotheads who evidently felt that if their feuding families were going to make peace a day or two hence, they should make the most of the time they had left.

Through it all, though, Dyllonna's accusation stuck in my head. I found myself keeping a particular watch for her and Rogros when I wasn't busy with something else.

I spotted Dyllonna first. She was telling jokes and reciting comical poems on a corner with her cap upended on the ground to catch coins. With her wide mouth grinning and her green eyes shining, her freckled face looked prettier than it had twisted with hate.

Unfortunately, I put an end to that myself, by moving to toss a silver piece in the cap. When she noticed me, the scowl came back, and I reflected that you know you truly have offended a busker when she spurns your money.

Rogros had no need to pander to the vulgar mob. Instead, he made a point of greeting the seven "high bards" when their processional marched into town to judge the first competition of the children who aspired to study under their tutelage.

Bards, you see, occupied three rungs on a ladder. At the bottom were wandering entertainers like Dyllonna. Above them were the elite who'd secured positions in noble households, like Rogros. But at the very top were the masters who preserved the traditions, trained the next generation, and exercised authority over the craft. Their enclave was by a grove outside Kreelan's Plaint, which was why it fell to Pivor to oversee the festival.

The youngest of the high bards looked at least as old as me, and I've entered my middle years. A couple appeared as elderly as my new and mostly useless ally the constable. But by all accounts, the music of each and every one was magnificent, and since I was going to be stuck in town anyway, I'd hoped to hear one or more of them perform.

For now, though, I eavesdropped as Rogros complained about Dyllonna's accusations. The high bards appeared to take his grievance seriously, but in the end, couldn't agree on what to do about it. Frustrated, the plump singer strained to remain deferential as he took his leave of them.

I felt vaguely pleased despite the fact that it might make my life simpler if Dyllonna's superiors sent her packing. But even if she was wrong about Rogros, it didn't seem to me that she deserved it. Perhaps seeing three of his ruffian friends attack her had made me sympathetic.

But not sympathetic enough to tolerate her causing any more disturbances. I caught up with her again that night, when she was regaling a cellar tavern full of topers and whores with jests more ribald than the ones she'd told on the corner.

I made sure she didn't notice me, and then, covering a yawn with my hand, shadowed her when she gave over the stage to a lute player and headed out into the night. I hoped to see her to wherever she was sleeping and then seek my own bed.

Instead, she slipped into the mouth of a murky alleyway and started watching a frame house with corbelled upper stories and a tiled façade that stood cattycorner across the street.

I had no idea why. As a sign proclaimed, the potter who lived there was renting floor space to out-of-towners, but Rogros surely wasn't one of them. He'd stay with the rest of Amseroth's entourage in the inn called the Harp and Tambour.

I decided I needed to keep watching Dyllonna. I circled around the block, came up behind her, and found a hiding place several paces back.

As time crawled by, the bard shifted from foot to foot and occasionally gave a sigh. She was either impatient for something to happen or dissatisfied with her vantage point. Spying on some place or person, I'd sometimes felt the same.

Suddenly there came a bang, and then a confusion of voices. I realized someone had thrown the house's front door open, and now people were spilling out into the street. "The physician's on Duck Lane!" a woman shrilled.

Dyllonna ran toward the commotion. I ran after her.

When I caught up, she was staring into the pallid, wide-eyed face of the black-haired lass who was the object of everyone's concern. The latter had blood oozing from a nick on her throat. Had she been a man, I might have thought she'd nicked herself shaving.

"Tell me what happened!" Dyllonna said.

The stricken woman—looking at her, you could tell she was stricken somehow—gaped back like a simpleton.

"Was it Rogros?" the redhead persisted. "Was it?"

The afflicted lass's mouth worked, but no sound came out.

"If *anyone* did this," I said, "someone needs to find him." I dashed on toward the open door, and after a moment, Dyllonna's footsteps thumped after me.

Despite the dozen people who'd brought the stricken woman outdoors, the floors were still littered with snoring folk who'd either decided whatever was happening was none of their affair or never wakened to begin with. Picking my way among them, occasionally stepping or tripping on one in the dark, I stalked from room to room until I found a casement with the oiled-paper leaves open wide.

Since Dyllonna had been watching the front door, it was a reasonable assumption the malefactor had entered this way, although how he'd passed through without disturbing any of the sleepers was a puzzle. It was a fair bet that he'd already fled this way as well.

I jumped out the window into the street beyond and turned right. The Harp and Tambour lay in that direction. Dyllonna kept following and we hurried along together, peering in the hope of seeing some suspicious soul scurrying before us.

"You were watching me," she said, keeping her voice low.

"What matters," I replied, "is who the victim is and why you were watching her."

"At every festival," Dyllonna said, "there are bards everyone expects to excel. Many people believed Olette would win the ballad competition."

"So you were waiting for Rogros to try to kill her, to catch him in the act."

"Yes. But he was too cunning for me."

"We'll see about that."

A moment later, we heard uneven footsteps clumping along in the darkness ahead. Perhaps Rogros had turned his ankle jumping out the casement and now was limping.

Dyllonna and I sprinted forward. Then I felt twinges in my calf. When I looked down, a rat was clinging above the top of my boot, digging its claws through my breeches to hang on. Discomfort exploded into pain as it sank its chisel teeth into my leg.

I yanked the rodent free and crushed the squirming thing in my grip. By then, though, others were climbing my body. I snatched out my dagger and stabbed. Twice I nearly put a hole in myself, but for the most part, I pierced the scrabbling, biting rodents instead.

Behind me, Dyllonna was no doubt engaged in a similar struggle, but she was also chanting.

A rat ran up my face. I closed my eye an instant before the animal's nails would otherwise have raked across it. Then it and all its fellows jumped off me and fled.

I turned. Dyllonna's small attackers were forsaking the fight as well, and though she was mottled with bloody bites and scratches like I was, she gave me a nod to signal that she could still function. We ran onward.

In fact, we ran the rest of the way to the coach gate of the Harp and Tambour, where glowing blue lanterns bracketed the entry. But we didn't catch up with our quarry.

Ignoring the porter, who seemed of the opinion that folk spotted with rat bites didn't belong in such a fine establishment, I threw open the tall azure door. Then Dyllonna and I followed the sounds of roistering.

They led me to a common room hung with black snake banners. A bushy-bearded, barrel-chested sort, the antithesis of Pivor and sophisticated patricians like him,

Amseroth was boozing and playing quoits with his
followers and friends, tossing the rings at the antlers of a
stag head mounted on the wall. I'd pretty much expected
such a scene. I *hadn't* expected Rogros to be there, too.

I started to warn Dyllonna to hold her tongue but was
too slow. "Murderer!" she shouted.

Everyone turned to stare at us.

"Tonight," she continued, "you attacked Olette!"

Amseroth frowned. "Rogros has been here all night."

Dyllonna hesitated. That gave me time to elbow her
in the ribs.

"Your pardon, my lord," I said. "Something unpleasant
did happen just a short time ago, and Dyllonna was in the
thick of it. She's understandably upset. But I see now it had
nothing to do with your man, so we'll take our leave."

"I want her gone!" Rogros said. "Gone or locked up!"

"I understand," I said, meanwhile more or less
manhandling Dyllonna out the door.

As I pulled it shut, she demanded, "How could you
do that?"

"What," I replied, "haul you out of there before
banishment or the town jail became unavoidable? Rogros
isn't our man. Even if Amseroth was willing to lie for him,
even if every other drunkard in the room had the presence
of mind to uphold the deception, our well-fed friend wasn't
out of breath, nor was he any more disheveled than an
evening's revelry would explain."

She scowled. "Then it was one of his cronies."

"The three who tried to hurt you this afternoon were in
the room as well, and if one of them had come rushing in
moments before us, there would have been some sign of it.
Somebody's eyes would have shifted in his direction when
you were making your accusation."

"Well, that doesn't prove Rogros didn't kill Evdel!"

"Not conclusively, but it suggests he didn't."

"He hated Evdel!"

"If my assessment of Rogros's character is correct, he hates everyone who sings better than he does. Let's find the physician who's tending Olette. With luck, she's recovered from the shock and can tell us what happened. Besides, we could do with some tending ourselves."

"All right."

As we tramped along, I said, "I take it that you and Evdel were close."

It took her a couple steps to frame her answer. Then: "I don't sing all that well. I barely passed my examinations. Evdel could have kept company with bards as gifted as himself, or fancy ladies. But whenever our paths crossed, he chose me."

"I like a good joke as much as a good tune."

"So do I. But the heart of the bardic arts is music, which means..." She shook her head, and her wavy hair swished on the collar of her stained old traveler's cloak. "It means I've spent the past three years brooding over Evdel's murder, and when Rogros and I came together again, I felt I had to do something about it. Now..."

"Now," I said, "we'll see what we can discover."

The physician was a scrawny fellow with side-whiskers and a needle nose. He didn't like being called away from his patient, but the sight of my badge of authority mollified him. Or maybe it was the realization that Dyllonna and I were likewise in need of care.

"See to my friend first," I said, "and while you're about it, tell me about Olette. Is she ready to answer questions?"

"No," the doctor said, "nor is she likely to become so."

"Why not?"

"It will make more sense if I show you." He then faltered as if realizing he couldn't do that and dab at Dyllonna's cheek with a swab at the same time.

"I'll keep." The bard gestured to the door the physician had just come through. "Olette's this way?"

She was, and she cowered as we entered. But the physician spoke to her gently, and, trembling, she allowed him to tug on her chin and open her mouth.

Her tongue was gray and withered. So were the gums and the rest of the tissue I could see. Dyllonna gasped.

"Acid?" I asked. "Or something hot?"

"If it had been," the physician said, "she'd be in pain, and that doesn't appear to be the case."

"Olette," I said, "can you write?"

She didn't seem to register that I was talking to her.

I turned back to the physician. "How long before she returns to her senses?"

He shook his head. "So far, there's no indication that she will. We don't know that only the mouth is shriveled. It's possible the brain is compromised as well."

I bit back an obscenity.

Dyllonna and I departed the premises greasy with salve and mottled with sticking plasters. I then cast about for somewhere to buy a drink. Fortunately, with the festival in full swing, a vendor's stall was easy to find.

When I finished my brandy and returned the clay goblet, I said, "So, magic."

Dyllonna wiped beer foam from her lips. "You're sure?"

"I had my suspicions when I saw how our culprit came and went without disturbing anyone but his victim. They became stronger when the rats attacked us, and certain when I observed the condition of Olette's mouth."

"I see what you mean."

"And plainly, bards practice a form of magic. You used it to drive the vermin away."

"Well, yes. There's magic in melody, rhythm, and rhyme, and it reveals itself as a bard advances in the craft. But only if you have the knack, and then gradually and perhaps just a little. I can only coax an audience that already likes me into being a little more generous with its appreciation. And occasionally influence animals to do my bidding." She smiled. "It's good for persuading bedbugs to leave you alone."

I snorted. "I've had nights when I could have used that trick."

"You realize, bards aren't the only folk who use magic."

"Of course. But if there were any wizards in town, I'd likely know about it."

If not, it wouldn't be for want of enquiring. It would be a canard to suggest that all such folk are troublemakers. But I had a knack for running afoul of the dastardly ones and had learned to keep an eye out.

"So what now?" Dyllonna asked.

"We go to Pivor's house. I'll find you a bedbug-free place to sleep, and we can consult with him over breakfast."

That turned out to be venison, stork, peaches, and cheat bread among other offerings laid out in a buffet. Pivor cocked his head when Dyllonna and I entered the room. "Isn't that...?" he said.

"Yes," I said, "the lass from the squabble in the square." I introduced them, and the bard bowed in a graceful way that somehow suggested a curtsey even though she was wearing scuffed leather breeches.

Pivor grinned at me. "I had a hunch you wouldn't be able to refrain from poking around."

"You wouldn't have wanted me to," I replied. "Another bard has been attacked. The assailant used magic."

Pivor's air of fashionable nonchalance fell away to reveal the responsible leader he could be when circumstances required. "Tell me."

Dyllonna and I seated ourselves, and then I gave my report.

Afterward, Pivor said, "It's different than the previous victim. Olette didn't have her throat cut."

"Her neck was bleeding. I think she was entranced but at the last instant found the strength to break away, and her attacker feared to pursue her through the crowded house."

Pivor frowned. "Hm."

"I also suspect the actual point of the attack on Edvel was to ruin his mouth and cripple his mind. Killing him simply hid what had befallen him beforehand. When you see a corpse that's manifestly dead of a slashed throat, you assume no further examination is required."

"But why would anyone bother to maim a person in such a way if he was going to kill him immediately afterward?"

"I don't know," I said. "Dyllonna?"

She shook her head. "No idea."

"Here's another problem," Pivor said. "If you're right that a bard did this, which bard? The Plaint is crawling with them."

"Somebody who was present three years ago," I said, "but I doubt that narrows it down very much. So, someone with a motive to harm two gifted singers. Maybe somebody looking to eliminate strong competition in the contests, as Dyllonna suggested. Although that still doesn't explain the maiming."

"It also strikes me as a weak motive," Pivor said. "The children's competitions are important. They determine who gets to study to be a bard and who doesn't. But the adult contests, not as much. The purses are modest, and a singer doesn't need to win to find a berth in a wealthy household. He just has to acquit himself well and strike the fancy of someone with a vacancy."

"There's considerable pride involved," Dyllonna said. "Still, milord, you may have a point."

Essentially, the point was that we understood very little. We glumly mulled that over for a moment.

Then I said, "I have a thought. What if the murders go back more than three years? Milord, would you remember that?"

"I should," Pivor said. "I've been coming here my whole life. Father dragged me along as part of his ongoing campaign to show me that nobles have actual duties and obligations. Let me think...yes! Or possibly yes. Six years ago, a talented singer was killed on the road into town. But that could have been bandits. This country has plenty. Including some of its lords, although you mustn't tell them I said so."

"If the same person," I said, "committed the same crime at the past two festivals, that narrows the field a little more."

"If that's the pattern," Pivor said, "one assault every three years, then at least the worst has already happened." His mouth twisted. "I realize that's a sour way of looking at it."

Dyllonna glowered. "Surely, milord, you aren't saying you intend to do nothing!"

Pivor scowled back. "No, singer, I'm not. My father's lessons took, and I understand I'm responsible for the folk in my dominions, to protect them whenever possible and avenge them when not."

The bard took a breath. "I beg your pardon. I spoke out of turn."

The apology cooled Pivor's temper. "It's all right. I confess, your sense of my priorities may not be *entirely* off. These deaths matter, but so do other things. So, Selden, I need you to investigate discreetly, without neglecting your other responsibilities, inciting a panic, or giving anyone who matters reason to take offense."

"I understand," I said, "and I know how to begin."

Dyllonna's attack on breakfast demonstrated that she knew how to make the most of a meal that was tasty, plentiful, and free. Then I saddled my mare, commandeered a second horse for her, and we rode out to the bards' school.

It was a collection of one-story structures adjacent to a stand of alders and elms. Students were weeding the gardens and drawing water from the well. Others were singing inside one of the buildings, breaking off when the teacher stopped them, receiving his criticism, and then attempting the same passage again.

Dyllonna and I repaired to the largest building. There I informed yet another pupil, this one playing doorman, that we needed to speak to the masters on a matter of urgency. On our first try, we got four of them, who met us in a room containing several large harps and a miscellany of other instruments.

"I'd hoped to consult with all seven of you," I said.

A woman with hair dyed a bright and unnatural shade of gold smiled as if I'd said something foolish. "Master...Selden, was it?...you've come at the least convenient time imaginable. We have to judge the competitions while also rehearsing the performances we'll give as the finale to the festival. You're lucky we four have even a little time to spare."

I stared her in the eye. "I respect you masters, but as long as you care to dwell in this place, Pivor is your lord, and as his representative, I'll have some respect in return. Especially since a bard is murdering other bards utilizing the secrets of your craft"—their eyes widened—"and I need your help to identify him. Now, please send for the others."

She dispatched the doorman, and they turned up one by one, including he who appeared to be the oldest of them all, wrinkled, white-bearded, and walking with the aid of a silver-handled cane. He still seemed fairly spry, though, with clear gray eyes that were shrewd and none too friendly.

"I'm Lendach," he said, "the leader of this circle. What is this nonsense?"

I told him, and at the end, I said, "I need to understand the purpose of this blighting magic and who knows how to use it."

The other masters looked to Lendach. Plainly, they believed he'd be the one to know if anyone did. But he shook his head and said, "There is no such song."

"Could you take a moment to think about it?" I replied. "*Something* unnatural befell Olette."

"Then look for a sorcerer or vampire. No bard could do such a thing."

"Did Olette have a rival who might have wished to do it if he could?"

"No."

We back-and-forthed a while longer, with Lendach providing the answers and his fellows endorsing them with their silence. Finally, Dyllonna and I took our leave.

Back out in the sunlight, I said, "Considering that Olette is one of your own, I find their level of sympathy unimpressive. They must have been a delight to study under."

Dyllonna smiled crookedly. "Especially if you were one of the unimpressive pupils. Seriously, they aren't all so bad. But once Lendach made it clear that in his judgment, we were bothering them with foolishness…"

"Yes, Lendach, who was ever so busy preparing for his concert. What would happen if he embarrassed himself with a bad one?"

"It would be a disgrace, obviously."

"What if the performance was bad enough to cast doubt on his fitness to be a master bard?"

"I suppose the other members of the inner circle might insist that he step down. But why are you asking? Lendach will do well. He may be old, but as you just heard for yourself, his voice is still melodious and his mind is still sharp."

"Yes," I said, "aren't they, though?"

I looked around and spied a lanky fellow of about my own age in a broad-brimmed straw hat. He was slouching in the shade of an alder watching the student gardeners. There had to be a couple such permanent workers here to make sure the young singers actually got their chores done.

I headed over to him with Dyllonna trailing after me. I gave him a smile and said, "It's a nice morning."

He grunted.

"Are you going to the festival later on?"

He shrugged.

"Perhaps you'd enjoy it more with some extra silver in your purse."

The suggestion didn't make him friendlier, exactly, but at least it moved him to speech. "What do you want?"

"A little information about the masters."

He frowned. "They wouldn't want me gossiping."

"Then we'll keep it among the three of us." I opened my belt pouch and scooped out several coins. "Do you want these or not?"

"Ask."

"Think back six or seven years. Was there a period when Lendach's health seemed to be failing? If so, did it affect his music or his thinking?"

My informant nodded. "He had a fit and wasn't himself for a while after. But then he got better. How'd you know?"

I gave him the silver. "Thanks. Enjoy the festival."

As Dyllonna and I walked back to the horses, she said, "I see what your idea is. But it's pure speculation."

"Remember that the person who attacked Olette couldn't simply outdistance us even though he had a head start. He limped. At the time, I thought that perhaps he hurt himself jumping out the casement, but it was only a short hop to the ground. Perhaps he was actually limping like an old man who carries a cane."

"Hm."

"Consider too that when discussing Olette's affliction, Lendach used the specific term 'vampire.' Not ghost or demon, 'vampire.' What if that was a slip?"

"You mean, what if, after his seizure, he couldn't bear the prospect of being less than he was and forced from his office? So he used evil magic to steal the physical and mental qualities that make a bard to restore his own powers? And needs to repeat the process at intervals?"

I nodded. "He'd likely be found out if he preyed on people here at the school. But he might well go uncaught at big, chaotic gatherings of all the bards and hundreds of other folk from across the southlands."

Dyllonna shook her head. "You make the notion sound halfway plausible, but it still just seems like guesswork. I don't want you to make a fool of yourself with a false accusation. Arrogant pig though he is, I'll be a long time living down my denunciations of Rogros."

I patted my mare's neck, then untied her reins from the hitching post. "Trust me, I have no intention of accusing the chief of the bards without proof. That's why I'm coming back after dark, to look for it. Will you help? You're the one who knows her way around."

Dyllonna pulled a wry face. "The order could cast me out if this goes amiss. But yes, of course."

I spent the remaining daylight hours keeping order in town and, without being obvious about it, making sure my men-at-arms were prepared to operate without me later on. Dyllonna and I rode back to the college after dark.

We left the horses tied at the back of the grove and skulked up through the trees. On first inspection, the school looked as deserted as I'd hoped. Still, it was likely someone was about, so we kept sneaking as Dyllonna led me to the cottage that was Lendach's residence.

To my surprise, given the bucolic setting, the door had a citified lock, and the master bard had engaged it. "I keep meaning to learn to pick these," I whispered, lifting my foot for a kick.

"Let me," Dyllonna replied. She knelt down, extracted a set of picks and torsion tools from inside her jerkin, and set to work. The lock clicked, and the door swung ajar.

"Nicely done. Is that part of the curriculum here?"

"It should be. Folk aren't always generous out on the road." She stowed away her burglar's kit and stood up. "Let's get inside."

We left the door cracked, opened the shutters just a little, and that provided just enough light to search by. Dyllonna examined a shelf of books and scrolls, carrying them to the window when that proved necessary to make out the writing. I looked for a hiding place, reasoning that if there was evidence of dark magic to be found, Lendach might not have left it sitting out in the open.

Eventually I rapped, heard a hollow sound, and fumbled open the hidden panel in the back of a wardrobe. Then I flinched as the sheaf of parchment inside the hitherto concealed cubby gave off a pulse of malignancy. If you've ever come into contact with accursed artifacts or the like, perhaps you know the sensation.

I swallowed and, when I was sure I wasn't going to puke, said, "Look at these if you can stomach it."

Dyllonna picked them up, then sucked in her breath as if they'd given her fingers a sting. After that, though, she was able to handle them without discomfort. She went the window and started to riffle through them.

Eventually she said, "I don't understand all of this. It's based on lore I was never taught and wouldn't care to be. But it's a collection of songs for hurting people, calling on devils, and doing other terrible things."

"That's a start. But a master bard could argue that it's proper for him to possess such papers as long as he doesn't actually cast the spells. We need—"

"I know." She skimmed three more pages, then came upon one that warranted a more careful reading. "This is it! The song for stealing another bard's abilities!"

"The song Lendach claimed didn't exist."

"There are even notes in a different hand and in darker, newer ink at the bottom of the parchment!"

"We should have no difficulty obtaining other samples of Lendach's handwriting to compare that writing to. Which clinches it. Evdel's killer is going to the gallows."

Dyllonna swallowed. "I knew I was going to try. But I didn't know if I could really...I mean..." She started crying.

I squeezed her shoulder. "This is no time for tears. This is the moment for joyous retribution."

"You're right." She snuffled and swiped at her nose and eyes. "If we hurry, we can denounce him in front of the whole town!"

That sounded satisfying to me as well, and I was eager to have at it as we hurried back to the horses and mounted up. Then I started to hurt.

My rat bites had been itching and smarting off and on all day, and at first I imagined the discomfort was simply more of the same. But it flowered in spots where the rodents' teeth hadn't pierced me, and as Dyllonna and I reached the road back into the Plaint, it erupted into genuine torment. I let out a strangled cry.

Dyllonna turned in the saddle to look at me. "Oh, no," she breathed.

"What's wrong with me?" I asked.

"Boils."

I raised a trembling hand and touched one of the newly risen bumps on my face. That was a mistake. The slightest pressure made it throb even worse.

"It's said," Dyllonna told me, "that in olden times, an accomplished bard could compose a satire against a lord or official, and the performance would raise boils on the target's face. Lendach must have taken to the stage tonight to ridicule you."

Because the gardener I'd questioned had tattled. Or maybe the things I'd said to Lendach himself had sufficed to make him worry I was sniffing too close to the truth.

"Well, if this is his best defense," I gritted, "he's finished. It takes more than a little pain to silence me."

"You don't understand. The real purpose of a satire was to make the victim an object of general dislike and contempt. Lendach's trying to fix it so no one will heed you." She hesitated. "Perhaps *I* should accuse him."

I shook my head, and the boils on my neck gave me pangs. "You said it yourself. You undermined your credibility by falsely accusing Rogros, and Lendach's an important man. If you denounce him, he'll brazen it out, the evidence notwithstanding. It has to be me, Pivor's deputy and friend."

She looked dubious, but she gave me a nod. We urged our mounts onward.

Haste too was arguably a mistake given the boils on my rump and inner thighs. But I thought a swift ride preferable to a more protracted, gentler one, especially as I planned to force Lendach to lift the curse he'd cast on me at the end of it.

The punishment wrung gasps, grunts, and the occasional profanity out of me, though, and after one such exclamation, Dyllonna sneered and said, "It's your own fault. If you were any good at your profession, you would have found the truth sooner, before Lendach had a chance to do this to you."

My pains urged me to respond with the same sort of spite, but then I realized what was actually happening. "Steady," I said. "The spell is corrupting *your* opinion of me."

She stiffened. "I...I think it was! I'm sorry!"

"It wasn't your fault. But keep your head straight."

We reached the edge of town not long after.

No doubt the greatest concentration of folk was in the square where the singers were competing, their voices intermittently audible even at a distance. But not everyone could squeeze in, and the streets radiating out from it were crowded, too, with revelers enjoying the antics of dancing dogs, jugglers, and puppeteers. Dyllonna and I had to slow our horses to a walk.

That gave people a chance to notice who was trying to ride through their midst. First, they glared, and then they catcalled.

"Coward!"

"Liar!"

"Pervert!"

Next, a flung rock hit a boil on my cheek. I jerked and cried out, and a sound went up from the mob that was half laugh and half roar. Certain more missiles would follow, I crouched down as best I could in the saddle and started to kick the mare into a faster gait. I still didn't want to ride over anyone, but I wasn't eager to endure a stoning, either.

Then a spearman with Pivor's coat of arms embroidered on his livery pushed his way through the crowd. Specifically, it was stolid, gap-toothed Beck, one of the soldiers my patron had placed under my direction.

"I need your help!" I said.

He spat. "After abandoning us to do all the work by ourselves? Where have you been?"

"Attending to Lord Pivor's business! I order you—"

Beck plunged his spear into my horse's neck.

The mare threw her head back, then fell. I kicked free of the stirrups and made an awkward leap.

That kept me from ending up pinned beneath the animal's convulsing body. But by the time I found my balance, Beck was coming at me. He'd left the spear in the mare's neck and drawn his sword.

I sprang back, and his first cut missed. I snatched out my blade, parried his second attack, started to riposte to with a stroke that could have crippled his hand forever after, and then remembered he wasn't to blame for his malice. I stopped the slash short of the target.

He hacked at my kidney. I parried, then, maintaining pressure on his sword, immobilizing it, shifted in close. I smashed my pommel into his jaw, and he reeled backward and fell.

Good. But when I looked around, other folk were converging on me with their knives or whatever makeshift weapon had been ready to hand. Turning, I balked the nearest with feints, a tactic that wouldn't hold them back for long.

Then Dyllonna forced her way toward me. Her staff rose and fell, cracking skulls. It was a clumsy weapon to use one handed or astride a horse for that matter, but aggression and the animal's bulk opened a path through my assailants.

I scrambled up behind Dyllonna and slashed someone's face. He would have caught hold of her belt and dragged her from the saddle if I hadn't.

The splash of blood and his squeal gave the other attackers pause, and Dyllonna managed to turn her horse and gallop back the way we'd come. Angry shouts and a shower of stones pursued up, but we made it back out of town.

When we felt safe, we dismounted, and Dyllonna crooned praise and reassurance to her trembling mount. By touch, I examined my cheek and found a mess of blood and pus. The first stone had burst the boil, which, to my disgust, didn't make the spot hurt any less.

At least the pain attendant upon my disfigurement hadn't hindered me during the fight. My focus on the exigencies of the moment blocked it out. That was something.

Still, I felt ill used, and my tone was petulant as I observed, "You said the satire would incline people to disrespect me. You didn't warn me it would turn them into mad dogs."

"That's not how it worked in the old accounts. Lendach must have found an especially poisonous version of the song."

"Well, how long is the effect supposed to last?"

Her mouth tightened. "Until the bard dissolves it, or something breaks his power."

"Plainly, we need to try for the latter. That means you need to sing a song to dilute its influence."

She blinked. "I told you, my music is only mediocre."

"A mediocrity that makes rats docile and crowds friendly. You know the necessary tricks."

"Do you want to gamble your life that I know them well enough to overcome the magic of the greatest bard in the southlands?"

"Lendach already performed his satire. The mob will be hearing your song as you sing it. Perhaps that will give you an edge. In any case, I can't stay as I am, and you can't let Edvel's murder go unavenged."

She took a deep breath. "Wait, and be quiet. It will take some time to put the song together."

She prowled around in the moonlight humming bits of melody and muttering under her breath. I pondered the advisability of lancing boils with a dagger point and decided not to make the experiment.

Eventually she turned to face me. "Just so you know," she said, "I don't really see you as the paragon the verses describe."

I chuckled. "I'll try not to take it to heart." I waved my hand toward the horse. "Shall we?"

She frowned. "I can ride, but I'm no expert. I've certainly never practiced singing while bouncing and swaying on horseback. If you want my song to be as potent as it can be…"

She didn't have to spell out the tradeoff. If her magic failed to calm the throng, accomplishing a second retreat would be more problematic on foot.

"We'll leave the poor animal to graze in peace," I said. "He's been through enough for one evening."

She started singing when we were twenty paces from the edge of town. Her vibrant alto voice seemed sweet and rich to my admittedly untutored ear. As promised, the song of Selden was a catalogue of stainless virtues and impossible heroisms that occasionally drew inspiration from my more notorious real-life exploits, like slaying the fire spirit and the undead magus Yshan Keenspur.

When people recognized me, their faces twisted. Fortunately, Dyllonna's song then touched them, and they faltered, some looking shocked at themselves, like they'd just awakened from a dream of doing something vile, others, perplexed and uncertain.

I still wanted to stride quickly but recognized that my companion couldn't do that and sing to best effect, either. She had to glide along in what amounted to a stately dance, turning from side to side to further charm the crowd with her gaze and her smile, and I had to hold myself to the same pace.

It wore my nerves to rags. Still, her tactics worked. We made it to the square without anyone else attacking us, although a number of scowling folk trailed along behind us as though the itch was still present.

Pivor, the mayor, and the high bards were all seated on an elevated platform for dignitaries. Lendach goggled at me, no doubt flummoxed that I'd made it here alive.

When the youth singing on the main stage realized I'd distracted everyone from his performance, he fell silent. Meanwhile, Dyllonna kept crooning her counterspell. But softly now, so I could make myself heard above the melody.

"Lendach," I called, "by the authority vested in me by Lord Pivor, I arrest you for murder!"

The master bard forced a laugh. "That's absurd! And in any case, Pivor now understands your incompetence and dishonesty, and he's stripped you of your position! Isn't that right, my lord?"

The nobleman looked back and forth between Lendach and me uncertainly. To some degree, he was still under the old man's sway. But, nudged by Dyllonna's power, he now recalled our friendship and all I'd done for his family and our city.

"I can prove what I say!" I held up the sheaf of parchments. "Songs of dark magic with notes appended in your hand! I ask the other high bards to inspect them!"

Lendach rose from his chair. "You insult me, and in so doing, you insult our sacred fellowship and its traditions. Rest assured, I will defend our honor."

With that, he started singing, if that was the proper word for it. It was a wail like a wolf pack howling together. He also stalked toward the edge of the platform, each pace surer and heavier than the last, and as he came toward me, he changed.

His upper body swelled, putting on muscle, until his robe ripped at the seams. His torso hitched forward, too, transforming him into something akin to a hunchback. His fingernails extended into jagged claws, his arms stretched longer than his legs, and the lower part of his face bulged into a slavering muzzle full of fangs. His ears sprouted points, the gray eyes turned yellow, and his body hair thickened into a coat of snow-white fur.

In short, he became a bestial horror that unquestionably looked capable of slaughtering a boil-ridden human swordsman. I assumed he meant to kill Dyllonna, too, and reduce the incriminating parchments to shredded, blood-soaked illegibility.

As I stuffed them in my shirt, I said, "You didn't warn me he could do this, either."

Dyllonna shook her head to say she hadn't known, hefted her staff, and started to move up beside me.

"No!" I snapped. "Stay back and concentrate on your singing!" If she hit a false note or missed a beat, the crowd might rush in to help Lendach rip me apart.

His transformation complete, the high bard sprang off the platform. I snatched my dagger from its sheath and threw it. A target can't dodge when he's in midair.

Unfortunately, he can parry. With more speed than I'd hoped to see, Lendach slapped the blade in midflight and sent it tumbling away.

As soon as his feet touched the ground, he came at me. I retreated before him until I had the broadsword out. He struck at the blade with a backhand swipe of his fist.

The blow nearly bashed the hilt from my grip. It did knock the weapon out of line, and he lunged and raked with his other hand. I jumped back just in time to keep his claws from ripping away my eyes.

Then we circled. The sword gave me an advantage in reach, but given his freakishly long arms, only barely, and his speed, strength, and unnatural hardiness offset it. He was willing to suffer cuts to his hands and forearms for the chance to beat my weapon to the side again, or better yet, disarm me, and I could see why. Though bloody, the wounds to his extremities weren't slowing him down.

I needed to strike him in the vitals. I was still pondering how when he grabbed my blade.

Without an armored gauntlet, no merely human combatant would do that for fear of losing fingers. But Lendach jerked me toward him and opened his jaws.

I couldn't use the sword, nor, without letting go of it, could I withstand the pull. As the beast-man's head shot forward to bite into mine, I stabbed my stiffened fingers into a yellow eye.

The shock of that froze him, and I floundered clear, dragging the sword free in the process. But it took me an instant to come back on guard, and that gave him time to do the same.

Panting, sweat burning in my eyes, I cut to the knee. Lendach smashed his fist down on my weapon, and I dropped it.

Goggling in what I hoped looked like panic, I recoiled. Lendach threw himself at me. Why not? I was defenseless.

I sidestepped, he plunged past me, and the momentum of that top-heavy, hunched-over frame made it difficult to stop. I had the sword back in my hand by the time he started to turn around.

My first cut sheared into his neck, and my second cut his spine. He pitched to the ground, and the third one split his skull.

Pivor gawked down at me. "Bright Angels! Did you drop the sword on purpose?" He was speaking to me as he would to a friend.

I grinned. "I had a hunch that if I didn't finish the fight quickly, it would end up going his way. So I tried a trick to get behind him." I pulled the parchments back out of my shirt. "You really should examine these."

With Lendach's curse broken, the other high bards affirmed that the papers proved his guilt. The only unsatisfactory thing about the end of the affair was that while everyone stopped despising me, the boils didn't instantly disappear. I had to return to the physician to have them lanced and ended up more covered in ointment and plasters than before.

The effect was more comical than seductive. Still, when I dined with Dyllonna the following night, I made bold to say, "I see why Edvel chose your company whenever your paths crossed. I'd be inclined to do the same."

"I'm afraid," she replied, her lips greasy and a chicken wing in her hand, "that will seldom happen. Lord Bluegarden offered me a place in his household. Apparently my performance in the square impressed him, and he too appreciates a good joke as much as a good tune."

I sighed. "He's lucky to have you."

She smiled. "But you and I are together now. Let's see where the night takes us."

Peach Tart

When the first fresh peaches of summer come in, the cook of the Black Dragon Inn can't help but to make them into tarts. The recipe he uses is the one taught to him by his father. It balances the sweetness of the fruit and sugar with the bite of red wine and ginger. He always boils the peaches first, before putting them into the tarts, to make sure they're perfectly tender to eat.

5 - 6 peaches
1/4 cup red wine
3/4 cup sugar
1/2 tsp. cinnamon
1/2 tsp. ginger
1/4 tsp. salt

Peel peaches, remove pits, and slice. Parboil in water until just tender. Drain peaches well and place in pie crust.

Make syrup of sugar, spices, and wine. Pour over peaches and cover with top crust, making a few slits in the top.

Bake at 425°F for 10 minutes, then reduce heat to 350°F and bake until done, about 30-40 minutes more.

HOW DAFT TEB BECAME KING

Daniel Myers

So you want to hear a story now? One about Daft Teb? Alright, I have a fine one for you. I'm sure you've heard about Teb and the talking sheep, and probably Teb and the golden chamberpot as well, but have you heard of the time he became king? Good! Get a pint - and one for me, thank you - pull up a chair, and I'll tell it.

Back about a dozen years ago, before the new governor was appointed for our province, Daft Teb was living as a shepherd in Bera-Temin. Now as shepherds go, Teb was far from the best. He was forever taking his sheep to graze in the oddest of places. It's no surprise, I guess. When the gods were handing out brains, Teb must have been off somewhere trying to remember which shoe went on which foot.

At any rate, one day when he was trying to graze his flock on the beach, he tried to count the sheep and decided that he had lost one of them. He looked up and down the beach, but the sands there ran in a long and narrow strip between the waters and the high bluffs, so there really wasn't much of a place for sheep to hide.

The problem is that when Teb looks for something, he looks everywhere. It doesn't matter if the thing he lost is as big as a horse, he's going to look in the hayloft and under the table and even in his belt pouch, because his mother always told him, "If you're going to search for something then you should leave no stone unturned". For the next hour he looked behind pieces of driftwood and around patches of seagrass and under suspicious shells, but he could not find the missing sheep.

That was when he looked across the waters to the island of Pelam-Sul and somehow got it into his head that his lost sheep was roaming somewhere among the ruins. It didn't matter that the island was a half-day's rowing away, or that a sheep wasn't likely to wade into the ocean. It was the only place he could see where he hadn't looked already, and his mother had always said, "You always find things in the damnedest places." So Teb herded his flock back to their pen next to his tumbledown house and went off to see his friend Big Bill who was a fisherman.

Teb walked all the way through Bera-Temin and down to the docks where Bill had just finished selling his morning's catch and was busy untangling the nets so they'd be ready for the next day's work.

"I need to borrow a boat," Teb told Bill.

Bill looked up from the nets to see Teb waiting impatiently. He didn't like loaning Teb anything since it rarely came back in the same condition, but Teb was always so earnest that it was hard to turn him away.

"What do you need a boat for?" Bill asked.

"I need to catch a sheep," answered Teb, and he was surprised to see Bill break into laughter. Then Teb remembered his mother telling him, "They're not laughing at you, they're laughing with you," so he laughed too.

When Bill stopped laughing enough breathe, he wiped the tears from his eyes and said, "Ok, you can take that little rowboat at the end of this dock. Will you need a net too?"

Teb thought a net would make it easier to catch the sheep when he found it, so he said "Oh! Good idea! Yes, please," and then Bill laughed some more and got him an old net.

Now as I mentioned before, Bill didn't like to loan anything to Teb for fear that it would be ruined, so it's no surprise that the rowboat was very old and rather leaky. But Bill also kind of liked Teb, so he made sure to toss an old pail in among the ropes in the bow, and he told Teb to bail anytime water got into the boat.

So Teb slowly rowed his way out from the docks and around Rocky Point and across the waters to Pelam-Sul, pausing every few strokes to scoop water from the bottom of the boat and dump it over the side. He was going so slowly that it took him all afternoon and all night to make the crossing, but his mother had always said, "You don't get out of a boat mid-stream." Teb knew that the ocean wasn't a stream, but he figured it was close enough.

Now as Teb was pulling the rowboat ashore the next morning he was quite thrilled with his good fortune, for he caught a glimpse of his lost sheep scampering among the trees. At least he *thought* it was his sheep. It looked more like a goat than a sheep really, but Teb remembered his mother saying, "Living alone changes a person," so maybe his sheep had gotten lonely and turned into a goat. It's no surprise, I guess. When the gods were handing out sense, Teb must have been off somewhere trying to stick his elbow in his ear.

Teb wasn't sure how to catch sheep in nets, or goats for that matter, but he'd seen fishermen using nets to catch fish many times. "How different could it be?" he said to himself. So he ran into the woods after the sheep-goat with the net trailing along behind him. It turned out to be a lot harder than he expected though as he had to keep standing back up after the net would snag on a branch or rock. He didn't give up though, because he remembered his mother saying, "You don't quit something just because it's hard." After an hour or so the net was so torn up that it was little more than a long, single line. That didn't bother Teb.

"Fishermen catch fish with a line all the time," he said to himself, "so it should work for sheep-goats too," and for the rest of the morning he chased the sheep-goat through the trees on the hills of Pelam-Sul, all the way up to the ruins at the top of mount Reshov.

I'm sorry, but I need to take a little break in the story to rest my poor voice. My cup is empty, you see, and my throat is so very dry. What's that? Another pint? Thank you *ever* so much. Very nice. Where was I? Oh yes.

You might remember that hundreds of years ago, Pelam-Sul used to be the fortress of Praskaam the Great, the most feared pirate of the northern seas. For decades Praskaam and his crew raided and sunk thousands of ships, merchant and military alike, collecting up all the wealth and weapons and sending hundreds of thousands to a watery death. All of that loot went back to Pelam-Sil where Praskaam used it to build his castle, and he lived there like a king. It was only when the Emperor decided to tame the seas that Praskaam and his army were defeated. The castle at Pelam-Sul was razed, but of the treasure nothing was found.

Teb, of course, remembered none of this. It's no surprise, I guess. When the gods were handing out memory, Teb must have been off somewhere trying to find his own house. You can imagine how shocked he was when he followed the sheep-goat behind a giant stone chair and through a small hole in a rock wall, and found himself in a large cave facing an enormous mountain of gold and silver.

Being a generally honest sort of person, Teb was worried that he had stumbled into someplace he shouldn't have. So he carefully looked around for any signs that the treasure before him belonged to someone. He looked for bars in the windows that would keep thieves out, but there were no windows in the cave. He looked for a heavy, iron-bound door to keep the treasure in, but there was only the small hole he'd crawled through. He even looked for big, strong guards to watch over the treasure, but there was only a sheep-goat. That thought made Teb laugh, because a sheep-goat would be a terrible guard. "It wouldn't be able to hold a big, scary-looking sword," he said to himself.

After checking a second and third time, Teb was convinced that the treasure didn't belong to anyone. Could it be his treasure? He wanted it to be his, but he remembered his mother telling him, "Always ask before you take something that isn't yours," so he knew he should ask for it. But just who should he ask? The only one there was the sheep-goat.

"Can I have this treasure?" Teb asked the sheep-goat.

The sheep-goat let out a quiet bleat and started to nibble on the hem of Teb's tunic.

"Did that mean yes?" Teb asked the sheep-goat.

The sheep-goat bleated again and wandered out of the cave.

Teb reasoned that a bleat from a sheep-goat must mean yes, for if it had meant anything else then the sheep-goat would have answered "No" to his second question. That meant that all of the great treasure was his.

Now anyone with even the smallest bit of wisdom would have taken home as much treasure as they could carry, and would sneak back later for more, trying to keep the hoard a secret for as long as possible. However Teb remembered his mother saying, "Go with the money." The treasure didn't seem to be going anywhere, so he decided he shouldn't either. For a full day Teb sat with the treasure and waited for it to go somewhere. It wasn't a comfortable wait. He sat all night cold and shivering, and all through the next morning hungry and empty.

Then it occurred to him that the ruins used to be a castle, and he remembered his mother saying, "A man's home is his castle." Since the treasure was his, the castle must also be his, for only a fool would keep his gold in someone else's castle. So he stood up and walked out of his cave to look at the front of his new home. That's when he realized that the island must also be his, for only a fool would have his castle on someone else's land. So Teb surveyed his castle that held his treasure and rested upon his island and noticed that it was in a sorry state.

Now Teb was not a vain man, for it takes a certain level of attention to personal appearance in order to support vanity and Teb often forgot to bathe for months at a time, but his mother had raised him to know that a good person always took care of their property. Since he owned the castle and the island, he would have to have things set straight. He also knew that repairing the castle would be much too much work for him to do on his own. He sat down on a fallen log to work out what to do, and after a few hours he remembered that when his mother needed help on the farm, she hired some neighbors.

"I will hire some neighbors to fix my castle," Teb told the log. Then he went back into the cave behind the throne and looked at the enormous mountain of gold and silver. There was an awful lot there, he thought. He couldn't count that high, but it was clearly enough. So he filled his belt pouch with gold, and then walked down to the beach.

Teb knew he could go back to Bera-Temin to hire some help but he did not want to leave his new home, for he remembered that when he was young his mother had often told him "Stay put." Instead he decided to wait until someone passed by and see if they could help him. That could have turned out to be a long wait for there aren't many ships that brave the rocky the waters near Pelam-Sul. Maybe it was luck, or maybe the gods were curious what Teb would do, but there was a boatful of fishermen working close to the island that day who weren't catching much. They saw Teb on the shore waving his arms wildly, and thinking he was stranded, they went to his rescue.

I'm sorry, but I think I need to stop for a bit. I haven't eaten at all today and I'm quite dizzy. Fish sausage? Yes, thank you! Just set it on the table here and I'll eat it as I continue.

At the time this story happened, things had been more than a bit thin. A blight had taken out many of the koba trees and the raids from the mainland to the south had made it difficult to get a crop in or keep a flock together. You can imagine then that with Teb suddenly hiring all manner of workers at the rate of four quadran a day, people came from as far away as Bera-Fehel to work. There were carpenters and carters, masons and mortarers, plasterers and painters, all working to restore the castle. Then to take care of them all, and to take care of Teb, there was a small army of bakers and cooks and kettle-washers, and stewards. Teb had even hired several guardsmen, because he worried that the sheep-goat might give away his treasure when he wasn't looking. Every day the workers all lined up before the giant stone chair, and Teb would pay each of them from a large sack of coins. He counted the coins out carefully, four to each worker, and it took all his concentration to get it right.

Teb kept the source of the treasure secret from all of his workers. At first he kept a pile of brush in front of the cave opening behind the giant stone chair, but later he found out quite by accident that the throne was cleverly rigged to slide back to conceal the entrance to the treasure chamber. After that he worried less, though he was still concerned about thievery. Eventually he bought a large, gaudy tapestry that a rug merchant had brought up from Thelera-Selor, and had it hung on the wall behind the chair where it would help to hide the source of his wealth.

After a season had passed Teb looked around and saw that he was living in a proper castle, and all was well and good until he remembered his mother saying, "It doesn't matter how much a man has, without a woman he has nothing." Those words worried Teb, and for the next week when he awoke every morning he expected all of his new things to have vanished. Finally he worked out a solution—he would get married and everything would remain everything.

Of course the question of who he should marry never even occurred to him. Rather he turned to the first woman he saw and said, "I need you to marry me or all this will be nothing." The laundry woman he asked, who would later be known as, "Her Most Royal Majesty, Queen Trixie," took a split second to weigh marrying a king against washing clothes for the rest of her life and came to the predictable conclusion.

Normally weddings in Bera-Temin are a simple matter of standing before the village elders and claiming marriage, but Trixie had other ideas. She demanded a fancy gown and three full days of sumptuous feasts. Teb was about to tell her no when he remembered his mother saying, "A smart man gives a woman whatever she wants," so he said yes instead.

That night Teb snuck into the treasure room to look at the very large hill of gold and silver. There was an awful lot there, he thought. He still couldn't count that high, but it was clearly enough. So he filled his belt pouch with gold, and then went to tell Trixie to find a dress-maker.

Did I just see a bowl of apple cobbler? I haven't had apple cobbler in years. Is it good? Why yes, I'd love some! Thank you.

The wedding was held in the throne room, and guests came from hundreds of miles around, some to wish the newlyweds well, but mostly it was for the free food and drink. Teb quickly adapted to married life. He knew exactly how married men should behave because the one thing his mother said more often than anything else was, "Shut up and do as you're told."

Like many new wives taking over a household, Trixie didn't care much for Teb's choice in decorations. In the short time he'd been king he had gathered an impressive collection of trophy animals, all stuffed and mounted and usually wearing brightly-colored hats. Teb kept them in every room of his now expansive palace, and greeted each one by name as he entered a room. But Trixie explained to Teb, using very short words, that this would not do. She asked Teb to let her have enough money to buy some proper castle decorations. Then he went back into the cave behind the throne and looked at the large mound of gold and silver. There was a lot there, he thought. He couldn't count that high, but it was probably enough. He scooped many handfuls into a sack and took it to his Queen.

Within days the castle's new trappings began to arrive. Paintings and wall hangings, fountains and fishpools, tables and cupboards, dishes and platters, all streamed into the castle, and each one was placed into the exactly right spot. Before long Teb's castle rivaled even that of the Emperor to the south, a fact that Teb would point out to the furniture that he'd taken up greeting by name whenever he entered a room.

All of this royal glory and marital bliss lasted exactly three weeks, for Teb had three very large problems, all of which were due to money.

The first reared its ugly head one day when it came time to pay the staff for their work. Teb went back into the cave behind the throne and looked at the small pile of gold and silver. There wasn't a lot there, he thought. He couldn't count that high, but it was probably *not* enough. He scooped the coins into a cloth sack and went to give the workers their due. The gold ran out halfway through, and the silver not long thereafter, and Teb made up the difference by giving away whatever he happened to find nearby. Before long, everything valuable in the castle was being carted away, bound for Bera-Fehel or or Bera-Temin. This was partly because Teb had a lot of people working for him, but mostly because he couldn't remember who he had already paid.

Trixie worked out for herself what was going on, and left on the first boat out with her family and a large, heavy wooden box. She left her crown with Teb, pointing out that the priests of Na-Lenas all agreed that if a King cannot keep his wife for a full year then the marriage is null and void. Teb shrugged and gave the crown away to a woodsman in exchange for a month's worth of firewood.

The second and third problems were due to the simple fact that when you pay someone, they don't just hold on to the coin forever. All of the carpenters and stonemasons and cooks and dishwashers that Teb had paid took their money and spent it to make their own lives better, which of course is a reasonable thing to do. The people they gave their money to spent it in turn, and the coins flowed outward, from hand to hand, and each of those coins bore upon its face the seal of Praskaam the Great.

When these coins reached the lands of the Yotan raiders to the north, and when they reached the desert of the Poshuan Empire to the south, both knew that Praskaam's hoard had been found, both vowed to take the majority of the treasure for themselves, and both sent out large armies to make it so. These two mighty forces arrived at sunset, just minutes after the last of Teb's former possessions had fled the island in the company of a baker.

Teb had been standing in the castle's tall watchtower, cheerfully waving goodbye to the receding flotilla of workers to the west when he saw the other ships to the north and south. Now, Teb may be daft, but he isn't completely stupid. These weren't merchant ships or fishing boats. They were the long boats used by soldiers. He remembered his mother once saying, "Nothing good ever came from a longboat," and then he said one of the smartest things he'd said in a very long time. "Uh oh."

Teb knew he would be best off if no one found him, and one thing Teb was surprisingly good at was hiding. He ran down the stairs and across the castle to his throne room. There he slipped into the cave, pulling the throne close to keep it secret, and there he sat and waited.

By chance the Yotan raiders and Poshuan soldiers arrived at the castle at exactly the same time, and each fighting force mistook the other to be castle guards. They engaged immediately, both intending to have the benefit of surprise. From inside the hidden cave, Teb heard the sounds of ferocious battle, screams and shouts, trumpets and drums, as the conflagration raged throughout the castle. He heard the Yotan raiders yelling, "Take no prisoners!" and he heard the Poshuan soldiers yelling, "Give no quarter!" The battle went on relentlessly for three full days.

When there was finally silence in the throne room, Teb came out of the cave to find that there were no surviving warriors from either side. The castle was once again in ruins, and the carnage was unbelievable.

Of course, since the carnage was unbelievable, Teb didn't believe it. Instead he wandered out of the castle and into the yard, looking for someone to talk to. There, in a surprisingly undamaged pen, was a single goat, also surprisingly undamaged.

Teb looked at the goat and smiled. "I used to have a sheep that looked like you," he told it.

He picked up the goat and carried it down to the dock, where he found a small rowboat. By the next day he had returned to his previous life as a shepherd, or maybe a goatherd—he tended to get the two confused.

Now you might be wondering how I know all this, and I tell you that I heard it from Teb's very own mouth. I met him the last time I was in Bera-Temin. He was there at the tavern of the Red Keg, amusing everyone because someone had bet him that he couldn't stick his elbow in his ear. He asked me if I would pay to hear his story, and I said I would if it was good enough. When he was done I laughed so much that I paid him a full sesterce, but he insisted on giving me this in change. Yes, it's a copper quadran, and if you look closely it bears on its face the seal of Praskaam the Great.

Fish Sausage

In the early spring, meats like beef or pork can be hard to come by, but the big river to the north of the Black Dragon Inn usually has enough slow-moving fish to take up the slack. The inn serves the fish cooked a number of ways, but the cook especially likes making them into sausage because they keep well all day. The customers especially like the fish sausage served with a sauce made from strong beer.

    2 lbs. salmon
    1/4 cup currants
    1/4 tsp. cloves
    1/8 tsp. mace
    1/2 tsp. salt

Remove and discard any skin from the salmon. Chop the fish finely and place in a large bowl with the remaining ingredients. Mix well and stuff into sausage casing.

Put sausages into a large pot of water, bring to a boil, and simmer until internal temperature reaches 165°F. Alternately, place in baking pan with enough water to cover and bake in an oven at 350°F until internal temperature reaches 165°F - about 45 minutes.

    Sauce
    3 slices white bread
    3/4 cup dark beer
    1/4 cup red wine vinegar
    1/4 tsp. cinnamon
    1/4 tsp. ginger
    1/8 tsp. cloves
    1 Tbsp. sugar
    pinch saffron
    1/4 tsp. salt

Cut bread in pieces and place in a bowl with wine and vinegar. Allow to soak, stirring occasionally, until bread turns to mush. Strain through a fine sieve into a saucepan, pressing well to get as much the liquid as possible out of the bread. Add spices and bring to a low boil, simmering until thick. Serve warm.

NIGEL THE BARD (CONTINUED)

Maxwell Alexander Drake

The warmth of the fire pressed against Nigel the Bard's back and he welcomed the heat seeping into his old bones. It'd been a long day, and his throat was beginning to tire. His belly, however, was full, and a cozy bed awaited him upstairs. He could ask for little more.

The sun-dried farmer sitting across the table from him harrumphed as he rose. "Praskaam the Great, pah!" The man's perpetual frown grew twice as deep with a quick shake of his head. "Never 'eard of 'em! Besides, dat coin's so warn, there's no tellin' what's engraved on it. Could be a king's likeness. Could be a horse's ass." He tossed the copper quadran back.

With a deftness belying his age, Nigel snagged the coin from the air before it hit the wooden table. "I am but a humble storyteller. It's not my job to convince you that my tales are true, just hope that you enjoy them."

"It's too late ta debate ya on that subject, as well." The old man waved a hand, turned, and waddled out the Black Dragon Inn's main door.

Everyone's a critic, Nigel thought. He might have been offended had it not been for the fact that the aged farmer had sat enthralled, devouring every word of every tale the bard told.

But that is as good an interruption as any, I suppose.

With an exaggerated yawn, Nigel rose from his seat and stretched. "It is late at that." Leaning forward, he nudged his upside-down hat an inch or two across the table. "And I'm sure I'm not the only one who must be up with the sun."

Without much fuss, the adults rose to a chorus of creaking chairs. A few even added a last minute coin or two to his hat. As the gathering moved to leave, Nigel emptied the hat into his money pouch without so much as a glance at how much he had earned. He found it rude to count coins in public, and would wait until he was in his room for such a mundane task.

Picking up his mug, Nigel drained its last swallow of mead then turned toward the stairs. As he did, his foot brushed against something and the distinct sound of a scuffling across floorboards reached his keen ears. He bent over, casting a wary glance under the table.

There in the shadows created by the few remaining candles burning on the table tops, sat a face he instantly recognized. "Why, Master Blackspoon, I thought you were sent home to bed hours ago."

A sheepish grin came to the young boy. "I was, sir. But I wanted to hear the rest of your tales." Edoard lost his smile. "I hope you're not mad with me."

"Not at all, lad." Nigel reached down and took the boy by the arm, helping him rise. "Not at all. Though, when your folks discover you're missing, they may have a different opinion." The bard brushed a few stray strands of straw from the boy's clothing. "Still, when I was your age, I did the very same thing."

"You did?"

"Most certainly." Turning the young boy around, Nigel nudged him for the door. "But the hour of sleep is upon us, and I do believe I hear your bed calling your name." He watched as the boy waddled his way across the now empty barroom.

Upon reaching the door, young Edoard stopped. He stood there for a time before glancing back over his shoulder, a solemnity sat in his eyes that belied his young age. "A farm boy I may be now, but one day you'll be telling tales of my deeds, sir." And with that, the boy disappeared into the night.

Nigel grunted. It had been a long time since Fate reminded him his stories could have an impact on those who heard them. "Perhaps I will, lad." He headed for the stairs that would take him to his room. "Perhaps I will at that."

INDEX OF RECIPES

Made in the USA
Charleston, SC
07 July 2015